THE STICKING PLACE

A Luke Jones Novel

T. B. SMITH

HELLGATE PRESS ASHLAND, OREGON

THE STICKING PLACE
©2011 T.B. SMITH

Published by Hellgate Press/Fiction
(An imprint of L&R Publishing, LLC)

Hellgate Press Fiction
PO Box 3531
Ashland, OR 97520
www.hellgatepress.com

Editing: Harley B. Patrick

Cover design: L. Redding

Library of Congress Cataloging-in-Publication Data

Smith, T. B., 1955-
The sticking place : a Luke Jones novel / T.B. Smith. -- 1st ed.
p. cm.
ISBN 978-1-55571-676-9
1. Police--California--San Diego--Fiction. 2. Street life--California--San Diego--Fiction. 3. San Diego (Calif.)--Fiction. I. Title.
PS3619.M5945S75 2011
813'.6--dc22
2010040432

Printed and bound in the United States of America
First edition 10 9 8 7 6 5 4 3 2 1

For Ben Limoli, the teacher that mattered and,
as with all things, for Miranda, my bridge to forever...

"But screw your courage to the sticking-place, and we'll not fail."

— Lady Macbeth exhorting her husband to murder the King of Scotland
Macbeth, Act I, scene vii

1

San Diego
Summer 1978

PHILLIP MCGRATH WAS ON HIS WAY TO KILL SOMEBODY.
He turned toward a home at the end of a quiet cul-de-sac where
rusted children's toys lay scattered in a puddle of oil in the driveway. A
dusty motor home rested near the stained stucco of the house and a
basketball hoop drooped over the crumbling asphalt.

The Toyota truck rolled to a stop beneath a tangle of power lines.

Sweat dripped down McGrath's neck, under his armpits and along
the sides of his protruding belly as he hobbled toward the door. He slid
the key from under the welcome mat and eased his way inside. A huge
German shepherd stood in the entryway, his tail thumping against the
door frame.

McGrath patted the shepherd's head and ran his fingers along its
muscular back as it panted along beside him. Dropping to his knees at
the open door to the study, McGrath muttered words of affection to
his only friend as he scratched the dog's massive chest and pulled gently
on his ears.

Struggling to his feet a moment later, McGrath blocked Max with his knee and locked the door behind him to ensure privacy in case someone came home. He limped to the stereo, pulled a record from its jacket and set the needle into the groove. Walking behind a large oak desk, he opened a closet door, lifted an afghan and clutched the Winchester rifle beneath it. Sinking backward into a heavy chair, he pushed against the floor with his feet and scooted toward the middle of the room.

Nothing could stop him now.

He swiveled to face the door and listened to the strains of Keith Jarrett's Köln Concert. As he closed his eyes, he envisioned the pianist's movements as Jarrett's chin slumped toward his heaving chest and his nimble fingers played a run of notes that peaked and waned in a series of mini-crescendos.

Where was the passion that used to drive McGrath's life? As he relived Jarrett's sweetly tormenting performance for the last time, a run of ecstatic moans escaped the pianist's lips and floated up to dangle in congress with the music.

As Jarrett's music filled the room, McGrath spread his legs, propped the rifle between them, swallowed the barrel and pulled the trigger. With no regard for who would deal with the mess.

2

TWENTY-THREE-YEAR-OLD POLICE TRAINEE Luke Jones, was one person who would deal with the mess.

None of his academy instructors had figured out what to make of him before graduation. His physical presence both impressed and confused them, but that was only part of it. His chin was as squared as pushed together bookends and his prominent brow made him a Dick Tracy look-alike. His chest looked like two anvils held together by builders' rebar that bent downward to join with an old fashioned washboard. He stood half a hand more than six-feet tall, could obviously bench press a bull elephant, and had barged into the academy classroom like his instructors owed him an accounting for all the world's injustices.

His hair covered half of his ears and touched his collar, stretching the limits of department regulations. So did his turned-down mustache since it crept past the edges of his mouth and sneaked onto his lower face. But the Shakespeare thing made him really stand out in the police crowd. He could quote the Bard faster than they could read a suspect his Miranda rights. He knew the sonnets better than they knew the California Penal Code and loved skewering them with an on-the-nose quote from *Hamlet* or an obscure tidbit from *Coriolanus* or *Titus Andronicus*.

The academy was as much a ghost as Hamlet's father now, though, and Luke had to impress his training officer to keep his job. The pair were talking in a police car in the parking lot of Jack Murphy Stadium when their call sign rang out over the radio.

T.D. Hartson interrupted his opening day spiel, acknowledged the call and stomped on the gas pedal.

Santa Ana winds bullied brittle blades of straw-colored grass on the surrounding hills and muscled their way into the cab that had no air conditioning. As Hartson sped toward the crest of the ravine, the engine pushed invisible plumes of heat through the open vents and whipped the officers' cheeks.

Hartson pulled to the curb and stepped into the gutter next to a row of dilapidated trash cans.

Luke waited for a break in radio traffic before announcing their arrival to dispatch and joined Hartson in the street.

A pale woman approached, the sharp wrinkles at the corners of her eyes deepening with the effort it took to smile. On the far side of seventy, she twirled fingertips through a mat of gray hair that stood out from her head in a spray of snarls. Trembling hands lowered to pick at a small patch of lint on the faded legs of her polyester pants.

"I got home and found the den door's locked," she said. "I think my husband's in there, but he won't come out, and he won't answer when I knock." Her volume trailed off. "Ever since he retired, he just sits in there and broods. But he never locks the door. You don't think he could've hurt himself?"

Hartson stepped onto the curb and supported the woman by her elbow. "What's your name?" he asked as he led her toward the house.

As they walked through the door, Luke heard her answer. "Martha McGrath," she said. Then she commanded Max to his blanket.

It surprised Luke that Hartson stood only a few inches taller than the squat woman walking beside him. Hartson's orientation speech in the stadium's parking lot had communicated a no-nonsense training officer who would demand his trainee's best efforts. The confident performance had made Hartson seem bigger. His full head of wavy white hair, moving in unison with Martha McGrath's gray mane, could have been the opening of a vaudeville act. His pudgy body dominated his skinny legs, but his self-confidence drew attention away from the avuncular physical attributes. Luke had to get down to business before Hartson mistook him for a typical first phase trainee.

He pushed through a swinging wooden gate to the backyard to look for a way to see inside the den. Sun glared off the glass as he leaned toward the window. An orange tree pushed pointed shards of shadow into the room, obliterating some of the room's contents. Luke made out the back of a chair and a pair of trousers stretching from the seat onto a circular rug in front of a large desk. Squinting allowed him to see the butt of a rifle before his gaze moved upwards. Shadows obliterated everything above the seat of the chair.

Luke had seen enough to know this encounter with Martha McGrath wouldn't have a happy ending. "I think we need to kick the door in," he said as he walked into the house. "Can I have your permission to do that?"

Martha McGrath processed Luke's request, appearing to come to grips with its meaning. She closed her eyes and nodded, the muscles in her neck twitching noticeably.

Luke's boot splintered the door and exposed a super-heated den packed with the surreal sight of a partially headless man and the sickening stench of heat and gore. Darts of pain pricked the base of his skull and settled behind his right ear. Shooting sensations turned into an iron fist that squeezed and twisted in his neck. He kneaded a growing knot with his fingers.

Hartson brushed past him looking every bit like a man on a rescue mission.

Luke couldn't let Hartson think of him as some punk trainee who needed coddling. A muscle jerked in his jaw. He fought the urge to bolt from the room as chunks of vomit spewed into his mouth. He swallowed hard.

Hartson pulled on Martha's elbow to turn and ease her from the room. "Is there somebody you'd like to call?" he asked.

Martha turned to Luke instead. "When I got home, his dog was standing right there, chewing on a piece of bone." She pointed toward the floor in the hall a little past where the shattered door used to stand.

Luke fought against his gagging reflex and reached for his radio. "It's an 11-44, self-inflicted," he said. "Notify the coroner and make sure they have the phone number."

The fist of pain at the back of Luke's head twisted and squeezed. As he headed toward the outside door to get the camera, he heard Martha's thready voice and turned to see her speaking into the telephone. "Son, your daddy's killed himself." Her legs gave way as she said it and she plopped in a heap to her knees, the telephone slipping from her hand.

Hartson lunged too late to stop her. He squatted close, rested his palm on her shuddering shoulder, lifted the phone and told her son to come home. "We'll take care of your mother until you get here," he said.

Martha kept talking; apparently unaware she'd already dropped the phone. "He's in the den and, oh, it's such a mess."

Luke stepped onto the welcome mat, sucked in a breath and looked up to the clouds punctuating the blank blue expanse of the sky. Then he remembered the box of cigars in his equipment bag. He needed one now. It couldn't smoke out the stink of the situation, but his roommate—a Viet Nam vet—had told him smoking cigars helped a little against the stench of heat and death.

Luke stepped over the forlorn dog stretched across the threshold as he reentered the house. Hartson kept Martha busy making coffee as Luke lit his White Owl and steeled his resolve to go back into the den for the photographs.

With the cigar smoke almost making him gag, Luke did what he always did in stressful moments. He searched his memory for something he'd read to reflect against his real life experiences.

Shakespeare's description of Macbeth's "weird sisters" stirring a pot in a dank cave matched the madness in McGrath's den. Luke puffed insistently on the cigar as he circled the chair, snapping photographs, his thoughts swirling in unison with his body's movements. The stench clung to his uniform and crawled up his nostrils. He remembered the witches' chanting as they circled round the spewing cauldron:

Round about the cauldron go;
In the poisn'd entrails throw . . .
Fillet of a fenny snake,
In the caldron boil and bake;

Without realizing it, he started muttering the words out loud.

For a charm of powerful trouble,
Like a hell-broth boil and bubble...

A noise behind Luke jerked him back to reality.

"Martha's son's here and wants to see his dad," Hartson told him. "I need you in the living room to keep him busy until the coroner gets here." Hartson shook his head. "And for Christ's sake, don't say any of your weird shit to him."

Luke crossed the hallway, wiping the rolling sweat from his mustache, his shoulders brushing the sides of the doorframe as he stepped into the living room. He awkwardly stretched his hand out for the introduction before sitting on a flower-printed sofa that rested beneath a faded Hudson Valley print.

"I should've known he'd do this," Phillip McGrath Jr. told Luke. "We actually didn't fight when he called me at work today."

Luke slid his department-issue notebook from his hip pocket, pulled a pen from his shirt and doodled, trying to find the words to engage the dead man's son while Hartson sat with the widow in the kitchen.

"Tell me about your father," he said. "What did he do for a living?"

A pause followed. "He was an engineer."

"What kind of engineer?"

"He worked at General Dynamics designing jet propulsion systems. He was a genius," McGrath said.

"How so?" Luke asked, hoping the topic would give McGrath a pleasant moment.

"He had seven patents to his credit," McGrath said, a tremor infusing his words. "But the company threatened to fire him if he insisted on keeping the profits. He hated himself for letting them get away with it. They kept all the money that should've made him rich in exchange for guaranteeing his job."

"Was he angry about not getting what he deserved?"

McGrath slumped into the couch. "It destroyed him. He wanted to buy a big house in La Jolla. Instead . . ."

"Instead of what?" Luke prompted.

"Instead of this." McGrath waved his arm to encompass the room and its contents. "He put all four of us kids through college and two of us through graduate school." McGrath's head and neck trembled.

"But our going to the best schools wasn't enough for him. He drove all of us until we hated him. Then he started in on his grandkids. That's when we stopped coming around to see Mom."

"Why do you suppose he did that?" Luke asked.

"He gave away his greatness thinking it guaranteed our success. And he hated himself for it. He retired last week and couldn't talk about anything but his worthless life."

Luke wanted to comfort this man whose father was doing the ugly imitation of the Headless Horseman in the other room and wondered what Hartson would advise. The answer came in an instant. Just do your job, he would say, and stay out of the way.

The sound of his call sign on the portable radio came as a relief, but its message did not. The coroner would be delayed.

Luke scoured the room, looking for some relief. The youthful face on the portrait of Phillip McGrath Senior looked identical to the sorrowful face of his son on the couch.

The hot room magnified the pain twisting at the base of Luke's skull and the intensity pushed his chin to his chest. He tried focusing his gaze on the throw rug under the coffee table. It matched the one in the den.

Luke wanted to scream, get me out of here!

He doodled in his notebook. He wanted to drive the freeway with the windows open, to snort fresh air into his lungs. The next radio call had to be better than this one, but he found himself stuck in this suffocating house waiting for the coroner who wouldn't show for more than an hour.

His doodles turned into words as he wrote a note and put quotation marks around it.

"*What's done cannot be undone.*"

Lady Macbeth was right about that.

3

TOM PLANTMAN SETTLED INTO THE RED LEATHER BOOTH at Bully's Steak House. He sucked his gut in, gazed at the velvet portraits of naked women above the heads of the two men across the booth, lit a match, and sucked hard against the end of his Macanudo cigar. He jabbed the ashes forward, each movement punctuating his point as he pushed the burning cigar tip closer to the chest of the man sitting opposite him.

Charles Henreid lifted his elbows from the table and pulled back into the booth. His crew cut carried the colors of coarse ground pepper. The gray flecks at his temples gave the illusion of wisdom, but the pronounced cheekbones that started where his sideburns ended and narrowed into a thin chin, created the noticeable contradiction of projected strength and weakness at the same time. It was the eyes that broke the tie and gave away Henreid's vulnerability.

"I'm not a guy who sells generic information," Plantman said. "Larry there'll tell you, that's not who I am." He nodded toward the beaver-toothed man who'd set up the meeting. "I'm a silent partner in a few racehorses who's just trying to take care of his family." Plantman settled back into the booth. "We've got a horse going today that can make us some serious money."

White wisps of smoke formed into exclamation points above Plantman's fingers as he poked the cigar forward. "We both win in this situation. You pay me the five hundred and bet as much cash as you can get your hands on." He took a puff and mirrored Henreid's posture.

He thought his injured horse would hold up for one race, but Henreid's five hundred, combined with the fifteen hundred he got from the three other guys would cover his own action. "Look. It's up to you. I'll only say this once. You can ignore the posted workouts and today's field is as weak as they come. Our horse'll go gate to wire at a good price."

"I don't have that kind of cash handy," Henreid said. "Why can't your share come out of my winnings?"

"Larry here says you could use a break, which is why I had him call you." Plantman pushed his glasses over the bridge of his nose. "I believe him when he says to trust you, but I got to look out for myself too. I'll end up with nothing to show for the work we've put into the horse if something happens. Besides, you know as well as me, whatever money you put down lowers my odds."

Henreid leaned forward.

Plantman dragged on the cigar, blowing a cloud into the cleavage of the waitress who leaned across the booth and poured another frosted Michelob into a sweaty mug. He found a direct view into Henreid's eyes.

Henreid would be back with the money.

4

HENREID TOSSED HIS NAVY BLAZER ONTO A NOTEBOOK with material about how to get rich on the real estate boom and pushed them across the bench seat of his half-ton pickup. There was an hour until the race, just enough time to withdraw the money for Plantman, get the name of the winning horse and make the bet that would give him his life back. But what if the horse lost? Losing that kind of money would destroy him.

He made up his mind. He wouldn't do it.

Still, what could it hurt to have the cash handy just in case?

No, placing the bet would turn him into a gambler again. How could he justify that? The solution turned out to be simple. He quit trying. This was an insider business decision. It was investing, not gambling.

Henreid parked beneath a towering palm. The pungent scent of ocean breezes hung strong in the air as he pulled open the glass door of the San Diego Trust and Savings Bank.

A series of bounced checks had prompted the bank to close his accounts, but he had a plan to come up with the cash. He handed over his MasterCard and asked for an advance.

"I'm sorry." The teller shifted nervously on spiked heels behind the counter. "It looks like you're at your limit." She fumbled with a pen and looked at the clock on the wall.

Henreid pulled his VISA Gold Card from his lizard-skin wallet and flipped it onto the counter. "There should be a couple grand available on this," he said as he twisted his wallet against the parquet counter. "Let's try for twenty-five hundred."

The teller disappeared into an inner office.

Henreid leaned against the counter with an unperturbed expression on his face and a pounding in his temples.

The teller reappeared a few minutes later and reached for the drawer. The smile playing across her lips relieved the tension for both of them. "Would you like large bills for this?"

"Large bills would be great." Henreid put the money in his pants pocket and pivoted on his heel.

He looked at his cowboy boots and pulled in a relieved breath as he stepped into the sunshine. His final credit card was now maxed out and he was on the verge of losing his business, but everything would be different after he put the two thousand down on a sure thing. The winnings would make everything wrong in his life right again.

He pulled the Chevy pickup into the valet parking area at the racetrack and handed his keys to the attendant with a five-dollar bill for parking. The crashing of the waves a couple furlongs to the west would've been audible on a quieter afternoon, but this was the middle of a seven-week meet at the Del Mar Thoroughbred Club, the place "Where the Turf Meets the Surf."

It was "Heaven by the Pacific" and had been since Bing Crosby and Pat O'Brien had founded it in 1937. According to legend, Bing and Bob Hope had come up with the road picture idea while clowning in the paddock between races.

Now, it was the place where Henreid would put his life back together.

The announcer introduced the horses with information about the owners, trainers and jockeys as mini-skirted women with manicured hands clutched shiny purses and ogled the thoroughbreds coming out for the post parade. The crowd of impeccably dressed socialites who needed to be seen, serious horse players, and the let's-go-to-the-races-one-day-a-year variety, had one thing in common. They all took the time to gaze at the photographs of Dorothy Lamour, W.C. Fields, Paulette Goddard, Edgar Bergen, Ann Miller and Don Ameche. The movie stars were denizens of the past and harbingers of the future.

The loud speaker boomed Bing Crosby's version of the Del Mar anthem as Henreid pushed his way toward the turf club.

He handed Plantman the five hundred dollars, learned that his horse's name was Wage Earner and muscled his way through the throng. He stepped up to the cashier at the large transaction window, heard the loudspeaker announce, "The horses are approaching the starting gate," and handed the cashier the last of his money. "Give me two-thousand to win on the eight-horse," he said.

The tote board flashed seven-to-one odds on Plantman's sure thing as the gates opened. The two horses vying for the lead with Wage Earner clipped heels rounding the first turn, giving the eight-horse an uncontested advantage as the rest of the field ducked in toward the rail or veered wide to avoid the trouble.

Perched on the concrete brim running along the base of the rail a few feet from the track, Henreid could feel the surging power of the speeding eight-horse as it ran by, its chest heaving and its hooves thundering into the dirt, each stride accompanied by a magnificent grunt. His chest pulsed with a thunderous pounding of its own as Wage Earner widened her lead to six lengths as she ran past.

The hot wash of the sweltering Santa Ana winds seemed to whip through the billowing manes of the other horses as they desperately tried running down the horse that would make Henreid's life right again. He tasted the salt in the air and could almost feel the pockets of his Van Heusens swell, momentarily forgetting that the $16,000 represented a pittance compared to what he'd already lost. He'd split the payoff between his late mortgage payments and his maxed out credit cards.

His reverie shattered as the crowd gasped.

"No!" Henreid shouted.

The right foreleg of the eight-horse had collapsed, sending her tumbling and rolling over the thrown jockey who lay in a heap on the track. Wage Earner was in a tangle, her leg splayed in the air like a turkey wishbone on a Thanksgiving platter.

"No!" The cry imploded in an internalized scream this time, a wail against the lost money and against being sucked into gambling again. The blood rushing to his head deafened him. He shredded his tickets and tossed them into the wind, his chance to start over as dead as Wage Earner would be when the vet administered the lethal injection. Adrenaline pounded his system and blood rushed through his brain, making his eyesight a red haze of confusion as he stumbled through the turnstile.

"You are such an asshole," he said to himself, more worried for the moment about the five-dollars he'd blown on the valet service than about the cash advance he couldn't repay.

Tipsters waved multi-colored selection sheets that promised future winners as Bing Crosby's voice crooned the Del Mar Anthem's lyrics over the loud speaker again. Henreid spit on the ground. "Fuck you Bing," he mumbled and climbed behind the wheel. The truck's tires pushed out a billowing cloud of dust and gravel in their wake.

Henreid pushed through the door of a liquor store on Camino Del Mar a few minutes later and snatched a pint bottle from the shelf. While the clerk busied herself with customers, Henreid stuffed the bottle under his jacket and walked out the door. It was the first time he'd ever stolen anything, but he had no money and he needed a drink.

He twisted the top off, tipped the Jack Daniels to his lips and stomped on the accelerator. The front bumper scraped pavement as he pulled into the street and lowered the electric windows.

For a fleeting instant he understood that nobody else carried the blame for destroying his life and swore to work hard and quit betting forever. Rational thoughts quickly got swallowed up by his growing hatred for Tom Plantman though, the man who'd seduced him into gambling again and taken his money from his pockets. "Damn, damn,

damn." The obsessive damns turned into a resounding mantra as Henreid sped south on Interstate 5 toward downtown San Diego.

He turned on the radio.

Rod Stewart's "Maggie May" faded away on station KCBQ as the talent's mellifluous voice launched into a familiar sign-off. "Rod Paige here, glad to have spent this time with you right here in beautiful San Diego, our very own Camelot by the Sea, old friend." The "old friend" dragged out in a long drawl that intermixed with Bing's crooning and Henreid's obsessive round robin of thoughts. *Get your hands on some cash, you can win tomorrow, you can win tomorrow and everything will be all right where the turf meets the surf in Camelot by the Sea, old friend.*

Flashing blue and red lights in his rear-view mirror interrupted Henreid's mantra. He pulled to the freeway shoulder a few hundred yards from the exit that led to the heart of downtown San Diego and squeezed the wheel as one police officer eased his way toward the driver's window and another took up position outside the front passenger door.

"May I see your driver's license and registration, sir?" the officer asked.

Henreid fumbled in his wallet for the license before plunging his fist into the glove compartment for the expired registration. A few months before, he'd stopped at the track on his way to mail a check to the DMV and threw it in the trash can along with the three losing tickets.

"Sir, are you aware that this registration has expired?"

Of course Henreid was aware, and wasn't that a stupid fucking question anyway? Yes, he knew it was expired and this arrogant bastard knew that he knew it. "Really? I didn't get any notice in the mail," Henreid said.

"Would you step out of the truck please, Mr. Henreid? Walk over there." The officer nodded toward the bank of ice plant near where the other officer stood. "Away from traffic please."

"Mr. Henreid, we intend to put you through a series of field sobriety tests. If you fail the tests, we'll place you under arrest. Please pay close attention to everything I say because part of what we're evaluating is your ability to comprehend and follow instructions. Do you understand?"

Henreid understood, or at least he thought he did. The instructions were simple enough, even if they were delivered by this highfalutin' son of a bitch who stood like he had a stick shoved up his ass.

"Mr. Henreid, I need you to count from seventy-five to fifty-five backwards. Begin now, please."

"Seventy-five, seventy-four, seventy-three, seventy, sixty-nine, sixty-eight," Henreid continued counting with no more mistakes. This was easy. "Fifty-five, fifty-four, fifth-three, fifty-two . . . how far did you say to count?" Henreid asked.

Luke Jones flipped a page in his notebook and started writing. He kept up the tests until Henreid stumbled against the police car while trying to balance on one leg. "Mr. Henreid, that's enough. Please put your hands behind your back with your palms together. You're under arrest for section 23102(a) of the California Vehicle Code, driving on a public highway while under the influence of an alcoholic beverage."

Hartson told Luke to handcuff their prisoner and escort him to the back seat of the police car.

Henreid watched from behind the cage as Hartson directed Luke to search the truck. Luke snatched the passenger door open, leaned across the length of the bench seat, put a knee on the floorboard and looked under the driver's area. That was where he found the mostly empty bottle of Jack Daniels.

Then Hartson directed Luke to call for a tow rig, to start filling out the tow report and to give the plate information to dispatch to check for wants and warrants.

The dispatcher's response resonated throughout the car a little later. Eight hundred dollars worth of warrants for failure to pay parking tickets waited at the Marshal's Office.

Luke handed the truck driver the tow slip just before the two officers piled into the car.

After they picked up the warrants Hartson eased the patrol car into the front lot of the police station as Henreid made up his mind. And this time he meant it. He'd go back to Gamon for sure and put his life back together, just like he'd done it before. He knew his screwed up life was entirely his fault.

Then he examined the real reasons for his predicament. First there was Plantman and then these two cops who thought they had the right to poke around in his truck and throw him in jail. They were why his life was all fucked up. No—not really—it was his fault.

He remembered the first time he'd stood in front of a group at a GA meeting, clutching the back of a hand-carved pew, forcing a smile. "My name's Charles Henreid and I'm a compulsive gambler."

A chorus rang out around him, "Hello Charles."

"This is my first time admitting I have a problem."

A new chorus of the voices of informed understanding sounded exactly like the holy-roller congregation of his childhood church, the ones that shouted Amen to the preacher's hell-fire and brimstone sermons.

"Sometimes it feels like killing myself is the only way to get control of my life back."

He was struck by how much this crowd understood and accepted his helplessness. They actually cared about him and listened to what he had to say.

Henreid was jerked back to the present when Luke started asking him the personal questions for the report top sheets while Hartson disappeared into an office near the front of the car. But Henreid had a few questions of his own. "What'll happen to my truck?" he asked.

"It'll be impounded," Luke said.

"How can I get it back?"

"I don't think you can get it out until you pay the parking fines and there'll be impound and storage fees tacked on," Luke said.

"I can't afford to pay. You're taking my livelihood away?"

"I don't know what to tell you," Luke said. "I don't have any choice."

"Mr. Henreid," Hartson said as he eased back on to the driver's seat. "You need to submit to a chemical test. The test can be of your blood, breath or urine. You have the right to choose which test, but not to refuse to take a test. If you do refuse, you'll go to jail and your driver's license will be suspended. Which test would you like to take?"

"Whatever. What difference does it make?" Henreid asked in disgust.

"Obviously, you have to pee in a bottle for a urine test and someone will stick a needle in your arm for the blood test," Hartson said. "Either test would have to be analyzed by the lab in the next day or two. The breath test isn't intrusive and you get the results right away."

"Can I think about it for a while," Henreid asked.

"We have reports to write," Hartson said. "We can wait a little before we book you, but the longer it takes to decide, the higher your blood alcohol level will go since you just stopped drinking a little while ago."

Henreid blew an exasperated sigh, pushing a cloudy fog against the window. "Breath," he said.

Then he blew a .18.

Once at the jail, Hartson held his palm over Henreid's head, protecting it from the top of the doorway as he slid out onto the concrete of the sally port. Henreid heard a loud click. A metal door slid open and the trio walked into the jail where Luke searched the prisoner for weapons one last time.

A second click reverberated. A grated door opened and Henreid stepped into a holding tank where a dozen other prisoners drooped lazily on the bolted metal benches or lay on the floor as far from the single toilet as possible.

As the heavy door slammed shut, leaving Henreid surrounded by hardened criminals and disheveled drunks he swore a silent oath never to do this to himself again. He'd decided to accept responsibility for his own predicament.

5

"OH, OH, OOOH, OOOOOOOH, OOH, MY GAWD..." Denny Durango's love-efforts generated a breathtaking moon-howl. It started deep inside the quivering belly of the woman writhing underneath him and scrambled out her pouting lips to echo throughout the lengthy hallways of the three-story apartment building.

Denny glanced at his Seiko runner's watch and let out a yelp as the moan subsided. He disengaged abruptly and rushed into the shower. "Let yourself out," he shouted above the sound of the water sputtering from the spigot. "I'm late for work."

Steamy water mixed with the creamy Dove soap that rolled along his legs, washing the sexual juices down the drain.

Once dressed, he slipped the badge pin into its clasp at the breast of the shirt. Putting on his uniform ranked right up there with an orgasm. "God!" he said into the mirror, watching his lips pucker as he formed the words, "I love being a pooooliceman."

His lean body resembled a bamboo shoot. A Boston Blackie mustache rode under his aquiline nose, and his four-inch afro looked like the bristles of a barbecue brush. As he formed his words into the mirror's reflection, he recalled his triumphant phone call to his mother in New York City to tell her he'd been hired and he smiled at the memory of her jubilant response.

He exulted in the prestige the uniform brought to a former street urchin who'd grown up prowling the alleys and rooftops of Bedford-Stuyvesant. He snatched a windbreaker to cover his shirt and bounded for the door. He'd find a locker when he got to the station.

He knew he faced a harrowing day, that every training shift loomed as dangerous as a La Salsa dance along the edges of a second story disco floor with the railing missing. If he didn't watch his step, his career would last about as long as a Donna Summer song.

Among those who'd graduated from the 89th San Diego Police Academy, Denny's test scores ranked dead last. But he took pride in knowing he stood out from the thirty-seven classmates who'd washed out during the six-month academy. Luke Jones, his up-tight bookworm of a roommate, had promised to keep tutoring him in report writing and Denny knew he'd be good enough at the paper work to survive by the time he finished his field training. He could really strut his stuff then.

He didn't know books, but he knew the streets. He could handle people. He could handle himself, and he exuded confidence as he scooted into the lineup room looking for the name tag of J.R. Shimmer. He found his man, extended his hand and announced, "I'm your new trainee, sir."

Shimmer stuck out his hand. "Don't sir me. I hate that shit. Sit over in the corner and we'll talk after."

6

THE THUD AND WHIRR OF MECHANICS' TOOLS surrounded Denny and Shimmer as they carried their equipment through the fleet garage. Denny surveyed Shimmer's hair from behind. It looked like Floyd from "The Andy Griffith Show" had cut it since it had the odd angles of a haircut from a shop where conversation was more important than how you looked when you got done.

Denny trotted up beside Shimmer. "Can I ax you a question?" he said.

Shimmer grunted his assent.

"Why do you go by your initials? Seems like a lot of you senior guys do it."

Shimmer's voice thundered above the noise of an electric air gun. "Yellow sheets say I got to wear a name tag. They don't say anything about using my full name. It's all this Community Oriented Policing crap. Brings us closer to John Q. Citizen the brass says. Bullshit! Brings us closer to the hairballs and assholes if you ask me."

Shimmer lifted his equipment bag toward a Ford van fitted out as an ambulance. "Ambulances are stupid. They should be run out of the fire department." He dropped his bag to the pavement, reached into his pocket, opened his nail clippers and slowly ran the file beneath dirty fingernails. "There's two assholes on this squad who actually like this thing, but you and me get assigned instead. That's how things work around here."

Denny gave a slight smile. "I kind of like the ambulance," he said. "I was a corpsman in Nam before they made me a dental technician. The experience might help. Besides, I won't have to write too many reports." There it was—he laid it out up front. His report writing stunk.

"Jesus H—a REMF." Shimmer spit out REMF like he'd spit out a wasp that flew into his mouth. "Like I need this. Babysitting some Rear Echelon Motherfucker who stayed in Saigon humping the gooks while I dodged bullets."

Shimmer looked like he was fighting for his composure and it looked like a daily exercise. "Always do a thorough job inspecting the equipment," he said. "It's bullshit when we got to come back to the garage because some lazy bastard didn't replenish our supplies."

Denny checked the splints, oxygen bottles, and plastic containers of saline solution, blankets and other first aid equipment while Shimmer settled into the driver's seat and went to work on his nails again.

"Hurry up and put us 10-8," Shimmer said as he stuck his clippers back into his pocket.

Denny hurried the inventory.

"Sit your ass down and put us 10-8," Shimmer insisted. "You can bet your REMF ass the dispatcher's itching to give us a call."

Shimmer was right. The dispatcher assigned their first call immediately after Denny announced their availability. "Unit 4-Frank, 11-41 at the Monroe Hotel, six hundred block of 5th Avenue. The reporting party is the manager."

Two minutes later, the ambulance rounded the corner from Market Street onto Fifth Avenue and eased against the east curb, parking in the yellow loading zone. Shimmer pushed the gear shift into park and looked at Denny. "Where's the call?"

Denny hadn't jotted the information down. "I don't remember," he said.

"We might have a guy dying right now," Shimmer said. "Waiting for us to save his ass and we're sitting on our keisters inside this stupid ambulance. You don't even know where we're supposed to go, do you?"

Denny didn't think his FTO would be such an asshole.

"Well, where are we supposed to go to save this guy's life?"

Denny gazed at his shoes.

"Don't ever acknowledge a radio call without knowing where we're going and why," Shimmer said. After issuing the order, he pushed his door open and stepped into the street.

A stench as pungent as Limburger cheese permeated the hotel entryway. The walls hosted grimy hand prints and the once salmon-colored carpets lay littered with greasy McDonald's wrappers and cigarette butts. A man with a scruffy salt-and-pepper beard limped toward them, offering Shimmer his hand and looking like a good candidate to borrow Shimmer's nail clippers.

"I'm the manager, officer." He wheezed out his words while puffing his way up three narrow flights of stairs before stopping in front of a room and reaching for the keys on his belt. "I can smell him. I know he's in here." He spit his words out through teeth that clenched the butt of his cigarette. "Claims he's some kind of college professor or something. All I know is he's probably unconscious—again—and I'm tired of it. He's been like this more times than I can count. Drinks himself into oblivion and pisses his pants. Shits all over himself and lays in it until I find him. He drinks enough to kill most folks, but he don't have the decency to die."

"I can't get the damn door open." The manager turned the key and pushed against the door to prove his point. He leaned forward with his shoulder, put his weight onto his front knee and pushed hard. The smoking cigarette bounced against his thigh and fell to the floor as the door gave way.

Denny saw the stain-spotted legs of khaki pants and bare feet inch toward the center of the room as the manager grunted and heaved against the door.

Another two-officer unit with trainee and FTO arrived as Denny squeezed through the aperture. He squatted, dragged the man further into the room to allow the others in, and knelt, searching for and finding a slight pulse. Denny knuckled his fingers and grunted as he pressed into the sternum hard enough to lift himself from his haunches. The drunk didn't respond.

Pulling a Bic pen from his shirt pocket, Denny shoved it between the drunk's fingers and squeezed so hard that the hand folded into itself and turned purple. Denny squeezed until he couldn't stand the pain himself and the drunk still didn't move or even grunt. This stuff hurt. Live people responded to this shit. Denny checked again for a pulse and whooshed out a surprised, "Damn," when it verified that the drunk was still alive.

Shimmer reached for the ammonia capsule beneath the leather flap covering his speed loaders and squatted beside Denny. Ammonia fumes filled the room as he snapped the capsule. Denny grunted in astonishment as Shimmer ground the capsule hard above the drunk's upper lip without getting a reaction.

"Shit," Shimmer said. "This is one for the record books. There ain't no telling how long he's been like this neither." Shimmer's knee joint crackled as he stood and turned to face the manager. "His pants sure give out a clue though. That must be quite a package in there."

Glossy gun belts and shiny boot leather rasped and creaked as Denny and the other trainee stooped to pick the comatose drunk up from the floor and strap him to the gurney. Denny puffed his cheeks and sucked in his stomach as he cinched the clasp until he lost the battle to hold his breath and the rancid stench raced up his sinuses. "Daaaaamn, he smells like rotten human being leftovers," he said.

The two rookies lifted the gurney.

The Monroe had no elevators.

The second rookie set his end of the gurney on the landing as Denny hefted the drunk's full weight above his head, agonizing to keep it from falling. They twisted the gurney onto the top step of the next level of stairs and started downward again, repeating the process at the next landing, leaving them slathered in sweat and sucking air.

"The bitch is turning blue," Shimmer rasped. The angle on the landing had set the drunk's body to sliding downward, forcing the waist strap against his trachea. "He's choking," Shimmer hollered. "Give him mouth to mouth."

The collective order hovered in the air like a death sentence for one of the trainees.

Denny stared at the other trainee for what seemed like forever, hoping he'd follow the order. Nobody spoke, but the body language was unmistakable. The other rookie had no intention of stepping up to the plate. Precious milliseconds passed as the trainees stood, bug-eyed and desperate for an alternative.

Denny dropped his end and the hard rubber wheels bounced against the concrete landing. Squeezing his body between the gurney and the wall, he bolted down the stairs, ran along a concrete hallway and hurled his body against a metal fire door that flung outward, brushing the shirttail of an unsuspecting pedestrian on the sidewalk. "Sorry." Denny panted, fumbling for his keys as he ran to the ambulance. He crawled inside, retrieved the oxygen dispenser and scuttled out.

His lungs flamed and his chest ached as he balanced the oxygen equipment. The other officers huddled silently as he reappeared on the landing.

Denny hadn't stuck around long enough to see that loosening the strap against the drunk's throat had allowed him to breathe again. He slipped the oxygen mask over a splotched face and turned the knob.

The other officers howled like kids in the front row of a clown show. Shimmer looked like the laughter might send him to his knees and the others held their sides, their faces turning various shades of purple, actual tears streaming down their faces.

Denny gushed sweat onto the landing, his breathing coming rapid and wheezy.

He leaned against the gurney and Shimmer stood upright from his doubled up position. "Tonight, you'll be the first trainee in history to get a perfect mark in judgment," Shimmer announced between jags of laughter. "The FTO office says to never, ever give out a perfect score but, son, that looked perfect to me."

7

THE EMERGENCY ROOM HOUSED A BUNCH OF SOUR faces when the officers wheeled in their bundle of joy. Doctor Knupp, who was busy sewing facial sutures, lifted a beefy face covered with a beard the color of a russet potato. "Is that piece of work here again?" he said. "Take him up to University. Anywhere but here."

Shimmer showed his teeth in a mock grimace that he followed with a suppressed smile. "Sorry, Doc," he said. "Department policy says to transport to the nearest hospital and Centre is it. Can you imagine the ruckus up at University if we sashayed in there and filled out the log listing the Monroe as our pickup spot?" Shimmer paused. "I'll try to bring something nice next time."

Doctor Knupp told him to "eat shit" and turned back to his patient.

"Sorry, Doc, but I got to do what I got to do." The words trailed behind Shimmer into the emergency room as he stepped onto the electric door pad and the glass doors opened.

Denny piled into the ambulance and reached for the microphone. "Unit 4-Frank, 10-8." He hooked the microphone and turned toward Shimmer. "You notice I did that on my own?"

"Yeah," Shimmer said. "I did. And don't do it again. I wanted to go to Denny's for some key lime pie and a cup of coffee. There's things can only be done when you're out of service."

The next radio call came within seconds. "Unit 4-Frank, respond to an 11-8 female, north side of five hundred Market."

Shimmer leaned across the space between the bucket seats, training his eyes on Denny's. "I want my pie and now I can't have it, thanks to you." He pulled the gear shift down and punched the accelerator.

Somebody lay prostrate on the sidewalk all right, but it was not a female. "Hey Kimmy," Shimmer said as he squatted next to a Vietnamese transvestite who had a line of sweat trailing down his cheek. "What the fuck happened to you?"

"Some John shot me for my money."

"I got to know more that that, but don't talk right now." Shimmer barked an order to Denny. "Fetch the gurney and get him ready for transport."

Denny turned Kimmy on his side to find three bullet holes and blood oozing through a white silk blouse. He sliced the taffeta fringe, running the blunt side of a scissor blade against Kimmy's side. Denny ripped the material away from the skin and poured a stream of saline solution over the wounds.

Kimmy's eyelids shuddered and his breathing got shallow. "Stop all the bullshit," Shimmer snapped. "Plug the holes and let's go."

Denny grabbed a fistful of gauze to force against the wounds and they lifted Kimmy onto the gurney. As the wheels snapped into place, Shimmer squatted to scoop up a wallet.

Shimmer tossed the wallet onto the dash, pushed the overhead light switch, turned the siren knob to wail and pulled away from the curb.

On the console rested two radio transmitters, the police radio connected to Station "A" and a second one connected to Station X, emergency medical services for the County of San Diego. Shimmer reached for the one on the right. "Station X," he said. "Unit 4-Frank is making code three 11-41 for a male with multiple gunshot wounds. Subject's unconscious and approximately twenty-one years old. Our ETA is three to four."

The Station X operator relayed the message to Centre City ER and patched them through for a direct conversation. "Centre City," Shimmer said into the microphone, "this is unit 4-Frank. We'll be 10-97 in less than one."

Shimmer shut the siren down as he skidded to a stop near the emergency room.

Dr. Knupp ran out, his shouts jerking with an uneven staccato rhythm. "Shit, Kimmy, what happened to you this time?" He grabbed the gurney and raised it in one motion, with a glare in Shimmer's direction. "This is what you call bringing me something nice?"

"No time to clean the blood," Knupp said as he jerked the curtain along its tracks. He cut Kimmy's abdomen with a scalpel and inserted a tube to siphon the blood. A blonde lab tech hurried beside him, set the intravenous apparatus next to the gurney and re-circulated Kimmy's blood into his body to keep him from bleeding to death.

A second technician propped Kimmy up on his side long enough to snap the oblique X-rays before rushing him into the operating room and closing the doors.

"Now's a good time to catch up on the journal and write the report on the ambulance transport," Shimmer told Denny.

Denny started the simple reports as Shimmer grabbed the phone in the officer's lounge and dialed. He tapped his fingers against the Formica counter, crooked the phone against his neck and started singing Blue Suede Shoes when someone had obviously put him on hold.

Shimmer leaned over, stretched the cord under Denny's nose, pulled a Styrofoam cup from the drawer under the coffee maker and started pouring coffee. "This could turn into a 187, boss," he said when the Watch Commander came on the line. "We had to scoot without preserving anything. Can you send a unit to rope off the crime scene and one to secure where we picked him up?"

If Kimmy died, a Homicide team would roll and 4-Frank's work would be done except for a quick One-Five-Three report about their conversation with the victim and how they found the wallet. A mound of work waited if Kimmy lived.

The officers sat stuck at the hospital. They couldn't go back in service until Kimmy either died or was stabilized enough for a real interview. Shimmer placed a few calls: to his wife, to his girlfriend, and to his poker partners to say he'd miss the weekly game if Kimmy lived.

Then he turned to Denny's reports. "You won't ever write easier reports than these two," he said. "And you screwed them both up."

Denny screwed his lips up into an expression of contrition.

"Holy fuck! I'm in for a long month!" Shimmer said as he suffered through the re-writes more than an hour later. He shook his head and glared at Denny as his head hinged back and forth, making sure Denny didn't doubt his disappointment.

"Fucking REMF," Shimmer said.

8

ONE PROPERLY COMPLETED REPORT, and two hours later, the nurse with a phalanx of red Medusa hair poked her face around the corner. "Kimmy's going to make it," she told Shimmer. "But he's lost a lot of blood." Her face disappeared and her footfall started to sound distant. The footfall stopped, followed by the sound of shoes against the linoleum coming toward the lounge before the nurse stuck her head into the room again. "Oh, by the way, that alleged human being you brought us from the Monroe? He'll make it too."

Denny marched into recovery behind Shimmer and listened from the foot of the bed. "Tell me what happened so I can get this bastard," Shimmer said.

"Will I have scars, J.R.?"

"The guy who shot you, tell me about him."

"I picked him up at the Chee Chee Club. He was cute. I might've done him for free, but I asked for money first. 'I'll give you a blowjob for fifty bucks' I told him and he said, 'Okay'. He didn't want a room, so we did it in the spot behind the Dumpster where you caught me last week?"

Shimmer nodded.

"He pushed his pants around his ankles and said, 'Go on ahead,' and started laughing. He thought he was funny. So, I took care of business." Kimmy nodded to Denny, almost apologetically, "If you know what I mean?"

"I know what you mean," Denny assured him.

"I knew he had a wad of money," Kimmy went on. "So I lifted his wallet while I was down there. He pulled out this little gun, which I thought was a toy and told me he wants my money. He's going to rob me with a little gun and he don't even know I have his wallet."

Shimmer exaggerated a whistle. "This is a bucket of worms. You got any idea how much work we just fell into? Tell me what we got here, what kind of crimes?"

"A whore deal and an attempted robbery," Denny said.

Shimmer tisked several times. "It's a lot more than that. First, let's talk about Kimmy. We got a 647 (b) for soliciting prostitution in a public place, and then he did the deed. Meets either test for that section. We got a 56.19 because he's in drag when he does it, then we got a 487.2, grand theft from a person, when he lifts the wallet. You with me so far?"

Denny nodded.

"On the trick's side, we got the same 647 (b), then we got a 12025 and a 12031 for the concealed and loaded gun. We also got an attempt 211 and a 217 because he tried to rob him and he tried to kill him."

Shimmer waited, apparently wanting the impact to sink in.

"Worst part is we got the other puke's wallet out in the ambulance so we have to go arrest him."

"You think I'm a puke?" Kimmy asked.

Shimmer rolled his eyes.

9

SHIMMER POUNDED ON THE SCREEN DOOR of an impeccably painted
California cottage. "Mr. Mortensen, I've got your wallet," Shimmer pronounced as the occupant stood from his fancy leather lounge chair and
ambled toward the doorway. "Found it down on Market Street. Funny
thing is there's a lot of money in it. Hard to imagine nobody took your
cash. Can I come inside and talk a minute?"

"Sure, come on in officer," Mortensen smiled with a chiseled face
that sported an immaculately trimmed goatee. It seemed he'd met this
attractive young lady at the Chee Chee Club, bought her a drink and
only noticed his wallet missing after he got home.

"Funny thing though," Shimmer said.

"What's that?"

"You meeting this honey at the Chee Chee. Drag queens and hus-
tlers hang out there. You didn't know that?" Shimmer asked.

"Are you sure?"

"You have any pets, Mr. Mortensen?"

"No. Why do you ask?"

"Just wanted to know if we needed to make any special arrange-
ments before I throw your ass in jail's all," Shimmer said. "Now let me
tell you what I know that you don't think I know, dummy."

Shimmer laid out the scenario. "There's good news, though." He
waited for Mortensen to ask the obvious question.

"You get to be listed as a victim for the grand theft," Shimmer went on. "Ain't that nice? Oh, by the way. You have the right to remain silent. If you give up the right to remain silent, anything you say can, and will be used against you in a court of law. You have the right to an attorney and to have the attorney present during questioning. If you so desire and cannot afford one, an attorney will be appointed for you without charge before questioning.

"Do you understand each of these rights I've explained to you?"

Mortensen nodded.

"I need you to answer yes or no, Mr. Mortensen."

"I understand."

"Having in mind and understanding your rights, are you willing to speak with me?"

"Yes," Mortensen answered.

"Good," Shimmer said. "Now, show me the fucking gun."

After retrieving the .22 from under Mortensen's bed, Shimmer called for a reserve unit to take their prisoner to jail. He handed the driver the booking slip and waved to Mortensen. Then he turned to Denny.

"Now, my REMF friend," he said. "You get to write a case report on the attempted robbery and attempted murder listing Kimmy as the victim. Then you write a case report listing Mortensen as the victim of a grand theft person. Next, there's the arrest report for Mortensen listing the prostitution caper and the shooting. Then there's the notify warrant requesting that Kimmy be issued a summons for lifting the john's wallet and you have to impound Kimmy's clothes. If you ever finish that, I'll be near dead of old age and you'll either be turning into a real cop or just a little closer to getting fired. Care to make any bets on which it'll be?"

10

LUKE AND DENNY PUSHED THROUGH THE DOOR of the One-Five-Three Club across the street from the police station. The bar's name came from a police catchall form with mostly blank lines that functioned primarily as a continuation for narratives from other report forms like arrests or crime cases. It was also the form officers used to document their actions when they were either being investigated as the result of a citizen's complaint or for internal probes initiated by someone further up the chain of command. Their supervisors almost invariably began the investigations by calling them in from the field and uttering the infamous words, "Give me a One-Five-Three about what happened."

In point of fact, "Give me a One-Five-Three about that incident the other night in the One-Five-Three Club" was a phrase officers heard altogether too often. So much so, that the watering hole's name had become a double entendre appreciated by nearly everyone who walked through the swinging doors of the dusty dump that was the opposite of everything the word "club" implied.

A busty redhead with amber eyes, spiked heels and skin-hugging Jordache jeans sat astride a stool near the end of the bar. She turned toward the entrance to check out the arriving talent and it looked to Luke like she fixed her gaze on his crotch before moving it up his torso. The enameled fingernails tapping against the bar, together with her cooing sing-along to Willie Nelson on the jukebox definitely advertised her availability.

Although he'd never really believed them, Luke knew the stories about cop groupies who thrived on copulating with cops, and this woman's attention seemed headed in his direction. But she couldn't be interested in him.

Luke wore snug nylon uniform pants and his XX T-shirt strained to contain his muscles. He ordered a club soda for himself and a Coors for Denny.

The groupie followed his movements. At least it seemed like she did. Luke's internal mirror still reflected back Moochie, the younger pudgy victim of his older brother's vicious attacks when they were kids.

Whenever girls came around, Tuffy had marshaled a gaggle together to surround Luke while they hissed epithets of hatred at the fat kid who stood with tears streaming down his cheeks and his eyes trained on his shoes. Tuffy would tweak Luke's ears, pinch his rolling belly and shout out the nickname he used when he was at his most vicious. "Moochie! Pull that shirt up and show us your fat."

The invitation signaled the others to yank Luke's shirt tail out, push him to the ground and join in the vicious pinching and kneading of his corpulent flesh while Luke clawed desperately, dug his heels into the dirt and pleaded for help.

The fairer sex always declined Tuffy's invitations to join in, but stood wide-eyed and giggly as Luke writhed on the ground, hating himself, hating his tormentors and hating the girls who watched in silence.

In the years since, he'd channeled his anger into pushups, stopping only when his muscles reached utter exhaustion. He started over again as soon as he could, his burning muscles an anesthetic for his pent-up anger.

He pounded out more than a thousand pushups a day and aimed his frustrations at his wrestling opponents. The muscle-numbing, body-exhausting, head-pounding matches forged a partial outlet for his seething rage.

"What a scum sucking bag of shit."

Luke heard the words coming from behind him. "Say Luke, what would your Mr. Shakespeare say about that asshole?"

Hearing the hint of camaraderie in Hartson's invitation to discuss the Bard was a surprise.

"What?" Luke asked.

"How would Shakespeare describe Biletnikoff?"

"I don't really know Biletnikoff."

"Humor me. If Shakespeare really hated some bastard the way we hate the Sarge, what would he say?"

Luke thought for a moment. "He'd say something like,

'*...that bolting-hutch of beastliness, that swoln parcel of dropsies, that huge bombard of sack, that stuffed cloakbag of guts, that roasted Manningtree ox with the pudding in his belly, that reverend vice, that grey iniquity, that father ruffian, that vanity of years...* '"

"What'd he say?" The question came from J.R. Shimmer who'd emerged from the bathroom with a glass of beer in his hand.

Luke sized up the slight man with chestnut hair, a Charlie Chaplin mustache, blood-shot cheeks and a nose like W.C. Fields. It made him a dead-ringer for Bardolph, a comic character in several of Shakespeare's plays.

"What'd he say?" Shimmer asked again. "What the fuck did he say?"

"Shut up and you might learn something," the groupie barked. Luke trained his marbled green eyes on Shimmer.

"My training officer asked for a Shakespearean insult," Luke said.

"Huh?" Shimmer asked. "What?"

"Never mind him," Hartson said to Luke. "Where'd you learn that shit anyway?"

"Books."

"I heard about you," Shimmer chimed in. "You used to stand on tables at the academy and quote poetry. What are you, some kind of faggot or something?"

"Well, my dear diminutive Bardolph," Luke said, "I'm an occasional pedagogue who chooses his words deliberately for the sole purpose of ameliorating the lives of others." Luke had developed his vocabulary with the same anger he'd utilized to develop his body. For years, he'd written every new word he encountered in his personal dictionary and added it to his arsenal against bullies. He pounded his words at Shimmer's ego like a billy club.

"What'd he say?" Shimmer looked around for help. "Will somebody tell me what the fuck he's talking about?"

"What'd you say, Luke?" Denny asked. "Tell him what you said."

Luke didn't know Shimmer was Denny's training officer and he wasn't giving Denny the chance to tell him. Luke certainly didn't know the little nebbish and he'd long since stopped taking guff from anybody. He craned his neck toward Shimmer and jutted his jaw forward, pouting his lips and enunciating every syllable. "I said I was being pedagogical."

Shimmer leaped from his bar stool. "Yeah, well fuck you. Shimmer's speech was thick and slurred. "You trainees got no business in a cop bar anyways. All you trainees need to get the fuck out of here."

Hartson stepped between them. "My trainee can't fight you," he said. "They'd fire his ass, which I can't let happen. Besides, he'd snap you like a teeny little twig. Then there'd be this huge investigation for which everybody in here'd have to write a One-Five-Three, and all's we want is to have a few beers. So leave him alone."

Hartson motioned for Luke to join his entourage and introduced him around as the group gathered several tables together and sat in a haphazard enclave. Luke pulled a chair next to Hartson and waved for Denny to take the seat.

"I think I should go," Denny said.

"You're not leaving because of him," Luke said, more in the form of an order than a question. He'd driven Denny to work and knew his roomie had to stay.

"Francie," Hartson said as Denny perched on the seat next to Luke. "Tell these guys about the Black Panthers in the Imperial Valley."

Hartson nodded to a beer keg of a man who responded with a high-pitched voice and a hint of hilarity in every syllable he spoke. "Okay," Francie said, "this is back in the late sixties and I'm a reserve deputy working in the Imperial Valley. My partner and I hear this all-units broadcast out of Los Angeles about some Black Panthers who'd surrounded an LA Sheriff's transport unit, blown the deputies away, snatched their pals who were on their way to prison, and hauled ass.

"Dispatch says a guy saw them getting into a dark blue van with side windows. The driver's a black male, twenty years old, with an Afro.

"So, three, maybe four hours go by and we're in the middle of the desert. We see this blue van with a driver who has an Afro and it's heading right for us. There were no black guys in the valley back then and enough time has passed for a drive from LA so we know this is the vehicle. The Panthers are armed with automatic weapons and have already blown two deputies away, so we're scared shitless. Some cars are following close to the van as it blows past so we're a few cars behind when we make our U-turn. We got time to make a plan, but we're the only unit for miles, so what the fuck are we going to do?"

The group shrugged collectively.

Francie continued, seemingly encouraged by the feedback and the roundness of the sweating Coors in his hand. "Out there, you call for help and CHP responds, Border Patrol comes, everybody, because nobody's close. We know nobody's around. We've got nothing but our piss-ant thirty-eights and figure we're dead meat.

"Anyways, there are four cars between us and what we're convinced is certain death. A few miles ahead is this humungous billboard at a traffic signal, so we have dispatch tell our cover units to stage behind it, thinking maybe we can surprise these assholes and live to tell about it.

"So, units from around the desert are scrambling for heavy weapons to save our asses. As we're driving along, one car in front turns off the highway. Now we're even closer to getting blown away, praying these guys don't pull over and take us on or we might as well eat our guns and save them the trouble. Then another car pulls off in front and there's only one car between us and the van so we're about to shit our pants."

Francie's congregation hoisted their glasses and drank in rhythmic unison with his lyrical delivery.

"We finally see the billboard in the distance and know we've got help waiting, but by now we're right behind the fucking van that reaches the intersection just as the light switches to red. Cops start crawling around the van like Japs at a two-for-one film sale. One guy flings the back doors open and falls out of the line of fire as other guys shove in their shotguns. There're officers at both windows and a dozen others surrounding the van and one of them has the barrel of a twelve-gauge screwed into the driver's ear. I mean to tell you, the dude's scared shitless.

"Problem is, it turns out he's just a kid with his girlfriend napping in the back who wakes up to a shotgun in her face. They're just driving to Phoenix, minding their own business.

"Our sergeant walks up, takes his sunglasses off and wipes them with a rag. Then he says to the guy, 'Son, you've got yourself a tail light out, and down in this here Imperial Valley, we take them things kind of serious."

Hartson dispatched Luke on a rookie's mission as the laughter resounded and Francie accepted a salute of clinking beer bottles for his story-telling ability. "You can buy the next round," Hartson said.

"I'm honored to provide the eleemosynary service," Luke responded.

"What the fuck did he say?" Shimmer implored from his stool near the end of the bar.

Everybody at the tables shrugged.

Luke sized up the One-Five-Three Club as he waited for the drinks. A musty odor pervaded and the lighting was low. The club had three rooms, including the small kitchen behind the bar. The back room housed two pinball machines and the front one held the busy pool table that stood surrounded by a few rickety booths and some tables. Cobwebs hung from the corners of the ceiling. The club exuded a nearly mystical simplicity, making it the perfect spot for cops to regale one another with their tales of the exotic and the bizarre.

Luke put the beers on a tray and returned to hear more stories of mayhem and hilarity. Every tale represented a sermon without a moral and the One-Five-Three Club was the church of the non-sequitur. Everybody inside held status as an eager member or a prospective parishioner.

"I'm stuck in Balboa Park on graveyard," Paul Devree started out. Devree, who sat directly opposite Luke, sported a sallow complexion and collar-length hair the color of shucked corn.

This started to become fun for Luke as he took slow sips of his club soda and sized Devree up. He constantly pushed his hair off his forehead and cocked his head to one side every few minutes, accompanying the movement with a quizzical expression like a German shepherd begging for a biscuit.

"I decide to go out on foot and see what's happening in the canyons and around the Fruit Loop," Devree said. "I turn my radio down and stick my keys in my pocket. I'm going to be a goddamn silent Indian tracker. So I'm walking along and I see this guy who I think's naked. Only it turns out he's not naked because he has a pair of socks on his feet and a heavy chain with a Master lock attached to his wrist. He looks around real sneaky like and runs over to this tree, throws his arms around the trunk and locks himself to it.

"This poor guy can't get buggered no matter how hard he tries." Devree leaned back, sucked a drag from his Kool menthol and looked around the table before leaning forward and lowering his voice to a whisper. "It's like they say, there's never a fudge-packer around when you need one. Know what I mean?"

Most of his table mates nodded as Francie added an emphatic, "No shit."

"Then, I swear this is true," Devree continued. "The bastard starts to howl. Just looks to the sky and howls like a goddamn she-wolf in heat because nobody'll abuse him. Here's this guy who's naked except for his socks, he's chained to a tree, he's got this huge erection and nobody'll come along and bugger his ass, the poor bastard.

"So, he fidgets behind the tree and undoes the lock. Then he looks around real furtive like and runs to another tree. He throws his arms around it, locks himself to the trunk and starts howling again.

"This is all I can stand now, so I walk up to the guy and tell him he's under arrest for barking up the wrong tree."

As Devree finished to a burst of laughter, a throaty voice shouted above the clanging sounds of the backroom pinball machine, "Hey, Francie, did you hear the one about the two gay Irishmen, John Fitzpatrick and Patrick Fitzjohn?"

Frances Patrick Eugene O'Malley laughed his deep belly laugh and hollered above the twangy sounds of the juke box. "Ain't no such a thing as a gay Irishman," he said as Hartson handed Luke a wad of singles and sent him to fetch another round of beers for the table.

Denny walked to the bar to get his own beer as the round of stories continued.

When Luke got back to the table, the group tried insisting that he tell a tale of his own, but he had nothing to say. He sat still and silent, fondling the outside of his glass.

Hartson broke the awkward silence. "That true, Luke?"

"Huh," Luke responded.

"What Shimmer said a while ago? God knows, I'm aware you quote Shakespeare, but that shit about standing up on the tables at the academy, is that true?"

"Damn straight," Luke said. "To use a crass colloquialism."

"Go ahead on then and quote us some Shakespeare."

Luke tried not to let his surprise register as the rest of the group started mumbling. "Do you want something from a history, a comedy, a tragedy or a romance?"

"Just give us some fucking Shakespeare before I change my mind," Hartson said.

Luke didn't mind being the side show. Side shows had a great tradition dating back at least to the Renaissance. Besides, he'd never pass up the chance to teach somebody about Shakespeare. "All right, but I can't do it from here. A man quoting the Bard needs room to pontificate." Luke bounded atop the bar to tower over his audience. "Here's something apposite to our lives in a modern constabulary."

"What'd he say?" Shimmer whined. "What the fuck did he say?"

"Shut up," a chorus of voices resounded to drown out Shimmer's whines.

Luke thought of Martha and Phillip McGrath, Jr. as he quoted the title character from *Richard II*:

Of comfort let no man speak:
Let's talk of graves, of worms and epitaphs;
Make dust our paper and with rainy eyes
Write sorrow on the bosom of the earth.
Let's choose executors and talk of wills:
And yet not so, for what can we bequeath
Save our deposed bodies to the ground?
And nothing can we call our own but death,
And that small model of barren earth
Which serves as paste and cover to our bones

Luke looked at Shimmer. "That one's dedicated to you Mr. Bardolph," he said.

A pall of stunned silence followed the speech until Hartson sliced through the tension with a light-hearted, "Jesus, Luke, you're some kind of a deep motherfucker, aren't you?"

Shimmer followed Hartson's theatrical review with, "What'd he say? What the fuck did the cocksucker say?" Then he turned toward the groupie. "What's a bardolph?" he asked.

His question was too late. The groupie was slipping out the front door with Denny's hand in hers.

11

NO ONE CAME INTO SIGHT AS Shimmer and Denny crunched breath mints beneath their boots and stepped over the shattered coffeepots in the 7-Eleven's doorway. Rolling beer cans collided with smashed Twinkie packages and the officers heard faint whimpering coming from behind the cash register.

Shimmer un-holstered his blue steel .38 Smith and Wesson and peered over the counter, finding a shivering, Slurpee-drenched clerk sprawled amongst malted milk balls, Jujubes and tattered Penthouse magazines. A topsy-turvy electric fan slapped magazine pages against the clerk's leg, exposing a random orgy of splayed limbs and lip-parted smiles.

Shimmer holstered his gun and walked behind the counter. He pinched the clerk's vertically striped shirt and tugged as a signal to stand.

"Security guard's locked himself in the office," the clerk spat out as he pushed his way to his feet. "Boss hired this punk for security and the son-of-a-bitch hides in the office while I'm getting the shit kicked out of me. He still won't come out." The clerk raised his voice to a shout. "I'M DYING OUT HERE, AND THAT SECURITY GUARD SON-OF-A-BITCH WON'T COME OUT TO HELP." The clerk lowered his voice and took Shimmer into his confidence. "You know, officer, I'm just trying to get through college, working for a lousy minimum wage. Look at the shit I got to take. Some freaking giant beats the piss out of me and ruins my clothes WHILE THE SECURITY GUARD HIDES IN BACK."

"What happened?" Denny asked.

Shimmer shot Denny a look that told him to shut up. The field training office didn't allow terminations this soon after the academy, but he sure as hell could make his trainee stay out of the way and keep his mouth shut. Not only could Denny not write a report, the way he'd let his roommate act in the One-Five-Three Club ranked right up there with insubordination. Not to mention Denny's leaving the bar with the cop groupie. Groupies were a side benefit for real cops.

"The guy's huge," the clerk said. "He left out of here about five minutes ago, headed toward the park. He acted real nice until I told him we're out of corn nuts. That's when he tore the place up."

"When you find him, don't get too close," the clerk went on. "He's scary, man. He scared the shit out of that punk-ass security guard, I can tell you that much." He raised his voice to a bellow again to goad the security guard hiding in the back room.

"What's he look like?" Shimmer asked as he yanked out his notebook.

"You can see for yourself, if you can get him to show his face," the clerk said.

"Not him, dummy. I'm talking about the guy who trashed this place."

The clerk shook his head in a gesture of disbelief. "His skin's as white as talcum powder," he said. "He must have been six-foot-eight, six-foot-nine and dressed all in white with a shaved head." The clerk thought for a second. "To tell you the truth; he's a dead ringer for Mr. Clean, only with tattoos on his arms. He's got a hoop in his left ear and everything."

Shimmer put his unused writing utensils away, passed the description on to dispatch and headed toward the patrol car to search for the tattooed incarnation of the Madison Avenue icon.

Denny trotted along behind him.

"Where the hell do you think you're going?" Shimmer asked, and his trainee actually acted like he didn't get the question. Judging from his expression, he thought he was going with Shimmer to look for Mr. Clean. He even started opening the door.

"I need you to stay here and get started on the report," Shimmer said.

An obvious question hung painfully in the air between them. Standing with one foot in the car and the other on the concrete, Denny finally put words to it, his posture representing the limbo of his situation. "Why do I have to stay here?"

Shimmer exploded. "You just don't get it, do you? You think you can let your friend treat me like some kind of pussy and then come to work and act like it's all good."

"I didn't let Luke do anything," Denny said. "He doesn't listen to me. You can't hold me responsible for him."

"It don't matter what your pal says anyways. You haven't finished one decent report since you started," Shimmer said. "What matters is that you learn to write reports and do what you're told, which is to stay here and get started on the paper work."

Shimmer decided to omit the outrage over his trainee's leaving with the groupie. He'd said too much already about being pissed at Luke. It was best to focus on Denny's job deficiencies.

Denny's face actually shot back an expression that said Shimmer wasn't being fair. Damn straight he wasn't being fair. The world wasn't fair.

12

SHIMMER REMEMBERED THE LOCAL HISTORY class he'd taken at City College. That fiasco happened a while ago, back when he tried learning about the humongous park in his area. Back when he actually tried fitting into the department's new community policing philosophy to maybe get promoted to sergeant. Before they screwed him over when he tried for detective for the third time.

His unspoken admission actually hurt his gut as he neared the middle of the original thirty acres of Balboa Park where Kate Sessions had built an "experimental nursery" in 1892. Kate Sessions was an amazing woman. She'd persuaded the city council way back then to grant the land use and water privileges necessary for the nursery's success. Then she dynamited the hard-plant earth, moved the dislodged rocks herself and hauled the water in, using barrels and horse-drawn carriages. Her agreement with the city meant annually ground planting a hundred trees of varying species where she chose, in addition to three hundred trees in planters where city officials decided.

A portion of the results of her efforts loomed as a stand of coastal Sequoias standing watch over Mr. Clean as he knelt by a circular sidewalk. The once idyllic nursery had morphed into "Queen's Circle," a trick-turning business locale for cross-dressing hookers. The queens serviced customers who knew they were men, but pretended to believe they were women. The queens pretended not to know their customers really wanted sex from men, and police officers feigned ignorance of the whole thing to avoid harassment complaints. The magical illusions would have made Harry Houdini proud.

The breeze whipped through the trees, separating the leaves enough to let moonlight peek through. Shimmer eased the front wheels over the curb and onto the curving sidewalk, barely making out a voice above the wind blowing through the open window.

"I couldn't find your corn nuts," Mr. Clean said. He tipped forward on his haunches, talking to an attentive squirrel whose tail twitched in the beams of Shimmer's head lamps. "I stopped at the store, but they were out. I'm sorry." He stretched a trembling palm toward the squirrel. The animal sniffed and recoiled.

Shimmer called, "I got Mr. Clean in Queen's Circle," into his microphone as he lit up his spotlight. He pushed the car door open and stepped onto the slippery grass. "Get me some cover here fast," he said as Mr. Clean stood and turned toward him.

Shimmer snatched his wooden baton from its plastic holder at the bottom of the door and barked out his orders. "You're under arrest. Turn around. Now! Put your hands behind your back." He expected resistance; a raging, braying, cursing and fighting crazy man. He got acquiescence.

"Yes sir," Mr. Clean said as he turned to put his hands behind him in the reverse prayer position. He'd obviously been handcuffed before.

Shimmer noted prison tattoos along the lengths of Mr. Clean's massive forearms as he moved forward. He was barely able to ratchet his cuffs one click around the giant's massive wrists as Mr. Clean stood perfectly still. Shimmer put his prisoner behind the cage and put a "code-4" out over the radio to call off his cover units. "I'll take my 10-16 back to the 7-Eleven for follow up," he told the dispatcher.

As Shimmer eased into the driver's seat, dispatch asked him to switch to a tactical frequency for another unit. "Hey John, you sure you're okay," Hartson wanted to know. "I'm only a couple blocks away. I could meet you at the 7-Eleven and my trainee can help out with the paperwork while I keep an eyeball on the 10-16."

"Nah," Shimmer said, trying to hide his surprise. "This guy's a pussy-cat. Besides, I can keep an eye out while my trainee attempts to do the paperwork." He wanted to be sure anyone who'd switched over to eavesdrop on the conversation wouldn't miss Denny's report writing struggles.

"Okay, meet me at Johnny's in a couple hours for some foot patrol though," Hartson said. "My trainee could use the exposure."

The last thing Shimmer wanted was to see Hartson's whack job of a trainee again, but the field training office would definitely frown on his refusal to participate in the training.

"Hey, I got to know something," Shimmer said to Mr. Clean. "You went berserk in that store, smacked the shit out of the clerk and scared the crap out of the security guard. You don't deny any of it, do you?"

"No, sir."

"Your tattoos tell me you've seen the inside of more than one prison and you're half off your nut judging from what just happened in the circle. Yet you did everything I asked you to. How come you gave up so easy?"

Mr. Clean's voice rang with sincerity. "Officer, I've been in and out of jails my whole life. The first time the cops busted me I called the officer a pussy. 'Just take these cuffs off,' I told him, 'and I'll kick your ass.'"

Mr. Clean settled back in his seat, sucked in a deep breath and looked out the window. "That was a big mistake on my part for sure. He took me behind a warehouse and put his gun, badge and stick in the trunk. Then he unlocked my cuffs, just like I asked him to. He didn't raise his voice or nothing. He just spoke like a gentleman. 'Now's your chance, son,'" he told me. "'Go ahead on and kick my ass if you can.'

"I clocked him square on the chin and he just sort of stepped back a little bit like he hardly noticed. Then he beat me near to death. Afterwards he told me he represented every policeman in the world and I shouldn't ever talk to a policeman like that again.

"Sir," Mr. Clean continued, "I never have since, and I never will again. Whenever I see a policeman now, I just sort of get my right mind back and do what I'm told."

The news gladdened Shimmer's heart and he muttered a silent prayer of thanksgiving to his anonymous benefactor as he jerked to a stop in the 7-Eleven's parking lot.

A banty-rooster security guard strutted in front of an ice machine and announced that the clerk was in the bathroom. "You know, Officer," the guard said as he stood tall on his toes and looked behind the cage at the cuffed prisoner, "I got me a black belt in Tang Soo Do. Truth is, I could've kicked his ass easy. But I didn't want to get the owner sued. A security guard hurts somebody these days—you know how it is. The asshole'd probably end up owning the store."

Shimmer kept his thoughts to himself.

"The clerk doesn't get it. He thinks I was scared, but I wasn't scared. I just didn't want a situation where I had to hurt some crazy bastard. If you talk to my boss, you be sure and tell him I was looking out for his interests. You know how it is?"

"I think I get the picture," Shimmer said.

13

HARTSON AND LUKE STOOD IN THE PARKING LOT behind Johnny's Restaurant. Johnny's, a pedestrian all-night diner, catered to downtown's night-time clientele of hookers, pimps, topless dancers, sailors, taxi drivers and police officers.

Hartson sipped oily coffee from a dirty Styrofoam cup, rested a worn heel against the front bumper and waited for Shimmer and his trainee to show up for their round of foot patrol. "Listen, Luke, I'm telling you, ninety-nine percent of success in this job is getting along with your superiors," he said. "Whether you like it or not, as long as you're a trainee, Shimmer's your superior and you better make up to him."

Luke groaned. "He's such a little nebbish," he said. "Can't I just avoid him?"

"A nebbish? Never mind. No, you can't. He could be your next training officer for all you know. You think you're hot shit out here because you're big and tough and you've read a few books, but I'm telling you, you'll never make it if you can't get along."

Luke sipped his coffee. "I don't think I can do it," he said.

"Getting along with Shimmer isn't a suggestion," Hartson said. "It's an order, and it'll show on your evaluations if you can't get it done."

Luke contemplated the chilly reality. "I'll make nice," he said. "But I don't like sucking up to jerks."

Hartson laughed out loud. "You better find another line of work then," he said. "Sucking up to jerks is in the job description. Besides, Shimmer isn't a total asshole."

"Whoa, wait a minute," Luke said. "I'll follow orders, but don't go expecting me to buy that line of crap."

Shimmer's car came into view before Hartson could answer. It turned past a trio of high-coiffed hookers and lurched to a stop in the parking lot. Shimmer pushed the door open and jerked a metal five-cell flashlight from between his legs. The door fell shut behind him as he made a production number out of ordering Denny to stay in the car to work on reports.

Denny shrugged as Luke looked in his direction for an explanation.

"T.D., my man, what's on the agenda tonight," Shimmer said.

"Contacts," Hartson told him. "My trainee's got to learn to generate numbers and nobody's better at that than you."

Luke nearly gagged at Hartson's effort to curry Shimmer's favor. It mattered not at all that the effort was intended for his benefit.

"I'm with you," Shimmer said. "There ain't none up on your beat, that's for sure, and besides, it's about time we started living up to Farnsworth's anthem." Luke knew Shimmer referred to a crotchety senior officer who constantly sung out his defiant credo against the department's conversion to Community Oriented Policing at line-up.

Shimmer did his best imitation of Farnsworth's deep belly laugh as he started imitating the anthem in a stilted reggae rhythm. "If it don't recap on your journal, mon, and it don't fuck up somebody's day, mon, don't bother with it mon."

Luke didn't bother to laugh. "The instructors at the academy told us numbers don't matter anymore," he said. "Don't you Neanderthals know the department's moving in a new direction?" Luke didn't really understand the friction between the brass and the work-a-day street cop, but he did know community policing loomed as the wave of the future for the San Diego Police Department.

It was more than Shimmer could stand. "You're too stupid for words," he said. "Sergeant Biletnikoff wants us humping our butts, putting people in jail and writing tickets. If he says to kick ass and take names that's what we do, or we get shitty evaluations. That's the real truth about the department's direction. And another thing, those morons in the corner pocket sitting behind their fancy desks and kissing the Mayor's ass think the sergeants are buying this C-O-P crap. Numbers don't matter no more? BULLSHIT! You don't know it's bullshit because you're a make-pretend cop who can't even make a decision without Hartson's go ahead."

Luke had dived head first into a thick soup without even knowing he'd been teetering on the edge of the bowl, but he had no idea how to retreat. Offense was the only tactic he knew. "You guys are refusing to change, and if you don't get with the program pretty soon, trainees like me will pass you by."

"We better get with the program?" Shimmer sputtered. "You better do what you're told and shut the fuck up. You don't even know how to stay alive out here, yet you're trying to tell us how to do our job?"

The air between them simmered with a nearly palpable tension. This was normally the time for Hartson to come to Luke's rescue, but instead he rhythmically tapped his flashlight against an open palm and advanced toward his trainee. "The brass don't know shit about what goes on out here," he said. "They didn't teach you that at the academy did they? If you're so smart, tell us how we can write tickets to everybody on the beat like Sarge wants, then rap on Granny's door for tea and crumpets like the brass wants. Granny's likely to show us the ticket we wrote her and shove it up our ass. Besides, I got 'Pill Hill' for a beat and, in case you don't know it—which I'm sure you don't—on the graveyard, all I got up there's Balboa Park, closed-up medical buildings and an occasional dirtbag pushing a shopping cart. The only numbers up there are in the park, but I can't go to the park because of the complaints I'd get, which means I have to poach downtown to fill my journal. But, if Sarge wants to, he can write me up for being off my beat which all adds up to me being screwed. See what I mean?"

"Why can't we go to the park?" Luke asked.

Shimmer clucked his tongue.

"The park's no place to generate numbers," Hartson said. "At night, the place is packed with perverts looking for anonymous sex. Now, I don't care who does what to who, but we're talking about a public place here and these guys have taken the park over because they keep complaining to the gay activists who lobby the politicians, who tell the brass we're all homophobes just out for a cheap thrill. It's a Catch-22 because we need recordable contacts for our journals to stay out of trouble and we're ordered to ignore the illegal shit that's going on in the middle of my beat. The result is, the sex stuff spills over into the ravines and bushes in the daytime and the family picnics and volleyball games are forced out of the area."

Hartson slapped his flashlight against an open palm again. The implication was pretty clear. He wanted to clunk Luke upside the head and knock some sense into him.

"I'm starting to see the problem," Luke said after a long deliberation. "But what can we do about it?"

"You're the smart guy," Hartson said. "You tell me. But do it straight from your head without any of your stupid quotations. If you're capable of thinking for yourself, that is."

This time Shimmer broke the tension. "The City Council, in its infinite wisdom, has declared that topless bars are police regulated businesses. We can do our part to keep them regulated and live up to Farnsworth's anthem at the same time. It don't get much better than that."

The truce was offered. Luke only needed to accept it.

He was no expert on police training, but he knew the only way to get trained was to actually do something. "Why are you making Denny sit in the car?"

Shimmer's eyelids fluttered like a porcelain top on a boiling teapot. "It's none of your fucking business, that's why," he shouted.

Luke thought Shimmer's head might teeter off his neck and crack into pieces on the sidewalk.

"Way to get along, Luke," Hartson said.

14

ONCE HARTSON GOT THE SITUATION CALMED DOWN, Shimmer explained the advantages to regulating Cindy's bar, the first destination for the peripatetic trio. Namely, that Cindy's boasted three stages with dancers performing two-song sets instead of the four-song sets at other clubs. Since the dancing girls only flicked off their skimpy tops during the last song, the shorter sets, combined with the three stages, meant Cindy's sported more naked tits per second than any of its competitors, making it a tit-rich environment.

Shimmer pulled aside the black leather entrance flap and the trio of officers saw a leggy strawberry blonde grasping a pole with both hands. She wrapped a thigh around it as her hips undulated in and out and up and down and her hands stroked the pole in front of an open mouth.

Their entrance into Cindy's was halted by a piercing shriek coming from a nearby sidewalk.

"Where's 'Yat?"

The shrieking woman stood in front of a bustling tattoo parlor around the corner from Cindy's. In her forties, she wore a faded maroon housecoat and corduroy slippers with holes at the big toes. Her hair did a Don King imitation and her caterwauls sent pedestrians scurrying around her and into the street.

"What the fuck is a Yat?" Shimmer asked.

The woman caught her breath and enunciated clearly. "Where is he at? Where is that sumbitch at? I know he be in one of these titty bars somewhere."

"Where is who at?" Shimmer asked.

"My good for nothing man be in one of these titty bars and I just know it, because it's his payday, and I ain't leaving until I find his tired ass and drag it home." The woman ran a trembling palm over her hair and pulled in a deep breath. "Then his ass is mine's. He think he can bring that tired-ass paycheck down here and drink beer and stare at them titties and buy him some ass until it all gone. I know exactly what he think he going to do but he ain't, because I'll drag his tired ass home!"

"Ma'am," Shimmer implored. "I need you to help me out here. You're creating a disturbance and I might have to arrest you. You don't want that now, do you?"

"But our money?" the woman pleaded. "He'll spend it all on whores and drinking and we got a grandbaby to feed."

Shimmer's demeanor instantly changed. His shoulders slumped and the timbre of his voice softened.

"Believe me," he told Mrs. Yat. "I understand your problem. You describe Mr. Yat for us and we'll bring him home. That's a promise from me to you. But only if you'll promise me you'll go home."

"The name ain't Yat, it's Brown. John Brown." The woman looked Shimmer up and down. "Okay," she said, a hint of hope infusing her words. "I'll let you figure out where he at. And just so you'd know, I wouldn't whup his ass like I said. I only want him back where he belong."

The three officers set off with Mr. Yat's description, address and phone number scribbled on the back page of Shimmer's notebook. He was tall and skinny and wearing a black Oakland Raider's jacket and cap, a virtual felony in San Diego.

The search for Mr. Yat would be incorporated into their quest for numbers to fill their journals.

They wrote tickets to pedestrians and filled out Field Interview Forms on prostitutes and drug dealers. They even tutored a batch of sailors who comprised the criminal element's most likely customers and eventual victims.

"Stay downtown and you might as well wear a shirt with a bulls-eye on it," Shimmer warned them. "You'll lose your paycheck to some Three-Card Monte scam or hand a wad of money over to some pimp who'll claim he'll be right back with the merchandise. You'll never see him or your money again. Then you'll call us and claim you were minding your own business and got robbed, and we'll figure out you're lying in about a nanosecond. So don't bother to call us for that shit, because we ain't a collection service!"

Hartson joined in. "Don't get fooled by that bull crap you hear on the radio that talks about San Diego's some kind of paradise. Trust me, boys, look around and you'll see. This is no fantasy land."

With several contacts under their belts, the trio finally got lucky at the corner of Third and Broadway where Mr. Yat teetered on the edge of the curb. His presence fulfilled two functions at once. He represented both a quantifiable citizen's contact and Shimmer's chance to keep his promise to the wronged wife waiting patiently at home for her wayward husband.

"You must be the famous Mr. Yat," Shimmer said.

"No, sir." The drunk slurred his words through tight lips and wobbled on shaky legs, hovering precariously close to the cars turning west onto Broadway. "Name's Brown."

"You live at 3213 Clay Street?" Shimmer asked.

"I do. Yes, sir."

"That makes you Yat," Shimmer said. "And it's obvious you've had too much to drink. But this is your lucky day because I intend to do you a favor. I won't throw your ass in jail if you let us give you a ride home."

The three officers walked a forlorn Mr. Yat the couple of blocks back to the rear of Johnny's. Once they got there, Shimmer surprised Luke by asking Hartson to take Yat home.

"I have to say," Luke said as they made the drive, "I'm a little confused by all this. Mr. Yat here's been drinking, but he's not really a danger to himself or to anybody else for that matter. Besides that, I know taking him home's a violation of department policy, so, I guess what I'm asking is, what gives?"

The muscles in Hartson's jaw worked a little. "It's about time I told you a little about Shimmer since you've already made up your mind about him," Hartson said.

The sharpness in Hartson's tone stung a little.

"A couple years back, Shimmer killed a guy who was holding his wife hostage and threatening to slit her throat. Shimmer did everything right, but the asshole still managed to separate her neck from her shoulders in the process. She bled out in front of him.

"That same week, his kid drowned in their pool. We were friends back then. His wife used to come to the One-Five-Three Club when she could find a babysitter and the three of us would have a blast telling jokes and knocking back a few beers. Now she hates his guts and I can tell its killing him. She's told me herself he used to be her hero. For Shimmer, taking care of Mr. Yat's like doing something he can't do for his own wife."

Luke sat, stunned by Hartson's insight and his willingness to share it. "Why didn't he take Yat home and get some of the glory for himself then?"

"He's a complicated guy," Hartson said.

The pair dropped Mr. Yat off and told dispatch they were back in service. The dispatcher responded with a call. "Unit Fifty-one-Frank, respond to a possible jumper at the top of the Community Concourse parking structure."

Luke acknowledged the call. Then a sudden thought struck him with all the wallop of a baseball bat to the gut. "I'm sort of wondering," he said. "How come you know so much about what Shimmer's wife thinks?"

"You're the smart guy," Hartson said. "You figure it out."

15

"IS THAT SOME KIND OF THREAT?" Francie wanted to know. "I don't care if you jump, but I'll need to know your name first to make it easier on me." Francie goose-stepped to the precipice and stood on his tip-toes. He pressed his belly against the concrete barrier and peeked over."

There was no answer.

"It's a long way down," Francie said. "I saw a guy jump from here once and his head popped like a water balloon when it slapped bottom. There'll be a big mess for somebody to clean up down there. That what you want, somebody else cleaning up your mess?"

The would-be jumper glanced down to the 1200 block of Second Avenue to see a police car rounding into the bottom floor.

Francie pressed on. "What's your name?"

Tense jaws and gritted teeth spat out an answer. "What difference does it make to you? You don't give a shit." The muscular man glowered down at Francie. He wore a tight rugby shirt tucked into polyester pants. His sturdy legs quivered atop a rectangular concrete slab that jutted several feet above the top floor of the structure.

Hartson's unit pulled next to the other police car. He joined Francie, and Luke took up a post with Francie's nearly apoplectic trainee. Her face looked as if it had just suffered a Bell's palsy with its two halves replicating the ancient masks of comedy and tragedy. Her name was Andee Bradford.

"I think my FTO's lost it," she said.

Luke combined observation and supposition with facts he'd learned from classmates as he sized up Bradford. Her first name was a female version of her grandfather's, and her dad's first signal of disappointment over his siring a girl child. She stood under five-feet-tall and her chest commandeered a bra with a cup size somewhere in the middle of the alphabet, which explained why Luke couldn't recall ever seeing a man look her in the eyes.

Although a trainee like Luke, she'd already earned a reputation for two noteworthy things. She held the academy record for timed pushups due to the short distance her arms needed to bend before her chest touched the wrestling mat. That really stung Luke who'd held the record for exactly two minutes before she took her turn.

She'd also single-handedly broken up a donnybrook at 25th and Imperial Streets on her first day of patrol when the pillow that allowed her to see over the dashboard fell into the gutter as she slid out of the car. The sight of her stooping to scoop the cushion up from the street sucked the tension out of the festering crowd and parted the combatants who found the situation too funny to keep fighting.

"What's going on?" Luke asked her.

"I've got paperwork," Francie said to the jumper, ignoring the arrival of the other officers. "It'll be easier if I know who you are. If you jump, we have to wait for the coroner before my trainee can check your pockets, but if you cooperate a little, we can get off on time."

"I'm supposed to be considerate of you, is that the idea?"

"Let me put it to you this way," Francie said. "I'd be willing to bet there's at least one moron out there," Francie waved his arm toward the horizon, "who loves you. When you jump, it'll be incredibly inconsiderate to them. If you do something nice for me, I can tell them about it and they won't be so pissed off."

Hartson pushed past Francie to take over the negotiations. "His name's Charles Henreid," he said.

Luke leaned toward Bradford and took her into his confidence. "We arrested this guy for drunk driving a couple days ago."

"Stay away from me or I'll jump," Henreid said.

"There you go with that threat again. Either get on with it or come down from there and quit wasting our time," Francie said.

Luke knew Hartson couldn't get close without risking falling or being pushed off and he and Bradford needed to stay out of the way to let Hartson establish some rapport.

"I'm a rational man," Hartson said. "I won't risk my life to save yours. Let's just you and me talk a few minutes."

Henreid squatted. Luke followed his gaze as he stared eastward toward the Presidio Tower in Balboa Park that jutted majestically above the Museum of Man in the distance. The bright floodlights at the base of the tower shone upward along its smooth façade, projecting an opalescent contrast to the dark night around it.

"What brings you up here tonight, Mr. Henreid?" Hartson asked.

"Maybe he took a cab," Francie said.

Hartson ignored the heckling. "What do your friends call you? Is it Chuck, Charlie, or Charles?"

Henreid didn't answer.

"My name's T.D.," Hartson continued. "My partner over there is Francie."

"You can call me Officer O'Malley," Francie interrupted.

For Luke, Francie's animosity was positively Shakespearean. There was just no rational explanation for how angry he was, just as there was no rational explanation for the hatred of Edmund in King Lear, Don John in Much Ado About Nothing or Iago in Othello.

"What do you really want from me?" Henreid demanded. "You want me to get down from here so you can throw me in jail again?"

"Let's start with why you want to kill yourself."

"You wouldn't understand."

"I don't understand much," Hartson assured him. "But I'm willing to listen."

"I just got out of jail and that truck you and your partner took from me was how I earned my living. How stupid are you anyway?"

"I was just doing my job," Hartson told him. "You were too drunk to drive, and you know it. You can't go blaming your problems on somebody else all the time."

Luke wondered if all his actions as a cop had such far reaching consequences for people's lives.

Francie interrupted his thoughts. "It's colder than my ex-wife's side of the bed up here with this breeze whipping through. Could you get on with this thing, so I can get in the car and turn the heater on?"

Luke couldn't tell whether the words constituted an invitation for Henreid to jump or to climb down and surrender.

"What's got him so pissed off?" Luke asked Bradford.

"It beats me," she said. "He was reading a letter from one of his kids over coffee and the next thing I know, we're answering this call and he's gone completely off his nut."

"It's the middle of August for Christ's sake," Hartson said to Francie. "Nobody's cold here in the middle of August."

"I am."

Hartson turned toward Henreid. "Ignore him," he said. "Let's just you and me talk and see if we can't come to an understanding."

Henreid stood tall again and edged closer to the brink of the concrete super-structure. "Why'd you have to impound my truck?" Henreid said. "I can't afford to get it back, which means I can't pay the rent."

"What else could I do?" Hartson asked.

"Turn your head," Henreid said. "I don't want you to see me jump."

"No." Hartson demanded. "If you go, you'll go, knowing you're taking my guts with you."

Henreid slid to the center of the slab. "I've lost everything," he said. He turned toward the Presidio Tower again. "My wife used to cup my face and tell me I was the best thing that ever happened to her. She won't even let me talk to my baby anymore. She says she won't let our daughter grow up knowing her daddy gambled our lives away."

Henreid heaved an enormous sigh that sounded like a train engine blowing steam into its silent surroundings. "I'm a gambler and I'd be better off dead."

"Ah, geez," Francie blurted out. "Is this shit supposed to make me cry? You used to have a wife, used to have a baby, used to have a this, used to have a that and lost it all to gambling. I think I'm about to puke.

"Let me tell you something, pal," Francie's pitchy voice piped higher as he tapped insistent fingers against his metal flashlight. He leaned toward Henreid who stood again. "I got kids too. Now, I live in a dump of an apartment with some other asshole whose wife dumped him. You don't see me crying and threatening to kill myself, do you?"

Luke's mouth gaped open. He knew Hartson was the other asshole.

"You think I'm kidding, but I'm not," Francie insisted.

"No," Henreid said. "I can see you're serious."

"Shut up and listen for once," Francie said. "I used to be a school principal who took care of other people's kids all day. Now, some other guy's raising my kids and I'm babysitting assholes like you in the middle of the night." Francie thumped his flashlight against his chest. "This fucking job is my addiction. This uniform yanked me away from everything I cared about. You think I care what happens to you?"

"Shut up, Francie," Hartson demanded. "Get in your fucking car and take your trainee out of here before I come over there and kick your ass."

"I got just one more thing to say," Francie insisted. "I had a life until I went on a ride-along. I bet everything on this job and tossed my career right before my wife tossed me and took the kids. This is everything now. Why else would I jerk off up here in the middle of the night? You got to find a way to live without anything else like I do."

"Are you saying imitating you's better than jumping?" Henreid asked.

Hartson lifted his palms toward Henreid in a gesture of supplication. "Don't let this prick push you over the edge," he said. "Let's talk this out. I'll deal with him later." He jabbed his thumb toward Francie.

Henreid sat on the edge, dangling his legs in the descending darkness. "I understand him." He made a fake gun with his hand and pointed it at Francie. "He doesn't piss me off," Henreid said. "Hey, O'Brien, one of us should join the other. You want to come up here with me?"

"I told you, it's O'Malley," Francie grunted. "Thanks for the invitation."

"Why would you want to kill yourself?" Hartson continued, ignoring the absurd antagonism between Francie and Henreid. "It sounds like you've got a great wife and kid."

"I can't figure out what else to do," Henreid said.

Hartson pulled a pack of menthols from his jacket pocket. "Now we're getting someplace," he said. He lit a cigarette and drew a lungfull of smoke into his chest, taking the time to figure out what to say.

"I don't doubt that I have to die," Henreid said. "I have to kill what's controlling me."

"What are you talking about?" Hartson demanded.

"I've lost control," Henreid answered. "I know you can't understand it, but it's like something's crawled up inside me that makes me gamble. If I jump, I'll take it with me."

"There's other things you can do," Hartson insisted. "There's Gambler's Anonymous, and there must be people who care about you who can help."

Henreid shook his head and his shoulders slumped. "I've driven everybody away. I've tried the twelve-step stuff already. All I've learned is that I'm too weak to control my life. But a swan dive from here puts me back in control."

"You won't be in control, you'll be dead, you jackass," Francie said.

Hartson agreed. "He's right about that much. Jumping would be the ultimate victory for whatever it is that makes you gamble. I'm not too smart, but one thing I know for sure is that death is final. If you try getting your shit together again, you can always come back and jump later if it doesn't work out."

Hartson shot a threatening glance at Francie. "Let me take you somewhere you can talk to somebody who knows more about this than me."

The sun peeked over the Presidio Tower as Hartson spoke and Henreid looked toward the sunrise. "I'll come down if you'll do one thing for me."

"Anything," Hartson said.

Henreid lifted his chin toward Francie. "Keep that O'Brien asshole away from me."

"It's O'Malley, you jackass," Francie said as he stomped toward his car and Henreid jumped down.

"Department policy says I have to cuff you," Hartson apologized.

Henreid turned his back to Hartson and put his hands behind him. "I'm getting used to it," he said.

16

"WATCH YOUR HEAD," LUKE SAID AS HE GUIDED Henreid into the back seat for the second time in three days.

"Okay then, let's get this show on the road," Hartson told Luke. "You might as well go ahead and drive while we're at it."

The circular trip down the ramp represented the first time Luke had driven a police car away from the academy. Its "Grinder" was nothing more than a big parking lot peppered by dilapidated police cars and traffic cones haphazardly placed to simulate traffic and parked cars. Simulation could never emulate the real thing.

"No driving with your head up your ass." Hartson's words competed with the noise of metal against concrete as the radio antenna thwacked against the ceiling.

"The only thing worse than a trainee driving with his head up his ass is D-W-O," Hartson said. He paused, giving Luke the chance to ask the obvious question.

"DWO?"

"Driving While Oriental," Hartson said. "That ought to be a felony, but it's not, so let's concentrate on you and save the bigger problems for later."

Luke nodded.

"Operating a police car's more than steering and braking," Hartson went on. "You'll need new skills that can only come with experience."

Hartson tapped his pen against the dashboard, Lawrence Welk conducting his champagne orchestra in a police car. "Listening to the radio's tough enough. Now you'll have to do it while playing car commander. At intersections, concentrate on more than stopping at the limit line. You need to stay far enough away to allow room for squeezing through in an emergency."

Luke listened intently, but glanced in the rear view mirror, making eye contact with Henreid. He wondered about their prisoner's response to Hartson's flippant racial slurs, but decided to avoid the topic.

"Mind if I ask you a question Mr. Henreid? Why'd you want to jump?"

"It's none of your business." Henreid spoke his words into the window. "I'm fed up with you cops, and the last thing I need's a grilling from a FNG."

"FNG?" Luke asked.

"A fucking new guy," Henreid said. "You've obviously never been in the military?"

Henreid's tone sounded a familiar note for Luke, oozing as it did with bitterness and anger designed to trumpet Luke's insignificance. Luke kept his anger in check, understanding that Henreid was the true target of his own boomeranging hatred.

"I don't mean any disrespect," Luke said. "I'm filling out the hospital admission paperwork and it'd help hearing your side of things. And to be honest, I'd like to hear more about what takes control over you?"

"That's a metaphor, you dip shit" Henreid said. "Ever heard of a metaphor?"

Luke laughed. "I know all about metaphors. Real life's what I'm trying to figure out."

"All I know is I can't stop gambling and it feels like something's pulling the strings and controlling me," Henreid said. A long paused followed. "You wouldn't believe what I've done to get money for a bet."

"I've done some reading that says addiction stems from body chemistry," Luke said. "I don't claim to really know anything, but I did a paper on addictions and I've read Dostoevsky's *The Gambler*. Between the two, I think I understand compulsions. The protagonist—the main guy in *The Gambler* I mean—lost everything playing roulette. No matter what good things happened to the guy throughout the book, they only put off the inevitable tragedy."

"All right, that's enough," Hartson blurted out. "You sound like a goddamn English teacher and I'm about to make you drive back to the Parkade so Henreid and me can both jump off."

Luke pressed his point. "There's a scene in the book where the guy risks everything he owns on one spin of the roulette wheel and wins enough money to completely turn his life around if he'd only stop. But he kept on playing until he lost everything. What amazed me was the total lack of suspense. I never for a second wondered if he'd stop gambling."

"Jesus H, Luke," Hartson interrupted again. "Leave the poor guy alone?"

"It's all right," Henreid said. "I didn't read his book, but I do know it's about the gambler, not the reader. Every spin of the wheel, every bet, it's all suspense to him. It's what drives his life."

"I told you I don't know anything," Luke reminded him. "I'm learning that books only have so much to teach."

"That's better," Hartson said.

"One thing to think about though," Luke told Henreid, "is a quotation from *Julius Caesar*: 'Of your philosophy you make no use, if you give place to accidental evils.'"

Hartson shifted in his seat. "Every time I think you're starting to get smart, you spout off again," he told Luke.

"All I know is, if you blame your problems on anything other than yourself, it's giving your power away," Luke said. "It's a cop out."

Luke turned to look in Henreid's eyes when he stopped at a red light. "The key to addictions is probably brain chemicals. Once you do whatever you're addicted to, the action sets off a cascading chemical process. If you know the cause, you can develop a strategy to stop it."

"You're way too naive to preach to me about anything," Henreid said.

Luke laughed, knowing no argument could win his point.

"Maybe I can beat this thing," Henreid said. "Just don't go saying you know how to clean up people's lives."

"The man's got a point," Hartson said. "You're talking some pretty heady shit and folks are bound to think you're an uppity son-of-a-bitch."

"I'm not preaching at anybody. I just think out loud sometimes," Luke said.

"Yeah, well, maybe you could figure it out better with your mouth shut," Hartson said and his upper lip twitched a little as things finally got quiet. "I should've made Francie write a One-Five-Three since he was the first officer on the scene," he said. "We might have some trouble with the admission."

"The report's simple," Luke said. "Mr. Henreid said he would've jumped if you didn't talk him down. That proves he's a danger to himself. What could be easier than that?"

"I see your momma didn't teach you anything about humility," Hartson said. "If you're so cock-sure, let's make it interesting. No errors and no liquid paper. If your report isn't totally perfect, you'll watch me tear it up until you get it right and you'll have to buy dinner. I'll buy if it is perfect. Sound good?"

"Seems fair enough," Luke answered as he jerked to a stop behind the hospital. He popped the trunk and tossed his mace, gun and baton beside the equipment bag resting against the spare tire. "I think I could go for some free Greek food tonight," he said.

Hartson chuckled as he followed suit with his weapon and equipment before opening the back door for Henreid to step onto the pavement.

Luke heard a raspy voice and sniffed ammonia as the trio stepped on to a once-brown vinyl floor that had faded to an ugly mustard color and was scarred with thick swaths of boot scuffs.

"I forgive you."

The magnanimous proclamation came from a man with a toothless grin and a plastic baggy full of goodies; pebbles, paper wads, toothpicks, baseball cards, clothes pins and shirt buttons. "Father, forgive him too," the man said as Luke filled out the intake form. "I'm pretty sure he doesn't know any better."

"Don't know any better than what?" Luke asked. But the man's attention lay with his bag of goodies, making his comment about Luke's nebulous culpability seem like a distant memory to him.

Hartson sat on a bench next to Henreid while Luke leaned against the counter, writing the admission report that needed to pass muster on three fronts. It had to convince the psychiatrist to commit Henreid for a mandatory seventy-two-hour evaluation and pass Hartson's initial scrutiny before he forwarded it to Sergeant Biletnikoff as the approving supervisor.

The bustling hospital ward made Luke's task next to impossible. Nurses and nurse's aides scurried around with clipboards held high and self-important airs that mimicked a vaudeville show on a set specifically decorated to depict institutional drabness. The metal chair legs supported torn Naughahyde seats whose cushions split at odd angles to display the escaping stuffing. The psychiatrist's office, behind a glass partition, allowed a universal view into the doctor's interviews. Empty gurneys with dangling arm and leg restraints littered adjacent hallways.

The little man with the bag of goodies stood up suddenly; sat under a gurney and curled up on the floor. He emptied the baggie's contents to construct a scene on a mound of sand and pebbles that he pulled from his pockets. The mound supported three clothes pins that had been broken and intersected into three crosses. Poked holes in the top of the baseball cards allowed them to hang from the crosses and touch the apex of the mound.

The intake nurse photocopied Luke's report.

She asked Hartson to take Henreid's cuffs off. Then she escorted Henreid into the doctor's office where the psychiatrist would decide if she agreed with the police assessment that Henreid's suicidal episode met the criteria for section 5150 of the California Welfare and Institutions Code.

"Listen, Luke," Hartson said as Henreid and the psychiatrist took their seats in the glass-enclosed inner office. "We can't leave until she's done, so you go ahead and wait here while I pop over to the ER to make a quick phone call."

Hartson took Luke's report with him, walked outside and sat in the front passenger seat. He lifted a blank report from the clipboard between the seats and filled out the blocks on the front. Once his bogus report resembled Luke's completed one, he hid his trainee's paper work beneath it on the clipboard.

The psychiatrist announced her intention to admit Henreid.

Luke walked to the toothless man who'd finished constructing his scene of Christ and the thieves on the crosses. The man squinted into the bright light above Luke's head. "This is where I died," he said.

"It's as good a place as any," Luke answered. "But you're not dead."

"I was before," the man said. He lowered his gaze and squinted pointedly into Luke's eyes.

Luke shook his head and went outside. He grabbed his equipment from the trunk and saw Hartson still reading his report.

"What's taking so long?" Luke asked the question as he slid into the driver's seat and turned toward the training officer who held the clipboard in front of his face. "It's a simple enough report."

Hartson made a show of lifting the report from the clipboard and slowly ripping it in half. "I'm afraid you need to write this piece of shit over again," he said.

Luke sat flabbergasted. Sure he'd been distracted. Things got a little crazy inside the nut house, but he'd made himself focus. This was more than needing to re-write a simple report. It called into question everything he thought he knew about himself. He needed experience, sure. Sure he needed wisdom, but he knew how to write a simple narrative. He knew that much.

17

"VERY FUNNY," LUKE TOLD HARTSON. "I thought I'd have a myocardial infarction for a second there."

"You see, that's your problem," Hartson said. "You can't just say 'heart attack' like a normal human being. Why can't you just say what you mean?"

"I did," Luke said. "I always do. My meaning just comes with a lot of syllables."

"You just talk like that to screw with people."

"I don't either."

"Jesus," Hartson said. "I'd give anything for a snapshot of your sockets when I ripped that report up. I thought your eyeballs might pop right out of your face."

"You'd like that, wouldn't you?" Luke enjoyed the developing camaraderie and nearly let loose with a few bon mots of his own about what an uncaring cretin his FTO was, before an all-units broadcast cut off his salvo. "A 245-shotgun in the Heights that could turn into a 187," the dispatcher said. "Victim's in front of the Welfare Office at Two-Five and Imperial Streets."

The call represented Hartson's first chance to expose his trainee to a potential murder scene. "Fifty-one-Frank, my partner and I'll respond to that one." It was Hartson's first reference to Luke as his partner.

Normally, training officers made their charges look up their destinations in the map book, but the call's urgency required an immediate response. Hartson called out the directions as Luke drove.

An angry crowd festered in the intersection as they arrived. Several drunks congregated near the adjacent doorways of Alejandro's Garage and Pepe's Carniceria, bottles of fortified Night Train wine bulging in their pockets.

Hispanic gangsters strutted between the drunks, inciting the groups of mechanics, grocery clerks and construction workers huddled nearby. "You pigs're gonna let this esse get away with it," an angry voice yelled above the confusion. "You couldn't care no less if somebody gets gunned down here in the barrio."

The pockets of people exploded into a mob and converged around the body. Hartson called for additional crowd control units and ordered Luke to check the victim's vital signs.

"Get those people away from him," Hartson barked to a pair of arriving officers as Luke knelt beside the victim. "This is a crime scene, not a damn freak show."

"Better call a supervisor and get Homicide started," Luke called, looking back over his shoulder at his training officer. "This guy's 11-44."

Luke ordered the crowd back as he stood and waded forward, his arms spread. "You want this murder solved? Then don't trample on the evidence," he said.

Luke saw Andee Bradford as more police cars arrived. He was already hearing what he knew were bogus rumors about her sleeping around to get ahead in the department. Being a trainee was tough enough for a man, but was obviously worse for somebody like her and he knew she'd almost certainly share his sense of feeling overwhelmed by the chaos of the murder scene. "Can you get me some crime scene tape?" he asked her.

"Don't have any," she called back. "I'll go check your trunk." It was something she could do easily enough since patrol officers carried a universal key for every vehicle in the fleet.

"We don't have any either," he called back. "The property room ran out. The clerk said an order got screwed up. Hey, anybody got any crime tape?" He yelled the question repeatedly to arriving officers before looking directly into the gray eyes of a pot-bellied veteran and asking again. "You got any crime scene tape?"

The officer shrugged, the up and down motion making his belly heave.

"I guess there's never any crime scene tape around when you need it," Bradford said, a wry smile playing on her lips.

Luke greeted the feeble inside joke with a weak smile of his own.

"I'll run in to the market at the corner to see if I can't borrow something," Bradford said. Sun-streaked bangs bounced against a tan forehead as she jogged across the street to find the owner who may have been the only person in the neighborhood not at the shooting scene. He ran his gaze up from the bottom of her boots and along her short body until it reached her breasts.

"Do you have any rope or something I can borrow?" she asked him.

"We sell string." The owner turned his back, lifted the string from the shelf and turned back toward her, exaggerating his disdain with a lascivious glare toward her ample chest. He clutched the wrapped ball of string tight and twirled it in his hands.

"That'll be $1.19," he said.

"I'll pay later," Bradford said. "I've got a police emergency outside."

"That ain't such a good idea. I could be gone when you get back."

"I have to contain a crime scene."

"That means nothing to me. I'm trying to run a business without getting ripped off by you cops," the owner responded.

Bradford reached for some money, forgetting she'd sewn her front pockets shut to break the habit of stuffing her hands inside them after Francie dinged her score on officer safety for the second day in a row. "You can't pull your gun with your hands in your pockets," he'd told her. "And you can't block a punch to the face either." She finally remembered the two quarters she'd secreted in her back pocket for buying soft drinks from the cafeteria vending machines. "This is all I've got with me," she said, palming the coins in front of her.

Galindo eyed her silently for several seconds. "I think we can work something out," he said. He pulled a knife from his hip pocket, using the blade to slit the plastic covering the string. He hauled some twine out and wrapped it around his hand and elbow until satisfied the allotted portion amounted to the fifty cents Bradford offered. "There you go, officer." He sneered as he snatched the quarters from her palm.

"Asshole," Bradford muttered the word through tight lips as she pushed the front door open and stepped onto the sidewalk.

Galindo called out exaggeratedly as Bradford exited. "Have a nice day, Officer."

"How's this for high-tech police equipment?" Luke hollered. He and Bradford ran string from the bumper of a police car around a street lamp and back again, establishing a flimsy perimeter around the body.

A portly man pushed through the crowd toward the victim. Alejandro was embroidered on the chest of his greasy coveralls.

"Keep away," Luke ordered, convinced that the authority in his voice, backed up by the badge on his chest would command obedience.

Alejandro ducked beneath the string and went to his knees. A puddle of blood soaked into his pants. "I already know what happened," he said.

Alejandro's sniffles evidenced his fight to control his tears. "One of the boys ran over to the house and told me. They just drove around on the streets and seen this *vato* who don't belong in the neighborhood. My *Kiko*, he got out of the van like a big shot and told him, what's he doing here? That he don't belong. The vato, he pulled a shotgun from under his coat and pulled the trigger. What's he doing with a coat on? He came down here looking for somebody to shoot to make a name for himself." Alejandro lifted himself from his knees and sat cross-legged in the middle of the intersection.

"Get that guy out of the crime scene," Hartson yelled.

"My Kiko, he had to be the first one to challenge him. Look at me," he said. His shoulders quivered as he lost his fight to hold back the tears that flowed into a pencil thin mustache with flecks of gray at the edges. "I was in Nam. They couldn't do nothing to hurt me there. But right here in my own neighborhood, somebody gunned down my boy. What am I going to tell his momma?"

Luke saw Hartson coming and there he was, just standing there, letting some guy sit in the middle of the crime scene. Hartson stomped through the crowd, apparently prepared to give Luke a tongue lashing only an incompetent trainee deserved.

"Sir, I wish I had a clue what to say to your wife about your son," Luke said, raising his voice so Hartson could hear. He reached under Alejandro's arms and started to lift as the burly mechanic raised a calloused hand and wiped a rolling tear away.

"Officer," Alejandro pleaded, another tear rolling through his mustache. "Can I hold my baby just one more time so I can tell his momma?"

"I wish I could, but I can't let you do that," Luke said. "We need to work together to protect the scene so we can catch who did this. Why don't you tell your wife you did the right thing, that you stayed strong?"

Luke helped Alejandro up, walked him to the curb and helped him sit. Alejandro tried to stand, but crumpled to his knees in the gutter and rocked on his haunches.

Hartson helped Bradford finish securing the scene and motioned for Luke to join him at the car since a supervisor had arrived to take charge. Only a few officers were needed to stay at the scene until Homicide got there and Hartson was hungry. He directed Luke to the drive-through at Roberto's, a small fast food Mexican restaurant that resembled a swollen pickle barrel.

"What kind of crap is this?" Luke asked. "I thought you were springing for Greek food tonight."

"There you go thinking again. I must've forgot to tell you, trainees should be seen and not heard."

Luke understood this type of macho banter only got tossed around by guys who liked one another and basked in his gained acceptance as he and his partner took massive bites from greasy tacos and deep swigs from aluminum soda cans. Luke wiped a glob of guacamole from his mustache, lifted his chin and pointed out a patch of salsa on the front of Hartson's shirt below the name tag.

"Shit," Hartson said. "Goddamn it. Wipe that grin off your rookie face."

"Pretty sloppy if you ask me," Luke said.

"Nobody asked you," Hartson said as he wiped at the spot with a napkin. The action left a greasy red blob that spread outward in a fashion sure to set with an irrevocable stain.

"A clean shirt's the sign of a clean mind," Luke said. "That mess is the outer evidence of the filth trapped inside that head of yours."

"I suppose that's Shakespeare," Hartson said.

"Actually, that one's courtesy of Grandma Jones," Luke answered. "But there're plenty of slobs in Shakespeare's plays to help make her point. They're always his lowlife characters, you know, the drunks and sluggards, the kind of folks you senior guys call pond scum and dirtbags."

"Fifty-one-Frank," the dispatcher said before Hartson could frame a response. "Can you clear your Code-7?"

"Affirmative," Luke answered into the microphone without checking with Hartson.

"We've got a six-year-old on the line who says her parents aren't home and she can't be late for school. The phone room operator has promised not to hang up until somebody gets there."

"Doesn't want to be late for school?" Luke said to Hartson. "It's the middle of the afternoon?"

"We'll just contact and evaluate," Hartson said. "What else can I say?"

The upstairs door that was ajar drew their attention as they walked beside a curving hedge lined at its base by Shasta daisies. Hartson nodded toward a set of keys in the lock after they trudged up the stairs. He grabbed the edge of the door, put a foot inside, and knocked, calling out repeatedly before leading Luke inside to find a neatly groomed woman dressed in a trim black suit. She was curled into a fetal position on the couch, the phone clutched close to her ear.

Hartson cupped her shoulder and nudged her gently. "What's going on?" he asked her. "Who else is here?"

Luke checked out the rest of the apartment as Hartson answered a curious radio dispatcher's questions through his handie-talkie. "Yes. We're inside. No, there's no little girl here. There's only a woman who's probably in her late twenties, but we can't get her to talk to us."

Hartson tugged the receiver from the woman's ear and spoke to the operator while Luke surveyed the room for clues to what had happened. "Unbelievable," Hartson said after hanging up. "The operator says he's been talking to a six-year-old girl for close to an hour now. He *swears* it's a little girl."

Luke eased onto his knees and stroked the woman's clammy forehead as her body quavered against the flowered print of the couch. "Are you all right?" he asked. "Why did you call the police? What's happened?"

"My daddy hurts me." The tentative answer came in the timbre of a young child. "My mommy won't love me if I tell. I don't want to, but I don't want him doing things anymore."

"Your daddy won't hurt you from now on," Luke assured her. "My partner and I'll see to it that nobody hurts you." His words triggered a memory and he smelled a musty odor. He'd forgotten being there until this moment, in the house of a childhood neighbor. He couldn't have been more than seven and pushed open a bedroom door to see Tuffy standing in the middle of the floor with his pants around his ankles and a man's face close to his crotch. Tuffy stood as still as anyone could stand.

"Smell that?" Hartson asked Luke as he walked to the front door, pulled the keys from the outer lock and closed the door in the faces of a gaggle of nosy neighbors.

"She's peed herself," Luke said.

Hartson eyed Luke as he whispered words of consolation to the attractive woman with a shivering adult body and the broken heart of a little girl. "You know," he said as he started looking around the apartment for some identification to figure out who to call for help. "Every now and then, something comes along that really gets to me."

Luke nodded.

A pristine kitchen, neatly placed knickknacks and a bedroom closet full of tightly pressed women's suits still wrapped in plastic baggies from the Fairlane Cleaners revealed that only one person lived here and that person was an adult female. A telephone answering machine on a stand next to the couch displayed a flashing red light. Hartson finally noticed it, walked back into the living room, and turned the knob.

"Laurie," an older female voice said, a tremulous urgency evident in every syllable. "I haven't been able to find you anywhere. Baby. Your daddy didn't make it through surgery. Can you come home right away? I need you here with me."

The question held a poignant silence together until Luke broke the tension with a question. "How often do you take two people in one shift to the mental hospital?"

From his answer, Luke knew Hartson's emotional center of gravity had been knocked askew. "This job's a lot like golf, the big difference is, somebody else tees off, and then we play everything as it lays."

"What happened to her?" Luke asked.

"It doesn't take a shrink to figure this mess out," Hartson said. "She was obviously molested by her father as a kid."

"I got that much," Luke interrupted.

Hartson took a quick glance around the room. "Look at the evidence, smart guy. Considering the keys hanging in the lock, she was obviously either headed in or out the door. She heard the phone ring, ran in to hear the message and snapped when she heard it. She got completely helpless again, like a six-year-old girl being hurt by somebody who should have protected her." Hartson paused. "I hope the old fuck was in a lot of pain when he died, that's all I can say."

"You know, Luke," Hartson said as the ambulance pulled away and they piled into their car to drive to the station. "You ran into a lot more shit today than some officers see in a month."

A grin spread on Luke's face. "That sort of reminds me of a quotation," Luke said.

"Aw Jesus, of course it does," Hartson said.

Luke let fly.

O that a man might know,
The end of this day's business ere it' come,
But it sufficeth that the day will end,
And then the end is known.

"I don't suppose that's Grandma Jones," Hartson said.

"*Julius Caesar*," Luke answered.

"Really," Hartson said. "I actually figured it was probably Shakespeare."

"Shit," Hartson spit the word out before Luke could say the quotation actually came from Shakespeare's play, not from Caesar himself. "I guess we're not done yet after all?"

"Huh?"

"Didn't you see that?"

"See what?"

"Get your head out of your ass and maybe you'll see something sometime," Hartson said. "You didn't see the turn that gray truck just made?" Hartson leaned forward to activate the emergency lights.

"I didn't see anything," Luke said as the truck with the personalized license plate of "Thor," yielded and pulled to the curb.

Hartson passed between the front of the car and back of the truck before Luke unfastened his seat belt. The truck's driver, who confronted Hartson in the street, completely personified the mythical name on his license plate. He was a gigantic man with shoulder-length blonde hair and his resentful gaze shot down toward the smaller man.

"What the fuck do you want?" Thor demanded to know.

"Sir," Hartson said as he craned his neck upward to look the towering man in the eyes. "I need to see your driver's license and the truck's registration papers."

"What'd I do?" Thor demanded. The slits of his eyes narrowed and his hands balled into fists.

"When you made that turn, you cut across a double yellow line, drove on the wrong side of the road and nearly caused an accident." Hartson spoke the words as he glanced to his side to make sure Luke understood the danger.

"Like hell!"

"I'll be right back with my ticket book," Hartson said.

"I won't sign shit."

"You'll either sign or you'll go to jail," Hartson said.

Luke knew the authority Hartson represented dictated the eventual winner in the battle of wills. The price of victory was the only unanswered question.

"I've been digging ditches all week," the Viking giant said, a slightly quieter tone to his voice. "And a ticket'll cost me three days wages. Can't you give me a break this once?"

"If you wanted a break, you should've asked before you came off like such an asshole," Hartson said.

"You can bet your pig ass you'll have a fight on your hands," the Viking shot back.

"Is that a threat? Are you threatening me?" Hartson demanded.

"You'll see when you finish writing that ticket."

The Viking behemoth, pulling himself deliberately tall in his square-toed work boots, stood two heads taller than Hartson. The size disparity obviously catapulted his confidence to immeasurable heights.

"I'll shove that stupid club up your ass sideways till it comes out your ears." The Viking shouted the words at Hartson before turning his attention toward Luke for the first time. "And you," he bellowed. "What the fuck are you going to do when I'm taking this punk's policeman toys away and kicking his ass up and down the street?"

Luke had trained for this moment for more than a decade. "That man's my training officer." Luke squared his feet into a fighting stance and delivered his responses with the calm of a Zen master surrounded by the serenity of an oriental garden. "And if he tells me to, I'll be kicking your ditch digger ass."

18

Winter 1978

BALBOA PARK'S BIG BANG MOMENT of creation came with the Panama-California Exposition opening on January 1, 1915, in what had previously been known as City Park.

It's impossible to calculate the cost in lives, human misery and personal tragedies among the workers who constructed Panama's canal so rich people who lived in rich nations could improve the quality of their already stellar lives. It is safe to say none of those thoughts stirred the minds in the park on opening day so many years ago.

The Expo was so big its most august participant performed his role from a stage twenty-six hundred miles away. Woodrow Wilson threw a Washington D.C. switch that ignited a stream of light bulbs suspended from a massive balloon. The flash illuminated three square miles on the ground and coincided with events several miles distant as Navy ships in San Diego's bay boomed enormous cannons at Point Loma's Fort Rosecrans. The explosions reverberated for miles around.

The exposition's Isthmus, a stretch on the east side of the park, spanned 8,000 square feet, encompassing twenty-five acres of ground. It housed Ferris wheels and merry-go-rounds together with the menagerie of exotic animals that would later blossom into the world famous San Diego Zoo. Other displays included a China town, a Japan town and a Hawaiian dance stage. Colossal dioramas of scenes from

20,000 Leagues Under the Sea and The Battle of Manila Bay, complete with a shipwreck and battle sound effects, dominated the landscape. The exhibit also boasted a replica of a mountain railway train, a .22 caliber shooting gallery and elictriquettes, small electric cars that carried two or three people at the fantastic speed of three miles-per-hour around the exhibition.

The exposition's magnetic appeal lured the rich and famous from around the country. Among the more celebrated visitors were William Jennings Bryan, Teddy Roosevelt, then Secretary of the Navy, and his nephew, Franklin Delano Roosevelt. Given the electric light opening, the attending luminaries had to include Thomas Alva Edison.

The west end of the park's layout included football fields, baseball diamonds, botanical gardens—courtesy of Kate Sessions—and a lily pond shimmering beneath a spectacular concrete and steel bridge named for Juan Cabrillo, its six arches emulating a famous bridge in Spain. Quail and rabbit skittered beneath the undulating trees and it seemed for all the world that nothing could go amiss in this magnificent park, the crown jewel of the city referred to by so many as, "This sun-splashed Eden by the Sea."

The exposition's more understated closing ceremonies were, by all accounts, a touch more elegant. A famous resident opera singer, Madame Ernestine Schumann-Heink, stood on the Organ Pavilion's magnificent stage, belting out Auld Lang Syne, tears streaming down her face as a splendiferous display of fireworks spelled out, "World's Peace, 1917." Congress declared war on Germany less than four months later.

No one at the exposition could possibly have predicted that, several decades later, a couple of other skirmishes would play out at a gathering going by the elevated sobriquet of the "America's Finest City Rally."

San Diego's cops were fed up. They were tired of working for a mayor who insisted on running the sixth largest city in the country like Podunk-town America. His strongman insistence on tight-fisting the city's budget while good cops quit for department's paying decent wages was straining the relationship between the rank-and-file and the almost universally respected Chief of Police.

Cops who stayed were grossly underpaid and forced to do more with less. Community Oriented Policing was touted as a way for fewer officers to do more efficient work by forging alliances with the public, but it wasn't working at the street level and the attempted transition added more pressure to cops on the beats. They weren't giving in without a fight.

"This is really stupid," Denny Durango said. "I know it's totally dumb."

"Shut up your rookie face," Shimmer told him. "You're a cop now and us cops got to stick together."

"Now, you say that," Denny answered. "But at work, all I hear is how I don't measure up. How come you need me all of a sudden?"

"He's got a point," Devree said from the back seat. "This is some serious shit we're getting into and a guy still on probation shouldn't be sticking his nose into it."

"The kid was my trainee and he does what I tell him," Shimmer insisted. "It don't get much simpler than that."

Shimmer's forest green GTO rumbled off the freeway exit ramp and headed south on Sixth Avenue toward Balboa Park as he lectured Denny on his upcoming participation in the labor demonstration.

"That's right," Francie interrupted. "If these guys think they can hold this America's Finest City Rally without us shoving their crappy pay raise up their ass, they got another think coming."

"Yeah, but we don't need to toss the rookie into the grease," Devree insisted.

"He's one of us now and he does what he's told," Shimmer said.

Francie waded in, ignoring Devree's protestations. "It started when the Mayor couldn't land the Republican Convention a couple years back," he told Denny. "He tried passing a measure to build a convention center so he could get one later on and give a speech on national television. The public went to the polls and told him to go fuck himself. So, now he figures the road to the Governor's mansion is through this 'America's Finest City' bull crap. You don't think he's throwing this party for John Q. Citizen to have fun, do you?" Although the question headed in Denny's direction, Francie's response came from Shimmer.

"Hell no, he ain't. He's using this as his ladder to higher offices and he's choking off our salaries like we're ninety-eight pound weaklings and he's Charles Fucking Atlas. This is a major city in the country and he pays us like hicks from Dogpatch." Red blotches formed on Shimmer's face and spread to his neck. "LA's the only city in the state bigger than us, but every piss-ant town up and down the coast pays their cops better."

"Yeah," Denny said. "If you guys say so. That stuff means something to you older guys, but I don't want to get fired."

"This ain't about you," Shimmer said. "The reason we're training so many recruits is because you guys leave after passing probation to work somewhere you can make decent money. The Mayor's gutting our department to prove he's strong enough to fight labor organizations, which makes him governor material, he thinks. We ain't standing still for it while our cops bail out of town for higher pay and he crawls over our backs to the Governor's Mansion by exercising physical restraint."

"I think you mean fiscal restraint," Devree said.

"Huh?"

"Never mind."

The car lurched to a stop and the four officers piled out at Balboa Park's Sixth and Laurel Streets near a gigantic Australian Sequoia tree. "Look at that," Shimmer said. "They're setting up a goddamned podium to tell everybody what a goddamn paradise we live in."

"Some of these morons'll buy it, too. That's the part that puckers my ass," Francie reached into the trunk for the picket signs. "Some more cops and their families are coming. Let's get ready to bust this faggot's balls when he starts his speech."

"Looks like there's about four hundred assholes here," Shimmer said.

He helped pass around the signs. "This'll really fry the Mayor's gonads."

Denny couldn't help but wince at his mental image of a guy watching his gonads fry in a crackling pan.

Carloads of off-duty officers started piling out and milling around, waiting for the action to start.

Denny could almost smell the trouble sizzling in the air.

He didn't know for sure that Shimmer could get him fired, but his former training officer's potential vindictiveness made it damn risky not to cooperate with him.

They'd come to an uneasy truce back in the training phases. Shimmer actually agreed to start training Denny again, but only because he couldn't justify turning in a blank evaluation every day. He'd gotten away with ignoring Denny for a while, but the FTO office would only listen to his song about focusing exclusively on report writing for so long. Shimmer could get fired if he made stuff up on the evaluations, so he finally gave in once Luke threatened to go to the training office.

Denny had every reason to fear Shimmer. On the other hand, even if Shimmer did have the clout to get him fired, he wasn't the only one, and a lot of people with that kind of clout would be at the rally. That bunch wouldn't like the sight of a rookie picketing the Mayor's speech.

The thought of breaking his mother's heart with a second transcontinental call announcing he'd failed as a cop really scared him. Apart from his mother's love, his new career mattered more than anything. Sure, he was a marginal employee, but he got better every day and he'd be all right now that he'd scraped through the training phases.

The Mayor stepped to the podium and tapped the microphone. "Ladies and gentlemen, it's a pleasure for me to…" His voice faltered as the picketers stomped toward the staging area, signs held high:

America's Finest City Pays Its Cops Diddly.
Veteran Cops Leave Every Week for Higher Wages.
Call the Mayor Next Time Somebody's Breaking into Your House.
Your Taxes Pay to Train New Police Who Go Away for More Pay.
It Costs Less to Keep a Cop Than To Train One.

Shimmer handed Denny a sign that read "Don't Send the Mayor to the Governor's Mansion on Money He's Ripped Off from Cops' Salaries," and pushed him into the lead.

Denny saw someone chugging toward him under a full head of steam. It was Aaron Goddson, chief assistant to the Mayor and the marketing guru who'd coined the "America's Finest City" slogan. As the picket line wended its way through the rows of metal folding chairs, Goddson worked his way around to the front of the platform and stepped into Denny's path.

"You're ruining this thing for everybody," he grunted through gritted teeth.

"Get out of the way," Shimmer yelled from behind Denny. "We got a right to be here."

The tips of Goddson's ears turned red. He grabbed Denny's arms and pushed him back. "You're ruining it for the good people," he said, digging his heels into the grass with the exertion.

"Let me go. Are you crazy or something?" Denny said, trying to free himself from Goddson's grip without dropping the sign.

"We're the good people, you dip shit," Shimmer hollered back. "That's a crime you just committed. Is that what *your* good people do in this town? Is that what makes this 'America's Finest City?' You just battered a citizen because you thought we were ruining your precious little rally. This is America you know. Arrest him, Denny," Shimmer insisted. "That's a crime and you're the victim."

"You people get out of here and let us have our rally," Goddson insisted. "You're ruining this for everybody." He dropped his hands to his side.

"You ain't everybody," Shimmer reminded him. "Arrest him, Denny. We're all witnesses to the battery." Shimmer canvassed the other officers to verify their support. Nearly all the heads were nodding.

"That's right," Francie prodded. "Go call a unit over here and arrest his ass."

"I don't think that's such a good idea," Devree said. He stepped behind Denny.

"Bullshit," Shimmer countered. "It was battery and we all seen it. Arrest him Denny. I'll go call communications to send a unit so you can arrest him."

"Arrest me?" Goddson said. "Arrest me for what?"

"It's a battery whenever you touch somebody without their consent," Francie bellowed. "You can't go shoving folks around like that just because you work for the Mayor."

Shimmer disappeared into the crowd, headed for the public telephone.

"I didn't punch anybody," Goddson blurted out. "That can't be a crime."

"You can't go putting your hands on people without their consent," Francie said. "You'll be sorry you did that, you sonofabitch, when Denny here arrests you."

"That's not such a good idea," Devree whispered to Denny.

"He doesn't have any bruises," Goddson insisted. "Look at his arms, look at mine." He held his arms out in front of him. "He doesn't have any bruises and I don't have any bruises."

"It's against the law to touch somebody without their consent," Francie insisted. "Didn't I just tell you that? Arrest him Denny."

"I really don't think that's such a good idea," Devree whispered.

19

DR. BRANDON FLECKMAN, A NATTILY DRESSED, Harvard trained neurosurgeon parked his spanking new charcoal gray Volvo GL against the east curb of the 2500 Block of Balboa Drive. A brilliant man, he'd blazed to his elevated station through hard work and attention to detail. On this particular day, though, he was oblivious to the platform, balloons, soft drink stands, television trucks and pickets at the rally a block away as he stepped on a bed of sorrel-colored pine needles at the doorway to the men's room.

The door-less stall inside passed for his home away from home, doubling as a rent-free love nest, a place he kept secret from his family, friends and patients. It was a place for the not-so-clandestine rendezvous that he shared with nameless sex seekers who used the park's public restrooms for sexual trysts uncomplicated by social or emotional attachments.

Patchy brown paint on the greasy concrete wall was streaked with congealing mucous spread there by previous occupants. An invitation to call Freddie for the blow job of a lifetime was scrawled in red ink beneath the slime. Fleckman noted the phone number as he unzipped his pants, pulled out a partially erect penis and held it in his palm. His gesture of faith was bolstered by numerous previous trysts that had convinced him someone would surely follow him inside.

The stench of overflowing toilet water and the fecal matter oozing onto the floor in the adjacent stall wafted out into the sun-baked air of "America's Finest City."

The stink greeted Dallas Cleveland, an approaching city councilman whose nose crinkled upward in disgust as he turned to step inside. He clutched his toddling grandson's hand, directing the boy toward the urinal. "Come on over here and show me what a big fellow you've become," Cleveland said.

As Cleveland reached for the boy's zipper, Fleckman shuffled into the open, thrusting a now fully erect penis in front of him.

The councilman reared in disgust and shoved his grandson behind him.

Fleckman nearly tripped over his pants. He tried shuffling backwards into the confines of the stall and fell into the toilet.

Although, he wasn't about to get his dick sucked like he hoped, Fleckman was about to meet the man who'd made it possible for him to be in this place without fear of arrest. Cleveland's office had been deluged with a letter campaign protesting "police harassment of the gay community in the park."

Fleckman had fired off his own unsigned missive about the San Diego Police Department's "jack-booted-storm-troopers" and his letter, one of three received that particular day, had morphed into the proverbial straw that drove the city councilman's camel to its knees. Cleveland decided then and there to protest the enforcement of specific penal code sections "in and around the environs" of Balboa Park.

"Don't your cops have anything better to do?" was Cleveland's question to the chief. He followed with an emphatic, "Let them live in peace," which really meant he wanted to live in peace.

Although this encounter stemmed from Cleveland's public political actions, his private reaction here and now approached apoplexy. His facial muscles twitched and his neck flushed the color of creamed tomato soup as he grabbed his grandson to drag him back to the rally where he saw the more than two-dozen off-duty officers in attendance. "But, Grandpa, I still have to go wee wee," his grandson cried as Cleveland hurried forward.

He clomped up to one of the officers, struggling to calm his panting so he could speak intelligibly. "Officer, you won't believe what just happened to me in that bathroom," he said. "I saw some pervert in there"—he paused to gulp a breath and look at his grandson—"holding his…"

"His peepee, Grandpa," the child said.

"He just stood there, holding it and staring at me," Cleveland whispered. "God only knows what he thought I'd do with that thing."

"God's not the only one who knows," Devree answered back. "He either wanted a blow job or to give it to you up the ass."

The time for more apoplexy had arrived. Cleveland covered his grandson's ears. "Don't talk like that in front of my grandson." Cleveland pushed the boy toward his mother who stood near the platform, holding a balloon and waving in their direction. The child toddled off with urine trickling down his leg.

The sight of it made Devree sick, sick of what Francie and Shimmer were forcing on Denny, sick of the political bullshit keeping him from doing his job; sick of working crappy hours for crappy wages, and sick of looking at Dallas Cleveland. What kind of a stupid fucking name was that anyway? "That stuff happens all the time," he said. "You told the chief to make us ignore it. 'You've got better things to do' he tells us, so we're leaving them alone."

"I want that man arrested," Cleveland insisted. "My grandson saw that pervert, for goodness sakes."

"You don't think other folks have grandkids?" Devree said. "It was kids like him I tried to protect when I enforced the laws around here."

"What I saw—it was disgusting. Nobody should be subjected to that," Cleveland said.

"They can do whatever they want," Devree said. "You've said so."

"IT'S NOT RIGHT!" Cleveland bellowed. "Not in such a public place. I want him arrested!"

"You're a citizen," Devree said. "Go make a citizen's arrest."

"I demand that you go in there right now and arrest this man."

"Sorry. I'm off-duty right now and I'm pretty sure you can't demand shit," Devree said.

"That's right," Shimmer joined in from behind. "You can't tell him shit. Go arrest the guy yourself if you want it so bad. We're busy exercising our constitutional rights to self expression."

"Why don't you take your other grandkids in the bathroom with you?" Francie said. "They can help with the arrest. Let them see what it's like to try and enforce the laws around here when you can't get any support."

20

"HELP, MASTER, HELP! HERE'S A FISH hangs in the net, like a poor man's right in the law."

"Ah, come on Luke," Denny said. "For once in your life, please just say what you mean?"

"Yeah, what the fuck are you talking about?" Shimmer demanded.

"It's a quotation from *Pericles, Prince of Tyre*," Luke said. Out of training now, Luke was working as a single officer unit and had responded to the radio call about a citizen's arrest at the rally.

"Jesus Holy Christ," Shimmer exploded. "What kind of crazy shit are you talking now?"

"I'm saying you're screwing my roomie. Is that plain enough?" Luke spun around, turning his back on Shimmer to look his friend square in the eye. "Don't get bullied into this thing. You know this is stupid, and you can't afford to do anything stupid."

"Luke's right," Hartson told Denny as he stepped next to Shimmer. "This is definitely dumb. You should let the whole thing drop. So should the rest of these guys." Hartson, off-duty, had attended the rally to participate in the picketing.

"What do you mean, he's right?" Shimmer insisted. "You don't even know what the fuck he said."

"He said you're using his friend as your chump," Hartson answered. "He said that clear as day and you'd have heard it if your head wasn't shoved so far up your ass."

Luke nodded in thanks for Hartson's support.

"Bullshit! Bullshit! Bullshit! And more bullshit." Shimmer bellowed the bullshits as he looked about for support from the crowd of officers surrounding them. "I'm not using nobody. This is bigger than our beef with the Mayor. We all seen the battery on Denny. This is about a crime." He looked around again and got signs of approval as several heads nodded. "Goddson can't get away with this shit just because he works for City Hall."

"If you all saw it, and this battery thing is so important, why don't you guys make the pinch?" Luke said. "I can carry Denny as the victim on the case report, but one of you geniuses can make the citizen's arrest and ride the heat."

"Officer," Councilman Dallas Cleveland interrupted, "I want that man in the restroom arrested, right now."

"I'll be right with you," Luke told him. "I can only do one thing at a time."

"But, he might get away!" Cleveland said.

"That's right Councilman, he might," Hartson interjected. "Officer Jones will do his best to help you in a few minutes. Right now he's got this other situation."

"Go ahead, Denny," Shimmer insisted. "Tell Goddson he's under arrest for battery and let's get on with it."

"Don't do it, Denny," Luke insisted. "Remember that quotation I mentioned a minute ago? In the same play, one character says to the other, 'Master, I marvel how the fishes live in the sea' and the guy answers back, 'Why, as men do a-land; the great ones eat up the little ones.'"

Luke stood looking at Denny, waiting for his words to sink in.

"What's your fucking point?" Shimmer insisted.

"Yeah, what are you trying to say?" Francie said.

"Come on, Luke, what are you talking about?" Denny's desperation showed.

"For cripes sake, put it in plain words so all this whining stops," Hartson said.

"What language am I speaking?" Luke asked incredulously. "Let me say it in plainer English. I mean Denny's a minnow and you other guys—with your tenure and your civil service protection—you're the big fish. Mr. Goddson and the Mayor's office, they're even bigger fish than you guys. Denny can't win, no matter who he messes with. You guys need to give him a break and fight your own battles."

"It makes sense what he's saying," Devree said.

"Shut up your face," Shimmer shouted to Luke, ignoring Devree. "You obviously don't understand how things work around here. You're just a rookie who does what he's told, and I'm telling you to keep your fucking mouth shut."

"See that man over there?" Luke lifted his chin toward T.D. Hartson. "He was my training officer, and if he tells me to keep my mouth shut, I might think about it. You're nobody to me but some jerk screwing my friend."

Shimmer tried butting in.

Luke cut him off. "Let me tell you the way things work with me. I say what I think is right and you find a way to live with it."

"Ah, geez," Shimmer said, total exasperation registering through the sweat that rolled along cheeks taking on the hue of dirty beets. "Tell this punk to shut up," he told Hartson. "Tell him to mind his own goddamn business and do what he's told."

"What do you think I should do?" Denny asked Luke.

Luke could see it was a rhetorical question—that Denny knew what he should do and knew what he was going to do and that the two were not the same. He could see the fear and anger in Denny's eyes. Denny just wanted to do his job and prove he could be a good cop and he was being railroaded by cowards.

This all appeared too much for the city councilman to endure. "Officer, I want that man in the bathroom arrested," he interrupted again. City Councilman Dallas Cleveland had obviously never been treated with such cavalier disdain in his entire life.

"Shut up and do what you're told, that's what you should do," Shimmer said to Denny, ignoring the councilman.

"Don't do it," Luke told Denny. "You're the only one who can lose in this situation. These guys want to hold a political fish fry to burn the Mayor, but you're the one getting cooked."

"Goddamn it, Luke, talk to me in plain English," Denny said.

This pile had risen to the level of all the rookie generated bullshit Shimmer could stand. "Arrest his ass," he insisted. He sidled behind Denny with absolute finality, pinched his back and breathed hot air onto his neck. "That's an order, and if you don't follow it, you'll be one sorry piece of shit rookie. You got me?" Shimmer obviously considered it irrelevant that he possessed exactly zero institutional authority to issue an order to anybody.

"Mr. Goddson, you're under citizen's arrest for battery" Denny said, the desperation obvious in his voice.

Francie jumped in and took the lead. "That's it," he said, stepping into the middle of the group. "You're under arrest, you sorry sonofabitch and Officer Jones here's going to write you a ticket for committing a battery. Isn't that right, Officer Jones?"

"It's a lawful arrest," Luke said. "You know I can't refuse."

"Officer," Councilman Dallas Cleveland blurted out as he stood on his toes, trying to see over the shoulders of the huddled officers. "I was accosted not fifteen minutes ago," he jiggled an extended finger up and down, pointing at the bathroom, "and I want you to go arrest that pervert."

"I'll be with you just as soon as I write this citation," Luke said. Then he started to write.

"Mr. Goddson, would you sign right here, please," Luke placed the pen to the line with an X for the suspect's signature and tapped it against the paper. "I'm issuing you a citation to appear in court at the time and place indicated at the bottom. When you sign, you're not admitting guilt, simply promising to appear in front of the judge."

"There are no bruises on his arms," Goddson insisted. "Neither one of us fell to the ground. I didn't punch him or anything. Battery sure sounds more serious than what happened."

"It's a battery anytime you touch somebody without their consent," Shimmer shouted. "How many times you got to hear that?"

"Damn straight," Francie joined in.

"That's something to save for the judge," Luke told Goddson as he tore the citation on the perforated lines. He pulled the pink defendant's copy off and handed it to Goddson.

Luke overheard a muffled conversation between Shimmer and Hartson as Goddson snatched the paper from his hand.

"What's up with your trainee?" Shimmer demanded. "First, he talks about some pair of cleats in a tire or some damn thing, like that makes some fucking sense to a normal person. Then the SOB tells me to shut up and you stand there and let him get away with it."

"Let me tell you something," Hartson countered. "When Luke was my trainee, we stopped this monster to write him a ticket. The guy bails out of his truck like a linebacker on steroids and I'm the quarterback. He tells me he's not signing shit and he'll kick my ass if I try taking him to jail. He's big enough to drive a Mack truck through and he's rocking back and forth, balling his hands into fists and sweat's streaming down his forehead."

"What's that got to do…?"

"I'm about to grab the radio and call for cover. The guy turns to Luke and says, 'What are you going to do while I'm kicking this pussy's ass?' Luke looks him in the eyeballs and tells him, 'I'll kick your ass if my training officer tells me to. That's what I'm going to do.' The guy looks Luke up and down. Luke's standing there like he's ready to fight and don't expect to lose. All of a sudden the guy decides, 'Hey, maybe signing this ticket ain't such a bad idea after all.' As far as I'm concerned, Luke Jones can speak his mind whether you like it or not."

Councilman Dallas Cleveland's exasperation started boiling over. "Officer," he said, pushing his way toward Luke again. "I'm a city councilman in this town and I insist that you go over and arrest that pervert."

Luke had never heard of City Councilman Dallas Cleveland, but he did know a radio call when he heard one. "Five-John," the dispatcher said, "A 211 just occurred near the El Cid statue on the Prado. Can you break and respond?"

"10-4," Luke said.

"I'm sorry, sir," Hartson told Dallas Cleveland as he guided Luke away. "A robbery just occurred on the other side of the park and Officer Jones has to go handle that right now."

Luke drove across the Cabrillo Bridge now spanning State Highway 163 to reach the eastern portion of Balboa Park that once hosted the Isthmus. It presently housed the Old Globe Theatre, Aerospace Museum, San Diego Museum of Art, the Natural History Museum and several other cultural complexes.

Luke pulled to a stop near the entrance of the Alcazar Garden. A woman sat against the base of an enormous black statue of the legendary Spanish champion who'd fought against the Moors. El Cid sat astride a rearing stallion and Luke knew statues had an abbreviated language of their own. Any statue of a person astride a rearing stallion had died in battle.

Pain registered in the woman's eyes and her trembling shoulders tilted forward. Her scraped hands massaged a swollen knee. "I'm glad to see you, officer," she said.

"What happened?" Luke asked. He squatted beside her.

"I was just walking to the El Prado when this goon came up behind me," she said. "He grabbed my purse and started running. I didn't know what was happening at first and I just held on until I fell down."

"What's your name?" Luke asked, trying to establish a little rapport.

"Emma."

"I'm Luke," he said. "Okay, Emma, go ahead."

"He just kept dragging me along the ground until the strap broke," she said. "He never got a thing." She lifted the strapless purse and held it in her lap like a prize. "Then he ran that way." She pointed toward the sidewalk that led along Park Boulevard toward the eastern edge of downtown.

"What did the guy look like, Emma?"

"Like a filthy bum, and he stunk something awful."

"Why don't we start at the top and work our way down? How tall?" Luke pulled his notebook to jot down the weight, hairstyle and color and type of clothing. He pulled his handie-talkie from its leather case next to his handcuffs to broadcast a description. "Unit 5-John, are you clear to copy an all-units?" he asked the dispatcher.

"Go ahead, 5-John."

"This is a 664-211 strong arm. Suspect is a white male about thirty-five to forty, with a scruffy beard. His hair's dark brown and extremely dirty. He's about five-foot-six, wearing sandals with no socks, dirty Levis and a blue and white Polo shirt with a hole in the back near the shoulder."

A few minutes later, a two-officer unit advised dispatch they had a suspect detained in front of a liquor store at the corner of 12th and Broadway just a few blocks to the south.

Luke asked Emma to take a ride with him to check out a possible suspect. "Let me explain a few things to you," Luke said as he drove. "The guy the other officers have detained may or may not be the man who tried to rob you. All I want is for you to take a good look at him and tell me directly if he's the right guy. I don't want you saying anything to him. Can you do that for me?"

"I can do that all right," Emma said as they turned south onto Park Boulevard from President's Way and headed toward the liquor store. "I sure would like to give him a swift kick, though."

Two officers stood on either side of the man who matched the broadcasted description. The neck of a Thunderbird wine bottle peeked over the top of a crumpled paper bag at his feet.

"Hey, that's the old biddy I mugged," the obvious drunk said as the police car lurched to a stop in front of him. "What's she doing here?" One of the officers stepped behind the prisoner to apply the cuffs.

"Well, geez," Luke said, overhearing the impromptu confession through the open window. "I guess that wraps this caper up."

As they pulled into the parking lot behind Balboa Park's Organ

Pavilion, home of free musical concerts, the annual nativity scene and the place where Madame Ernestine Schumann-Heink had sung "Auld Lang Syne" for the closing ceremonies of the Panama-California Exposition, Emma leaned toward the dash and clucked her tongue. "Officer, that's my Civic over there," she said. "See it, the one with the drunk leaning against it?"

"I see it." Luke stepped onto the pavement. "Come on now. Get up," he said, kicking the sole of the drunk's dirty Converse tennis shoe. "Get up and move along."

The drunk grunted, pulled his legs toward his abdomen and curled up beneath the front wheel-well. He never loosened his grip on a bagged can of Olde English 800 malt liquor.

Luke tapped the soles of the drunk's shoes with his wooden baton. There was no response. "Okay, that's enough," Luke said. He squatted, placed his left knee on the pavement, grabbed the drunk's hand and lifted at the wrist. He pulled the unconscious man from the pavement and twisted his wrist, pointing the fingers downward in an Aikido pain compliance maneuver. With a firm hold, Luke applied downward pressure, folding the drunk's elbow against his own abdomen directly above the gun belt as he stood and pulled the drunk along with him.

"Owowowowowow. Owowowowow. Owow. Ow," the man bellowed. He awoke to find himself standing tall on his toes next to a fortress of a man in a police uniform.

With his free hand, Luke searched the drunk's pockets for weapons or contraband. Finding neither, he rolled his prisoner's wrist behind his back. He reached to the left side of his gun belt and pulled out his cuffs before rolling one onto the trapped wrist. "Put your other hand behind you," he ordered. The drunk complied between cries of pain as Luke cuffed the loose wrist to the shackled one before kicking the can of malt liquor over.

"Ah Jesus," the man cried. "What did you have to go and do that for? Ah Jesus. Ah Jesus."

Luke swung the front of the car onto Park Boulevard for the second time and headed south toward the Detox Center at the end of the long downward slope leading from Pill Hill north of the park to the portion of San Diego's Harbor spanning the gulf between downtown San Diego and the Isthmus of Coronado.

A plane zoomed overhead and a school bus full of screaming children pulled beside the car at a red light. As the light turned green and the cacophonous noises settled into a bearable roar, Luke heard muttering sounds coming from the back seat. The words were only slightly louder than the rattling of the radio traffic suddenly emerging in the background after being drowned out by the roar.

The "Ah Jesus" chorus had evolved into the lyrics of one of Luke's favorite poems:

Where Alph, the sacred river ran. Through caverns measureless to man...

Luke turned the radio down and looked in the rear view mirror. What he heard was a baritone voice delivering the lilting lyrics of exquisite poetry. What he saw was a drunk with a wad of drool hanging from his upper lip. He joined in unison—"...down to a sunless sea. So twice five miles of fertile ground, with walls and towers were girdled round..."

"Hey," the drunk interrupted. "I didn't know cops knew anything about Coleridge."

"That's funny," Luke said. "I didn't know skuzzy old downtown drunks knew anything about Coleridge either."

"I know, huh." The two men laughed together.

Luke pulled into the lot. The front desk clerk, one of a group of recovering alcoholics who ran the center, flung the entrance door outward to wade into the parking lot. He clutched a clipboard. "Sorry, Professor, you know you can't stay. It's already been five times this month. Sorry, Officer, he's reached our quota for the month. He'll have to go to jail this time." The clerk hurriedly signed the bottom of a form, tore it from the clipboard and handed it to Luke. "Here's your rejection slip."

Luke put the man back into the car. "What did he mean calling you Professor?" Luke asked.

"I used to be a literature professor up at UCLA, but the bottle sort of got the best of me," the man said.

"No kidding," Luke said. "I got my master's in Renaissance Literature before I started the academy."

During the short pause that followed, Luke marveled at how a shared love had bridged the obvious chasm between him and the intoxicated and handcuffed man behind the cage. He briefly wondered what the Professor was thinking. Then the two men simultaneously started the poem over and went through to the end.

"Hey, Luke," the Professor said as the car headed into the jail's sally port. He leaned forward, pressing his face against the cold metal. "I'm thinking of the perfect Shakespearean quotation for this occasion. Any idea what it is?"

"No," Luke said.

"It's from Richard II."

"I'm still not with you," Luke answered.

"Here goes," the Professor said, "*I have been studying…*"

"Hang on," Luke interrupted. "Now I think I'm with you. Start it over."

The Professor began again.

Luke joined in to quote part of Richard the Second's lament before his death. "*I have been studying how I may compare the prison where I live unto the world.*"

"You're right. That's just about perfect," Luke said. Then he walked the Professor in to the jail.

21

POLICE CHIEF BOB COLEMAN'S SECRETARY opened his door, poked her streaked bangs through the widening opening and interrupted the meeting. "Chief," she said, "Mayor Pillson's on line one, and he doesn't sound happy."

Coleman took a long puff from his cigarette and smashed the tip into the ashtray. A swirl of smoke rimmed the indented edges as ashes smeared into the gold badge embossed at the bottom of the thick glass. His team of assistants took their cue, stood away from the mahogany conference table and filed toward the door as he reached for the phone. "Hi, Pete," Coleman said. He reached for the lighter and stuck a white filter between his lips. "What's up?"

"What's up, is one of your officers just arrested my chief assistant for battery and I want it taken care of," the Mayor said.

Coleman was incredulous. "I don't know what you're talking about."

"I'm talking about your officers coming to my America's Finest City Rally and arresting Aaron Goddson for a little push. That's what I'm talking about."

"I don't know anything about that. What happened?"

"Nothing happened. That's my point. Some of your officers showed up to picket my rally and Goddson simply asked if they wouldn't mind moving on so everybody could have a good time and one of your guys arrested him. Your people had no business being there to begin with.

It was a false arrest and an abuse of police power and I want it taken care of."

Coleman knew his cops were righteously pissed at the Mayor. Their march on the city council meeting a few days before had proved that.

He also knew Pillson had a tough job trying to run the city even if his ambitions were no secret. Coleman believed Pillson had his eye on an eventual run for the White House and had to prove himself in San Diego before he could take his next logical step. His ambition didn't make him a bad guy, but it did make Coleman's job harder.

Coleman genuinely liked the Mayor. But Coleman was a cop at heart and his troopers' respect really mattered. He certainly respected anybody who wore a badge and didn't automatically believe the worst about them, no matter who made the accusations.

"I don't know what went on," Coleman said. "But calling it a bogus arrest sounds a little over the top."

The gap spanning the cosmos between an ill-advised enforcement action and false arrest could be either miniscule or gargantuan. A tiny gap meant small problems. A huge gap could spark an explosion big enough to topple an entire police administration if mishandled. Coleman paused, giving the Mayor a chance to respond.

No response came.

Coleman's secretary peeked into the room again, exaggerating a wincing movement with her cheeks and eyebrows. It clearly indicated more trouble was coming Coleman's way as she tiptoed to the edge of the enormous mahogany desk and slipped a yellow piece of paper onto the blotter next to the Chief's glasses.

"Goddson got arrested for not doing anything. What else would you call it but police harassment?" the Mayor said.

"I'll check into it," Coleman promised before hanging up, picking up his silver-rimmed bifocals, and reading the message written in the bold ink of a red felt pen. Call Councilman Cleveland as soon as you can!

"Just a second," the secretary at the other end of the line said. "He'll be right with you, Chief." She lowered her voice to a whisper. "Just thought you should know, he asked me to hold all his calls until you got through."

"What's up?" Coleman asked.

"I really don't know. All I can tell you is he's hopping mad."

"What can I do for you, Dallas?" Coleman asked when the councilman picked up the line. Cleveland, a constant pain in Coleman's ass, sometimes tried to run the police department and the chief sometimes gave in to his ridiculous demands just to keep his sanity.

"I was accosted by some pervert in Balboa Park in broad daylight and your officers refused to help me. That's what you can do for me."

"I just got off the phone with the Mayor," Coleman said. "He tells me Goddson got arrested for not doing anything, now you tell me my officers wouldn't help you arrest somebody who committed a crime. What the hell's going on out there?"

The answer was silence.

"How were you accosted? Who were the officers involved? What exactly are you talking about?" Coleman asked.

"I'm talking about walking into a public restroom with my grandkid, in broad daylight, and having some pervert standing there with his prick in his hand and your officers refusing to help me. That's what I'm talking about." The councilman's sputtering words sounded like a verbal Gatling gun spitting out bullets.

"Slow down and tell me exactly what happened," Coleman said.

"I had my grandson with me, for goodness sakes."

"What happened to him?"

"Nothing happened to him. You're not listening."

Coleman tapped a cigarette filter against his desk.

"I went into the bathroom at Pete's rally and found some guy standing there holding his erect johnson in his hand with his pants down around his ankles. That's what happened. I told several of your officers about it and they refused to help. How much more do you need to know?"

"You led the brigade telling me to have my troopers lay off those guys. Now you want me to discipline them for following orders. Is that what you're telling me?"

"Cripes, Bob, that's different and you know it. I was talking about guys being hassled just because they're gay."

"That's not what we're talking about at all," Coleman said. "Just how did you think these guys make their desires known in a public place in broad daylight? They do it how you described. Sometimes they get a taker and sometimes they run into folks who get the shock of their lives. It's not a pretty sight, but you asked me to have my officers lay off because of the complaints you kept getting, so don't lay all this crap on my guys."

Coleman listened to Cleveland's heavy breathing and involuntary clucking noises. Recognizing the signs of anger building to the exploding point, he adopted a more conciliatory tone. "Do you know who the officers were?"

"I didn't get their names."

"Do you know where they work?"

"No, I don't."

"Were they patrol officers or detectives?"

"I don't know."

"Were they in uniforms or suits and ties?"

"Flip flops and T-shirts mostly, but one of them wore a uniform."

"What?"

"What did I just say?"

"That doesn't make any sense."

"That's how they were dressed."

"Wait a minute," Coleman said. "Are you telling me these officers weren't on duty?"

"The one in uniform was, I guess. What's that got to do with anything? Besides, what do you mean telling me I'm laying crap on somebody? All I've got to say is it must be a hell of a lot worse out there than it used to be. I mean—the guy just stood there holding his johnson in his hand like—like he wanted to hand off a football. That's a public park and I want a stop put to that kind of foolishness."

"I'll see what I can do," Coleman said, resisting the impulse to say what he really thought. The buzzer rang the instant Coleman hung up the phone.

"Chief," Coleman's secretary said. "Tom Murray from the San Diego Union's on line one."

Coleman realized Murray's call would probably be the least painful of the press calls he'd have to take. Murray, a journeyman police reporter, was genuinely too nice a guy to move up the reporter's ranks. He lacked that certain killer instinct necessary to sniff out a story and follow it through to its ruthless conclusion in spite of the consequences to people's lives. He ran stories down by utilizing the personal relationships he'd cultivated with the men and women of the San Diego Police Department, up and down the ranks. They genuinely liked him, and didn't consider him a threat.

"Chief," Murray asked as Coleman picked up the phone again, lighting the cigarette in his hand. "Can I ask you to comment on the arrest of Aaron Goddson at the America's Finest City Rally earlier today?"

"I don't know much yet," Coleman said. "But I can tell you this much. I don't like what I see."

"Exactly what have you seen so far?"

"Well nothing really but…"

"Have you read the arrest report?"

Coleman took a deep breath. He'd already committed a tactical error saying he didn't like what he'd seen. "Not yet but…"

"Have you spoken to the officers involved?"

"I don't know who they are. But I can tell you this, I intend to press this investigation fully." This represented a much smarter line to take.

"Well, let me ask you this," Murray insisted. "Was the arrest warranted?"

"I'll have to let the investigators make that determination," Coleman said.

Most reporters would've pressed their advantage once Coleman said he'd seen something he didn't like. Coleman was grateful Murray let it pass.

Coleman hung up, but immediately picked up the receiver to dial the Homicide Lieutenant's extension. "Jim," he said. "Mayor Pillson's hot under the collar right now and I don't blame him. He says one of our officers arrested his chief assistant just for asking him to leave a picnic. I want one of your teams to start investigating this thing right away."

"Chief, I'm a little strapped right now," Lieutenant Berend said. "We had two murders over the weekend with two suspects in custody and a forty-eight-hour deadline to finish the DA's packages. Crimes Against Persons usually handles this sort of thing, or Internal Affairs maybe, if you think that's appropriate."

"I don't care what you've got on your plate," Coleman said. "I want a Homicide team investigating this thing because I want all the bases covered, and I want you briefing me on every move. Is that clear?" Coleman made sure his voice signaled his sense of urgency, the kind of urgency that could make heads roll.

"Yes, sir, I'll take care of it," Berend said.

Coleman next dialed the extension to his academy classmate and good friend, the Captain of Central Division, to demand that something be done about the "increasing problems around the men's rest rooms at Balboa Park."

"Problems? What problems?" Captain Mahler asked. "Didn't you say we don't have any of those? Didn't you tell me to leave those people alone?"

"Councilman Cleveland walked in on some pervert tripping over his pants and holding his stuff in his hand," Coleman said. "All of a sudden, we've got an issue again and he wants something done. What I need is for you to handle it so he gets off my ass. Could you do that for me?"

"Okay, Bob. I'm all for enforcing the laws Cleveland used to tell us to leave alone, especially since you're saying something has to be done.

But we should have never stopped in the first place."

"It's not me saying it."

"Then who is?"

Coleman hesitated. "Okay, it's me. You had to make me say that?"

"I told you when we gave the orders to stop enforcing those laws we had a problem on our hands."

"All right," Coleman said. "You can go ahead and say I told you so if you want, but I still need this thing handled."

"It'll be a little tricky, getting the troopers motivated since we kept telling them to lay off," Mahler said. "What should I tell them?"

"Tell them the truth," Coleman said. "Tell them the councilman walked in on some pervert and wants something done."

"That's not such a good idea, Chief. It's sure to piss the guys off, knowing Cleveland made us lay off for political reasons, but changed his mind because he was personally offended."

"Maybe you're right," Coleman agreed. "Tell them whatever you want. Just find some way to deal with this thing and get Cleveland off my ass."

"What about the complaints we'll start getting? My supervisors will all be tied up with personnel investigations," Mahler said.

"Goddamn it, I'll tell you what," Coleman insisted, "how about I just give the order and you figure a way to get it done?"

"Seems fair enough, considering I don't have any choice," Mahler said.

"It's good to hear you're finally seeing things my way. By the way," Coleman said before hanging up, "the shit's really spattering against the walls and dribbling down to the floors around here. I better pass on happy hour."

Coleman's secretary called him on the intercom as soon as the phone's light went dark to tell him a crowd of reporters were swarming his outer office with microphones, note pads and cameras in hand.

In no mood to confront a pack of reporters, Coleman lit a cigarette and dialed the extension to the Press Relations Office. No one picked up, so he cleared the line and started calling his deputy chiefs in order of preference. All lines went unanswered until he called his last choice, Hal Browner, the one deputy chief he'd inherited when promoted to the top position a few years before. The officers in the lower ranks referred to him ironically as "Hal, the patrolman's pal" because of his reputation for visiting harsh punishment on mistakes or violations of department policy. Coleman didn't like Browner any more than his patrol officers did.

"Hal," he said when he heard Browner's voice at the other end. "I've got a pack of reporters over here and I need you to come down and deal with them. I'm up to my ass in alligators and I need you to wrestle a few for me."

"What am I supposed to say to them?"

"All I know is Pete tells me one of our officers arrested Aaron Goddson at the America's Finest City Rally because he didn't like Goddson's attitude," Coleman said. "It hasn't been looked into yet, but it sounds pretty bad. Just tell them there's an ongoing investigation and we'll have some sort of comment later."

Hal Browner closed the door to his office on the way to Coleman's waiting room. "Ladies and gentlemen," he said as he strode in, "Chief Coleman has asked me to answer any questions you might have."

"Hal," Murray jumped in. "What's the name of the officer who made the arrest?"

"I'm not at liberty to tell you that just now."

"What happened out there?" another reporter asked.

"We're looking into that. I'll be able to tell you more as the investigation moves along."

"Let me ask you this," Murray pressed, "was this a legitimate arrest, or did the officer arrest Goddson because he didn't like his attitude?"

Browner thought for a second about holding the company line; that the incomplete investigation inhibited further comment. But it was the

Mayor himself making the accusations after all. Pillson would love seeing this quote in the morning paper. "Since you put it that way, if you want to talk about an attitude arrest, this exemplifies it to the hilt." Browner smiled.

Satisfied he had the makings of a provocative headline, Murray hurried into the press office situated next to the SWAT armory. Murray, the *San Diego Union's* reporter officially assigned to the police beat, warranted the office along with his counterpart from the afternoon *Tribune.* Since the *Tribune's* reporter wasn't at work yet, Murray could get the jump on the story. He picked the phone up and called the Mayor's office.

"Mayor Pillson, can you tell me about the arrest of Aaron Goddson at the America's Finest City Rally earlier today? I understand you've filed a formal complaint with the Chief."

"To me, it's an abuse of police power, even if it is a small one," Pillson said. "It's unfortunate that a respected citizen, who's given so much of his time to this celebration, can be treated this way."

"Can I speak with Mr. Goddson?" Murray asked.

"This thing shook him up so badly, I sent him home for the day."

"Can I have his home phone number?"

"I'll tell you what," Pillson said, "give me your number and I'll have him call you back within a few minutes."

Murray set the receiver down to fill his stained coffee cup with five-hour-old black coffee. Before he could manage his first sip, the phone rang with Goddson on the line.

"Mr. Goddson," Murray asked. "As the Mayor's chief assistant, aren't you a little bit embarrassed at being arrested?"

"To tell you the truth, the officers should be embarrassed," Goddson answered. "I just asked if they wouldn't mind moving along since we were having a picnic. Times are pretty scary when that's enough to get you arrested, wouldn't you say?"

Murray hung up the phone and pondered the question he'd decided not to ask. When had the America's Finest City Rally the Mayor orchestrated to gain the political will to build a convention center turned into a simple picnic?

22

A MAN POUNDED AT THE APARTMENT'S DOOR for more than a minute. "Criminy," Lt. Berend said. "This Durango kid has to be at work in about an hour. Where else could he be?"

Luke set his dog-eared copy of *Nietzsche's Human, All Too Human* on top of his bedroom copy of *The Complete Works of William Shakespeare*, slipped out of bed and pulled a pair of gym shorts over his BVD's. He started rehearsing his response, assuming the insistent knocking was coming from one of Denny's persistent women who showed up at all times of the day or night.

Denny already had a woman in his bed on the opposite side of the living room. Luke intended to lie about his roomie's whereabouts and to politely, but firmly, refuse to let the knocking woman inside the apartment.

Luke walked to the refrigerator before heading for the door to buy some time to decide on what he'd come to call his *prevarication du jour* about Denny's sexual activities. His naked feet crunched the sunflower seeds dropped by the cockatoo Denny kept in a cage where the living room's shag carpet merged with the canary-colored linoleum.

Luke grabbed the orange juice from the top shelf and padded toward the door, deciding on the easiest lie possible. He'd say Denny had left for work a little early.

Luke shook the orange juice as he peeked through the security hole.

There was no woman standing outside the door this time, just two men wearing the white shirts and ties that made them look like Mormon missionaries intent on saving somebody's soul. The man in front straightened his tie.

Luke opened the door.

"Are you Denny Durango?"

"No," Luke said. "He's in bed."

"Who are you?" the man in front asked.

"What do you mean, who am I? Who are you?"

"I'm Lt. Jim Berend with SDPD Homicide and this is Sgt. Bob Farren. We're here to see Denny Durango."

"What does Homicide want with Denny?"

"I think we should save that information for Officer Durango, don't you?" Berend put one foot inside the apartment as he said it.

"Sure thing," Luke said. "Come on in and I'll get him up. He needs to get ready for work anyhow."

Berend glanced at his watch. Luke could tell his thoughts by his perturbed expression. Damn straight Denny needed to get ready for work. The rookie should already be at the station looking up crime trends on his beat and preparing a patrol strategy for his upcoming shift.

A silky white pair of thighs that wrapped around Denny's ears impaired his hearing as he nibbled and licked a swollen clitoris through moist silk panties. Rounded hips and an abdomen as smooth as brushed Egyptian cotton undulated above the mattress of the king-size waterbed as Denny's tongue slow danced in unison with the thrumming sounds of Donna Summer's singing "Love to Love Ya Baby" on the stereo.

Luke pounded harder and got no response. He knew his knocking was loud enough for Denny to hear him and assumed his roommate believed he'd eventually go away and get rid of whatever woman had showed up unannounced. Denny was wrong.

Luke pulled the door open, pushed his way across the room and flipped the switch to the stereo down. "There's some people from Homicide here to see you," he said and walked away without giving Denny a chance to ask any questions.

Denny stood robed in the living room within two minutes, rubbing his eyes. "You guys are from Homicide?" he asked. "Who died?"

"Nobody's died," Berend said. "We need you to come down to the station so we can get to the bottom of what happened in the park today."

Denny looked at Luke, but spoke to Berend. "What's Homicide got to do with anything?"

"The Chief's asked us to look into this thing for him. Don't you work graveyard tonight?"

"The Chief?" Denny asked incredulously.

"Yes, the Chief," Berend said. His lowered voice added gravity to his words. The added impact was unnecessary.

"It'll take me a few minutes to get ready," Denny said.

"Fine. Just go ahead and get into uniform. We'll drive you to the station."

"I don't need a ride," Denny said.

"You can ride with us," Sgt. Farren said. "You can start your shift after we get through with a few questions down at the station. We'll see to it your Sergeant finds a way to get you home in the morning."

Denny and Luke split off in opposite directions, Luke glaring over his shoulder at Denny as they disappeared into their respective rooms. He hoped his eyes conveyed the, I told you so message he wanted so badly to shout across the room.

Luke despised anyone who victimized other people and he hated situations when he felt helpless. His brother Tuffy had made him feel that way often enough, but Tuffy was six years older and Luke had been too helpless to fight back in those early days, but not anymore. He'd long since vowed never again to let anybody abuse him or take advantage of anyone he cared about.

Protecting victims was one of the main reasons he'd become a cop.

But he'd let Denny down at the rally. Francie and Shimmer had manipulated his roomie into doing something stupid enough to jeopardize his career. To top it off, they'd seen to it that Luke got stuck with writing the ticket after their act of cowardice. That made Luke an unwilling Judas and the thought of it made the back of his head hurt and his stomach ache.

As Luke heard the living room door slam shut, he pulled a folding chair from behind his desk and set it in the center of the room. He faced downward, lifted his feet to the front of the chair, stretched his arms out and started doing pushups. It was the only way he could stem the rage that was building toward Francie and Shimmer and all the other people who turned good people into dupes to further their own agendas.

23

"HAVE A SEAT FOR RIGHT NOW," Lt. Berend told Denny. "We'll be with you in a few minutes."

As Berend and Farren disappeared into an inner office, Denny glanced down at the front page of the *San Diego Union*. It carried the eye-catching headline, "Mayor Calls Incident Abuse of Police Power". A grainy copy of Denny's personnel photo rested under a larger picture of a beaming Aaron Goddson taken at Pillson's swearing in ceremony. Next to the newspaper sat a familiar pink piece of paper judiciously placed at the corner of the receptionist's desk. Denny stared at Goddson's copy of the citation, mouth agape as Berend and Farren shuffled back in to usher him into the interrogation room.

Third watch lineup was finishing up on the other side of the headquarters building about half a football field away, its officers filtering into the parking lot. "Anybody seen Durango?" Shimmer asked. "Where the hell is he?"

"I saw him going toward the Homicide office," Devree volunteered.

"Homicide?" Shimmer said. "What the hell's he doing in Homicide?"

Devree glared at Shimmer. It clearly had something to do with the arrest at the park earlier in the day and Shimmer knew it as well as he did.

Devree headed toward the suite of investigative offices on the far side of the courtyard and it looked to him like Shimmer was slinking away in the opposite direction; a hyena padding off toward a decaying animal.

Devree couldn't see anyone in the Homicide reception area as he looked through the glass, so he tried the door. It was unlocked.

He popped his head in, looked around, and tip-toed inside, trying to overhear anything that might be going on behind the closed doors to the rear of the suite of offices and cubicles. He found the newspaper and Goddson's copy of the Misdemeanor Release Citation on the table.

The only reasonable conclusion seemed impossible to believe. The charges against Goddson must have already been dropped. How could Homicide drop the charges when they were still in the middle of the investigation, and if they weren't in the middle of the investigation, why would they be interviewing the arresting officer? If they'd already determined that Denny had screwed the pooch, he'd be in the Internal Affairs office now, not Homicide. He slipped the citation beneath his shirt and hurried out to find an envelope and inter-office memo before rushing off to the locked press office.

He couldn't afford to get caught and he stood in the hallway, prancing around like he had to pee as he hurriedly scribbled an anonymous note on the inter-office form. "This is Goddson's copy of his citation," he wrote. "I found it in the Homicide office and it can only mean one thing. The Chief's squashing the ticket before it goes to court." He put the memo inside the envelope, sealed it and slid it beneath the door.

"You should send someone over to your offices at police headquarters right away," he told the *Union*'s copy editor over the phone. "There's an interesting little something in an envelope inside the door."

It took Sgt. Farren a few minutes to remember the copy of the citation he'd left beside the newspaper. The beautifully staged touch had to make Durango spill his guts. The Chief hadn't directly ordered any intervention in the arrest, but any knucklehead could see Coleman wanted the arrest to go away and wanted Durango to pay for his stupidity. Deputy Chief Browner had made that clear enough when he asked the Lieutenant to pick up the ticket.

Farren stood over the desk without moving for a full minute. What had happened to the citation? It couldn't just disappear into thin air.

He checked the trash cans. He looked under the newspaper. He opened the paper and shook it. He flipped through each and every page, hoping it had somehow gotten wedged into one of the folds. It was still on the desk when he and Berend had escorted Durango into the interior office. He'd made sure of that.

Bob Farren couldn't have been more flummoxed at that moment if Lieutenant Berend's wife had walked naked into the room and sat on the edge of the desk the way she did at night in his dreams.

24

THE NEXT DAY'S HEADLINES SQUIRTED as much juice as the ones about the arrest from the previous day: "Favoritism Evident in Pulling of Ticket." The accompanying article said an anonymous police source had turned Goddson's citation over to the paper.

Coleman called a meeting of his deputy chiefs and press relations people as soon as he flipped the lights on in his office. "Did you all see this?" he asked, holding the newspaper in front for all to see. "Who's responsible for this?"

"Responsible for what exactly?" Deputy Chief Montano asked. "For pulling the ticket or for leaking it to the press?"

"For pulling the ticket, that's not how we do things around here. Who pulled the damn ticket?" Coleman glanced around the room waiting for a confession.

"I had the ticket pulled, Chief," Browner said. "You said yourself it stunk of attitude arrest and it seemed like a darn clean thing to do."

Coleman waited a few seconds, something he only did when struggling to control his anger. "The press'll have my ass for this, Hal, and you know it," he said. "We have systems in place for this sort of thing. What in the world were you thinking?"

Browner sat silent.

Coleman knew everybody present understood Browner's anger about being passed over back when Coleman skipped a rank for the

Chief's promotion. Browner thought he should already be the chief and wanted to be the next one. Having the Mayor on his side would certainly boost his chances, especially if Coleman laid an egg on this thing.

Browner leaned back and folded his arms defensively. Coleman kept the focus in Browner's direction.

"How are we going to play this?" Coleman asked his press liaison after glaring at Browner long enough to make him fidget. "This thing's got stingers."

"Well, first, Chief, you better say you pulled the ticket," Will Roberson said. "We can't let it out that somebody in the ranks takes it on himself to do something like this without your permission. Just play it like a normal thing to do and let's see if the reporters let it all die down in a few days."

"All right," Coleman said, the slight tremor in his voice giving the lie to his calm exterior. "When we're through here, let's just everybody go about our business like it's no big deal. I'll handle the damage control as best I can. Hal," he said as he pushed his chair away from the table, "you don't talk to the press about this thing anymore."

Everyone filtered out of the conference room, Coleman bringing up the rear. He squared his shoulders, wiped the scuffed toes of his Ferragamos against the back of his pants, ran a comb through his coal black hair and walked into the reception room outside his office. It was standing room only.

"Chief, who pulled Goddson's citation?" Murray demanded as Coleman stepped in.

"When I was informed of the circumstances, I had it pulled."

None of this sounded like Coleman's style and Coleman knew that Murray knew it.

"Why would you do a thing like that, Chief?" Murray asked. "Isn't that what the courts are for?"

"We held it up, but we didn't tear it up," Coleman said. "We're still looking into this thing."

"Still, don't you think it looks like there's two standards of justice in play here?" Murray pressed. "One for the Mayor's Office and another one for everybody else?"

The reporters spotted a stunning woman in the corner, her arms folded across the front of an elegantly tailored jacket. They shifted their attention toward the President of the Police Officers' Association before Coleman answered.

Nearly every officer on the department was a member of the association that negotiated salary contracts with the Mayor and city council and provided legal and administrative support for officers in trouble.

Sgt. Caroline Rood was a highly visible and striking spokesperson for the organization. She sported neck-length hair the color of the stars twirling in Van Gogh's *Starry Night* and her lips glistened with a discreet amount of peach-colored lipstick. In addition to being a savvy politico with ambitions to climb the ranks, Rood's status as the department's lead instructor in arrest and control techniques boosted her reputation among the rank-and-file.

"Sgt. Rood, what's the POA's position on the Chief's pulling Goddson's ticket?" Murray asked.

"Aaron Goddson's a bully." Rood strode into the crowd of reporters to expose Denny who stood hidden behind her. "People go to jail every day for less than what he did. Officer Durango here should be congratulated for his professional restraint."

"What do you think about all this?" Murray asked Denny.

"It embarrassed me," Denny said, beginning his coached statement. "I'm angry that this happened. I simply wanted to get the message out at the rally that San Diego's losing a lot of good cops and Mr. Goddson attacked me for no reason. His behavior could only be described as rude and aggressive and he's saying really bad things about me and the other officers. I had the police called like any other citizen would do and had a citation issued. It's too bad someone like him has the clout to commit a battery and shift the blame onto the victim. The Mayor's complaint is totally unwarranted, but I'm confident the investigation will be fair."

"We're here to see that it is," Sergeant Rood said.

25

"W-W-W, ONE JOHN GO AHEAD," Officer Pat Randolph told dispatch.

Even though it meant working for the infamous Sgt. Biletnikoff, Luke and Denny were living the dream they'd talked about so often in the academy. A recent shift change saw them assigned to the same squad and occasionally partnered up.

"Oh, crap," Denny said. "There goes Nine-John-Randolph again. Man, its painful hearing him talk over the radio." The merciless Nine-John epithet dogged the unfortunate Randolph, who usually took around nine try's to stutter out his call sign.

The sky had been spitting out a waterfall for three days.

While it was almost literally true it never rained in Southern California, for a few days every fifth decade or so, the skies spilled out torrents of water sufficient to conjure up images of Noah and the Old Testament.

In meteorological terms, San Diego's latitude and longitude made it a near desert and protracted rainfall invariably brought severe flooding to the streets. Nearly every police unit in the city was out of service, handling crashes, providing traffic control around fallen branches, and setting barricades up at flooded intersections to stop unwitting motorists from driving into the raging waters.

"One-John, all the Heights units are out of service," the dispatcher said. "Can you respond from downtown to a report of a child who's fallen into the flood channel at 28th and Marcy Streets?"

"W-w-w-w-w-w, One-John, 10-4. I'm r-r-r-r-r-, responding from First and Br-Br-Br…"

"We can get there before this guy acknowledges the call," Luke said, speeding away from Detox toward the freeway. "If you can ever get through, let her know we'll be covering."

Denny Durango reached for the microphone.

"Broadway," Nine-John-Randolph said.

"Unit 5-King," Denny said. "We're 10-8 from our run to Detox and covering that call in the Heights."

Sheeted rain pelted the windshield as Luke turned eastbound onto G Street and slowed to twenty-five to assure catching all green lights. As G Street merged with State Route 94, Luke punched the accelerator for a few hundred yards, maneuvered into a partially controlled skid, rounded onto the next exit ramp and turned south onto 28th Street. "Get on the air before Nine-John does and let dispatch know we're in the area," Luke said.

"W, w, w,"

"Crap," Denny said. "He beat me to the radio."

"W, w, w, w, w, One-John, I'm ten n, n, n, 90-7 in the area."

"Unit 5-King, we're 10-97 in the area," Denny sputtered as fast as he could, not giving the dispatcher time to respond to Randolph and, more importantly, not giving Nine-John-Randolph a chance to say anything else.

"Good going. That's the fastest I've ever seen you do anything," Luke said.

"Ask around," Denny said with a smirk. "Fast isn't always good. Some things I do real slow."

Luke shook his head.

"You know what I'm talking about," Denny said.

"Next thing I know, you'll be lecturing me about how size matters," Luke said.

"It doesn't actually," Denny said, "unless that's all you're offering.

Me personally, I like getting them so hot, it's a bonus prize when they discover what a huge dick they've got coming their way." Denny laughed at his own pun.

Luke couldn't help but join in. "What about a woman's mind?" he asked. "Does that hold any interest at all?"

"Course," Denny said. "It's the mind that tells their bodies to follow me into bed."

"That's not what I meant, and you know it," Luke said.

"W-w-w-w-w-, One-John, a citizen just saw the k-k-k, kid being s, swept under the bridge at F-F-Fortieth and Market."

Luke reached down and flipped the overhead lights on. "This flood channel's a damn river," he said. "How could he float down there so fast?"

Rainwater poured through a crack at the top of Denny's door and soaked his leg as Luke made the sharp left onto Market Street and stomped on the accelerator. "There he is," Denny panted a few seconds later. "Let me out." Denny leaned into the door, preparing for a running start. He stumbled into the raging current of waters that poured along the gutter and down the grated drain to the raging channel twenty feet beneath them. Luke sped off to get ahead of the child who swirled uncontrollably in the angry whirl of rapidly flowing water and floating debris.

"Five-King, let my partner know I've lost sight of the kid," Denny panted into the radio as he ran the banks of the channel, watching the roiling waters for any sign of a flailing child.

"One-John," Randolph said. "I just saw his head and then he disappeared again."

"What's your location?" the dispatcher asked.

"I've got One-John in sight and my partner's right behind him," Luke said. He pushed the door open, leaped over the flooded gutter and ran to the fence. His thick-toed boot slipped as he tried lifting a leg over the top. The jagged edge of the twisted top links of the fence ripped his pants near his crotch and gouged his flesh before he belly flopped to the ground. He skidded to a stop after sledding along the top of the ice plant for several yards, then scrambled to his feet and burst into a sprint.

"Tell One-John, I just saw the kid's head again," Denny said into his handie-talkie.

Nine-John-Randolph slogged into the billowing torrent. "I think I see him," he yelled.

Denny ran to the bank beside him, holding his baton out for Randolph to grab as a support while he reached down with his other hand and scooped out a rag doll body. A tree branch slammed into Randolph's back, knocking him head first into the water. The torrent sucked him into a vortex of waters as Denny snatched the child onto the bank.

Luke leaped and hopped over tree stumps and assorted garbage in pursuit of the tumbling officer.

Denny started CPR on the boy.

No way I'm going in the water after this guy, Luke thought as he ran. For all his athleticism, Luke's hydrophobia had prevented his learning to swim. For the first time in his life, he truly regretted the lack of the important skill precipitated by his near drowning in Denver's Sheridan Lake as a boy. He'd have drowned for sure had Tuffy not jumped in to grab the scruff of his winter coat and pull him to safety. Tuffy was a hero that day, but Luke knew the hero's secret. Tuffy had pushed him off the pier to set up the heroic rescue.

Ignoring his self-advice, Luke scooted toward a thick metal pipe jutting out from a concrete support and into the raging channel of waters. He clutched the pipe and waded in to extend his arm, grabbing wildly as Randolph tumbled in his direction.

Luke first saw a head, then an arm, then a series of flailing appendages, but never the whole officer at once as he grabbed for a handful of curly auburn hair. He snatched a solid hold and yanked Randolph's tumbling body from the wild waters and into a shallow eddy near the pipe.

Both officers lay on the bank, Luke's legs in the water with Randolph's head bobbing against his hip. Nearly too exhausted to move, he remembered the child, struggled to his haunches, and crawled to Denny who knelt beside the boy about a hundred yards away. As Luke inched toward them, he saw Denny pushing down on the boy's chest, then moving to the head to give a couple quick breaths into a gaping mouth.

"I can help," Luke sputtered as he got closer. He took a position near the boy's head, pinched off the nostrils and breathed into a mouth with a gouge that extended into the left cheek. Blood spewed with every compression, but the officers kept up the rhythm until the ambulance crew arrived.

The crew took over the CPR as they snatched the boy from the ground to throw him onto the gurney. They called a second ambulance to transport Randolph.

Two rookie officers bailed out of the second ambulance. With a conscious and responsive patient, the officers started a primary first aid survey. Starting at Randolph's head, they worked toward his feet, searching for any obvious broken bones, hemorrhaging or noticeable pain. Randolph let out a voluminous "ouch," when the ambulance attendant touched the top of his head.

"Sorry," Luke said. He opened his hand to find several strands of hair pasted between his fingers and palm.

Probing hands palpated toward Randolph's knees. Randolph grimaced as fingers squeezed the left knee joint and howled in pain when they reached his lower back. "Can you move your legs?" the officer conducting the survey asked.

Randolph moved his legs.

"Things look pretty good," the officer said. "Let's just take you over to the hospital and let the doctor have a look."

Randolph nodded his appreciation and assent as his gurney was shoved into the ambulance for transport to Paradise Valley, the same hospital treating the boy.

Luke and Denny walked briskly into the emergency room, soaking the floors and counters around them.

Minutes passed before a doctor emerged through the swinging door to announce the child's death and insist on examining the bleeding gouge in Luke's crotch. He ordered a nurse to clean and bandage it and demanded that the officers go home for a shower and change of clothes before resuming their shift.

"Th-th-th-th, thank you," Nine-John Randolph said to Luke as they passed his gurney on their way to the car.

Luke patted his hand.

Neither partner spoke. A constant chatter of police jargon escaped the radio speaker and rattled throughout the cab. The metal of the car protected Luke from the rain pelting against the exterior, but couldn't protect him from the parasitic pain eating away at his insides.

Denny drove. Luke sat beside him, staring into the night, seeing nothing. The radio chatter rose like a wall between them. Luke felt physical pain gnawing at his insides. He knew Denny felt it too. They'd lost the kid. And now they were headed home to do—what? How did you let this go? The car seemed like a giant vacuum that sucked up time and any good feelings about saving Nine-John Randolph. Underscoring the point, the radio fell silent too.

Once inside their apartment, Luke showered quickly and ran a cotton towel through his hair after putting on his spare uniform. His cracked and soaked gun belt had no replacement, but the warmth of the fresh underwear, neatly pressed uniform and dry boots felt good against his skin. He found Denny sitting in his robe on the couch. "Let's get going," Luke said.

"My uniform's in the washer," Denny told him. "The other one's in the cleaners."

"Want some hot tea?" Luke asked. Although irritated by Denny's lack of preparation, he decided not to challenge him under the circumstances.

"I'll just sit here for a while," Denny said.

Conversation seemed impossible.

Luke reverted to his bedroom, leaving Denny alone with his thoughts. He took off his uniform, squatted to the floor in his underwear and started a set of leg-lifts. He held his legs six-inches off the floor, refusing to lower them as a piercing pain seeped into his abdomen and seared his lower back. Sheer mental force kept his legs in defiance of gravity for several minutes. His teeth gritted and beads of sweat seeped onto his face until the pain reached a crescendo too intense to bear. He let his legs fall to the ground, but turned onto his stomach and pushed himself up from the ground. He grabbed a deck of playing cards from the top of his dresser and prepared himself for the ritual he'd initiated the night before his victorious wrestling meet against the Soviet World Cup Team.

He'd assigned a point value to each playing card, fifty points for each of the two jokers, fifteen for the aces, ten for face cards and the other cards at face value. He set the deck face-down in front of him, pulled the top card and, when the Ace of Clubs appeared, started a set of fifteen pushups, one for each point value of the card. Each rest period lasted only long enough to turn the next card over. He worked his way through the deck and started another set of leg lifts.

After a second shower, Luke walked into the living room to meet up with Denny who emerged from his bedroom, in full uniform this time. Denny announced their in-service status to the operator as the duo trudged toward the elevator fifty-feet down the carpeted hall from their third floor apartment.

"Unit 5-King," the radio dispatcher said. "All my beach units are 10-7. I've got a 415, possible 647 (f) male pounding on the front door at 1615 Garnet Avenue, refusing to leave. Subject is a white male about thirty-five to forty, wearing a gray suit. Can you handle that?"

26

A BESOTTED MAN LEANED AGAINST THE WALL. Pressing his forehead against a windowpane, he repeatedly slapped the screen door and bayed to be let inside as the police car pulled up. "Let me in. I got a question." His head bisected a pink and blue neon sign with the words *Palm Reader and Psychic* in the front window. A second, painted sign, written in elegant calligraphy announced, *Ten Dollars for the First Reading. Madame Gloria has the Answers to All Life's Questions.*

"I got an important question," the man repeated. "Open up."

"Get lost." The dismissive words came from a doe-eyed woman with hair the color of charcoal. She had opened the door to the extent the security chain allowed. "Here come the cops." Open slightly at the top, her robe exposed portions of a bountiful chest.

"What seems to be the trouble, mister?" Denny asked.

"She won't let me in to ask my question." The man's speech slurred with noticeable sibilance and his breath and body reeked of metabolizing alcohol. "I got the ten dollars right here in my pocket, but the bitch won't let me in to ask my question."

"What's the question?" Luke asked.

"Where did I park my car? Can you ask her that for me?" the drunk said.

"Sure," Luke agreed, too tired to tell a sure-to-be-irritated Denny how the situation reminded him of a scene from Macbeth. He walked silently to the door, jerked his thumb toward the drunk and told Madame Gloria, "He wants to know where he parked his car."

"How the hell should I know where his car is?" the psychic asked.

"You tell me," Luke said. "I'm just the wing-footed messenger."

"I can't tell him where his car is, but I can predict his future," the psychic said. "He's soon to be arrested and taken away from here."

"Yes ma'am," Luke said. "That's just about the most accurate prognostication it's ever been my pleasure to witness."

Madame Gloria reached into a pocket in her robe, pulled out a business card and handed it to Luke through the crack in the door. "How you do talk," she said. "Come by for a reading anytime. On me."

"I don't need her to predict your future," Denny said as Luke cuffed their prisoner. "If you ever have the good sense to accept her invitation and come back here, that is."

"Really," Luke said, playing the straight man for what he knew would be a joke at his expense. "What might that be?"

"You'd get fucked is what," Denny said. "She was letting off so much steam in your direction I could feel the heat from ten feet away."

"No way," Luke said. He looked toward the business. Madame Gloria still stood in the doorway. The front of her robe had opened a little more and she waggled four fingers in a confident wave.

"Are you blind, or just stupid?" Denny said. "'Come by for a reading ON ME,' she says. She wants something on her for sure, and that something is you."

"I just wanted to find my car," the drunk interrupted. "Why couldn't the bitch open up and tell me how to find my car?"

"This works out almost as good," Denny said. "Your car'll be safe wherever it is, and you won't have to stand out in the rain all night."

A few minutes of silence ensued until they pulled into the parking lot of the Detox Center. "Hey, Luke," a man's voice called out from the corner as the trio walked through the open door and headed for the sign-in sheet. "Luke Jones, wait a minute."

The Professor, who lay supine on one of the two dozen or so rubbery pallets littering the floor, propped himself up on an elbow, rested briefly, and rolled over onto his knees. He pushed himself upright and started toward Luke, a folded piece of lined paper in his hand. "I wrote this for you."

Luke straightened the paper. It contained an original poem scribed in number two pencil. Written in bold capital letters, the title dominated the top of the page: NEW PRAETORIAN GUARD. "That's you, a member of the new Praetorian Guard," the Professor told Luke.

"Wait a second," Denny said incredulously. "I know you. I took you up to the hospital from over at the Monroe a few months back. Man, I thought you'd die you were so…"

"I don't remember that," the Professor said as Luke soaked in the contents of the poem.

27

WITH THE WEEK'S DELUGE FINALLY OVER, Hartson just wanted to finish his shift. This pistol of a hangover was bad enough to turn him into what the troopers called a "cherry picker." Cherry pickers were cops who haunted specific locations to find easy numbers to fill up their journals so they could keep their number hungry bosses off their backs.

Sergeant Biletnikoff wasn't much different from Hartson's other bosses when it came to numbers. He wanted a minimum of eight contacts a shift and the numbers had to represent what he called "well-rounded activity." An ideal journal would list at least two "hazardous" traffic tickets for violations like going through a stop sign, and two "non-hazardous" tickets or traffic warnings for violations like driving with the front license plate missing or with a tail light out.

The tickets needed to be accompanied by two or more misdemeanor arrests together with the occasional felony pinch when the opportunity arose. The remainder of the journal should indicate a minimum of two citizen's contacts and two crime investigations.

The truth was that getting eight numbers on most second watch shifts was like playing pickup sticks against a blind man. There was very little resistance, nothing to it except for the shifts when Hartson had to chase from one radio call to the next and never had time to do anything else. Tonight, he intended to spend an hour or so picking up his contacts with a spurt of enforcement activities on Horton Plaza and then go up to his beat to hide and sip coffee.

The Plaza was the perfect place for cherry picking.

If the City of San Diego could magically transform into a human body, Horton Plaza would definitely be the asshole and, tonight, like any other night, it positively crowned with opportunities for cops to generate numbers. It was a tiny park situated between the 300 blocks of Broadway and Plaza Street and boasted an art deco fountain that worked about as often as it was out of order. The two underground restrooms constantly flooded and oozed human excrement.

Across the street, two adult movie houses stood next to a busy hot dog stand and a Western Union storefront where the chicken hawks liked to ply their trade. Chicken hawks were that disgusting genus of human being who recruited and trafficked in juvenile prostitutes. They'd find their "employees" among the runaways and stranded kids who waited near the Western Union for money arriving from home.

Right at the moment, Hartson had his eye on the busy bus stop with the posted "No Right Turn" signs that were more than mere signs. They doubled as bonanzas for cops who needed to write hazardous tickets and as nightmares for the unsuspecting motorists who had to sign the bottom of the citations. City buses constantly idled in front of the signs and blocked them from the motorists' views.

Hartson's headache pounded worse than usual as he rested a cheek against a sweaty palm. When he'd resigned from the Chicago Police Department, he'd hoped to support a new tee-totaling lifestyle with San Diego's sunny skies and moderate climate. He knew his drinking was a mere by-product of working crappy hours in crappy weather.

He'd quit drinking again when his wife came out and brought Ted Jr. with her. Until then, he'd let the amber glow of his tumblers of scotch and soda and San Diego's golden sunshine provide the analgesic he needed for his psychological pain.

A man approached and extended his hand through the open window.

Hartson didn't bother to look up. He assumed the guy was just another foot soldier in the rude infantry of citizens who believed wearing a police uniform was an invitation to ask stupid questions and make rude comments. His bellicose grunt was supposed to be a signal to this particular version of John Q. Citizen to go away and leave him alone. He picked his clipboard up and started writing an entry in his journal.

Charles Henreid either missed the cues to go away or ignored them. "I've wondered about your name. Should I call you Officer Hartson?" Henreid asked.

A taut smile tugged on Hartson's lips. "Mr. Henreid," he said. "It's good to see you're still alive."

"Can I buy you a cup of coffee?" Henreid asked.

"I don't see why not. I could definitely use some," Hartson said.

"I'd also like to talk to the officer who was your partner that night up at the parking garage. Is that possible?"

Hartson called for Luke, who was working an adjacent beat, and started across the street with Henreid. They happened to cross directly in front of a sign that hung from a waist-high chain declaring "No Pedestrian Crossing." Hartson definitely felt guilty about walking in front of the same sign he'd used as justification for writing so many tickets, but not guilty enough to trek all the way to the corner. His headache could only withstand so many of the thundering reverberations that started at the soles of his feet, shot up all the way through his body, and rattled around in his brain with every step he took.

The duo marched in tandem into the busy Carl's Jr. Restaurant. Hartson staked out a table while Henreid headed for the counter.

"I wanted to say thanks," Henreid said as he handed Hartson a cup.

Luke heard the comment as he approached.

"Thank me? I didn't do anything," Hartson said.

"Actually, I wanted to thank both of you for saving my life."

"We just told you not to be in a hurry to off yourself. You did the rest," Hartson said.

"Arguing about taking credit for my magnificent existence isn't why I'm here," Henreid told him. The irony in his voice was palpable. "I'm in a twelve-step program again and need to fix the hurt I've done to other people."

Hartson's incomprehension showed on his face. "You didn't do anything to hurt us," he said.

"You might not think so," Hartson said. "But it feels like it to me. I couldn't let it go after you guys threw me in jail and took my truck that night. Hell, I don't know—it just seems like after you save a guy's life, he should be grateful, not pissed off."

"I appreciate that, but…"

A look of exasperation flashed across Henreid's face.

"You're welcome," Hartson said. "So, how are things?"

Luke settled into the booth to listen, showing the maturity that accompanied his six months of patrol duty. With that experience under his belt, he found listening infinitely preferable to talking.

"Better."

"Better than what?" Hartson asked.

"I didn't come here to bare my soul," Henreid said. "Just to say thanks."

"You can thank me by telling us about yourself since you insist on giving us credit for saving your life," Hartson said. He looked to Luke to support the assertion.

Luke nodded. He could see that Henreid had come to bare his soul and he honored the struggle he saw behind the man's eyes. He was intent on trying to do the right thing and take responsibility for his own bad decisions and actions. Luke had been on the job long enough to know almost nobody did that. People usually tried shifting blame onto somebody else.

Henreid pulled a pack of Kools from his hip pocket. Hartson accepted his invitation to join him by flicking both cigarettes alight with his Bic.

Luke flinched at the smoke, but kept his mouth shut.

"It's not totally true saying I wanted to fix something between us,"

Henreid said. "It's more like I needed somebody to talk to."

His confession belied his earlier statements, but verified what Luke already knew.

"Does that make sense?"

Hartson blew smoke rings over Henreid's head.

Henreid seemed to accept the action as an affirmative response. "I did decide to die that night, but you stopped me by saying I'd take a piece of you with me. I couldn't do that to another human being."

Henreid blew a line of progressively smaller smoke circles across the table that joined with the ones already dissipating in the air above them.

Luke marveled at the modern smoke signal language the two men were inventing as they accepted the give and take of conversation and the billowing circles of expanding and contracting smoke. The circles slowly melded into a mist, drifted through the room and sneaked outside in willowy clouds as people opened the side door and made their way into the busy restaurant.

"Unless I could've gotten a bet down on the outcome," Henreid said. There was obvious shame in the timbre of his quavering voice. "Still, things worked out for the best."

"How's that?" Hartson asked.

"You helped by treating me like a human being instead of a piece of shit the way O'Malley did. Officer Jones here talked too much, but he cared whether I lived or died. The shrink convinced me to call my sponsor who treated me like a man. I thought I'd betrayed him, but he told me the only way to betray somebody's to give up on them."

"Based on that definition you almost betrayed yourself that night," Hartson said.

Henreid nodded and lit another cigarette. How much should he tell Hartson? Should he reveal how he'd manipulated people into making bets when he couldn't cover the action? How understanding were these police officers facing him? What would they say if they knew he'd taken his own daughter's piggy bank money to lose on the daily double? Henreid knew the Fifth Step called for admitting his wrongs, but he was on a roller-coaster of ups and downs that might never settle into a level life and his guts were held together by a tether of thread.

"So," Henreid continued, "I kept insisting that I loved my family more than anything, all the while sacrificing their needs for mine, telling myself I only needed one big score to get us out of debt.

"I'll win them back, though." Henreid made the proclamation about his wife and daughter and genuinely seemed to mean it. "My wife's name is June," he said. "She used to call me Ward, like we were the perfect couple." Henreid settled back into the booth and the monstrous gravity of his words shook through his body like a temblor. "I ruined everything, but I know she loves me and we'll work things out."

Hartson puffed and blew smoke while Luke compared the situation of his companions in the booth to the lyrics of a popular song. They talked about a guy who needed to make just a few changes to his life and circumstances. Then he'd be the same as the king who used to be a frog. The lyrics were an anthem to impossible dreams coming true that left the dreamers feeling empty and hopeless inside. It was a declaration that happy endings did not exist.

The smoke drifted out into the room and made a meandering turn toward the salad bar.

Should Hartson tell Henreid how he understood everything; that he'd lost his own family to booze? Should he warn Henreid that winning his family back wasn't a likely benefit of stopping his gambling; that changing his life couldn't erase the accumulated effects his selfish actions had had on others?

"That's all really good," Hartson said.

"I have a good job again and things are getting better," Henreid told them.

"Doing what?" Hartson asked.

Luke saw a red-faced man of about forty hurrying toward the table before Henreid could answer.

"Officer, there's a guy over at the Plaza. I just dropped him off, and he's refusing to pay his fare."

The two officers, Henreid and the cab driver walked outside. "He's over there," the cabby said. "See him, the one with the crack of his ass showing?"

"Dos Tacos," Hartson said in disgust.

"What?" Henreid asked.

"Dos Tacos," Luke said. "Every couple days we get a radio call about this guy. He goes in to some dive, orders two tacos and walks away without paying. We've arrested him at least fifty times."

"If he doesn't pay the fare, I have to pay it," the cabby said.

"I can guarantee this asshole doesn't have any money." Hartson said it as he witnessed one of Dos Tacos' other favorite criminal specialties. "Hey! Cut that out," Hartson yelled.

A woman with a filial resemblance to a beached sea lion was sleeping on the grass near the Plaza's fountain. With her knees high and the soles of her bare feet planted firmly into the turf, the strained elastic waistband of her sweat pants afforded Dos Tacos the opportunity to slip his hand inside. Like his previous victims, this one could only aspire to a better life as trailer trash. The others had all gotten just outraged enough to raise a ruckus about the disgusting state of Dos Tacos' humanity, but not outraged enough to show up in court when the time came.

"Hey," Hartson shouted again as the quartet jogged across the street. "Get your hands out of that woman's pants."

"Huh? What?" Dos Tacos toothed a hyena grin. "I don't do nothing." He heavily accented the O in the word "nothing," making it sound like a prolonged "NO" before drawling out the "thing" that followed. "Officer T.D., I swear. I no do nothing."

"You goddamned prevert," the woman shouted as she rolled over onto her stomach to start the difficult ascent to her knees as a prelude to the ever-so-much-more-difficult task of standing. "Just what the hell do you think you're doing?"

"Nothing," Dos Tacos insisted. "I promise you, lady. I no do nothing."

"Do you want this asshole arrested?" Hartson asked, confident of a negative answer.

"Damn skippy," the woman said. "Put his ass in jail."

Shit. Luke could see that Hartson's hangover had robbed him of any desire to write a case report for sexual battery and an arrest narrative on a case that would never make it to court.

"You know you're going to have to testify," Hartson said.

"I know."

Hartson took a long look at her, obviously deciding how much effort to put into dissuading her from generating the work that would surely die somewhere up the prosecutorial chain when the victim withdrew her participation. "Just a minute, I'll go get my clipboard," he told her. He collected Dos Tacos and took him to the car.

"Why don't I take the case report," Luke told Hartson as he followed along. "You can take the 10-16 to jail and we can hook up later to put the package together."

Hartson ordered Dos Tacos to put his hands on the trunk and spread his legs. An uneventful search followed until Hartson reared back in disgust.

Luke sniffed the unmistakable stench of urine. Dos Tacos' peeing took the form of a silent protest against the indignity of his being arrested.

"I no do nothing, Officer T.D.," he insisted as Hartson backed away.

"Put your hands behind your back," Hartson told his grinning prisoner.

"Maybe next time you remember. Maybe next time you no arrest me for doing nothing."

Hartson pulled a fifth of cheap whiskey from a pocket in Dos Tacos' windbreaker and poured it into the gutter. "Maybe next time you remember," Hartson said. "Maybe next time you no piss your pants when I arrest you for nothing." The accent was on the O in the word "nothing" as Hartson's way of declaring Dos Tacos' status as a raging asshole.

Dos Tacos sat behind the cage, stewing in the warmth of his percolating urine as Hartson filled out the top sheet for the arrest report.

The impatient cab driver waited on the sidewalk. "What about my fare?" the driver finally asked.

"There's nothing I can do about that," Hartson told him.

The forlorn cabby shifted his weight from one foot to the other, emanating his status as the victim of an injustice somebody needed to set right. "This'll come out of my paycheck," he said. The financial devastation was etched on the cabby's face.

Luke tried to ignore it. "Couldn't you tell he wasn't a decent fare when you picked him up?" Luke asked, trying to divert the driver's attention so Hartson could get out of there.

"It's my first day on the job," the cabby said. "I'll go broke at this rate."

"We're sorry," Hartson said. "You'll need to be more careful next time."

Hartson walked to his car, put it in gear, drove to the corner of the Plaza, shook his head, put the car in reverse, got out of the car and reached into his pocket for his money clip. "How much does he owe you?" he said as Luke and Henreid watched in amazement.

Andee Bradford parked her patrol car behind Luke's and walked up to the two men in time to hear Luke making plans to take Henreid on a ride-along.

28

THE DAY AFTER HENREID'S RIDE-ALONG with Luke it was the Professor's turn. "Do you always start your shift with dinner?" the Professor wanted to know.

"This is a special occasion," Luke said. "You kept your promise to stay sober for two weeks so I could take you on a ride-along." The Professor was such an infamous downtown drunk the Lieutenant had ordered Luke to verify the two weeks of sobriety and promise the Professor would be properly groomed and wouldn't stink like an outhouse privy as he sat in the front seat of a police car.

Luke took in the skittering activity inside the dining room as he lectured the Professor on appropriate behavior for ride-alongs. The walls of the dingy restaurant were covered with faded brown wallpaper stenciled with Chinese teapots, bamboo shoots and Pandas sitting in rows about an inch apart. The ambient light camouflaged the age of the bamboo chairs and frayed carpet. The delicious and plentiful fare assured a loyal clientele and a pungent odor wafted out from the kitchen and into the crowded dining room.

Luke picked at his food, mumbling under his breath. "What are these cashews doing in my Kung Pao chicken?" The presence of the cashews totally exasperated Luke, who wanted peanuts.

"What's that?" the Professor asked.

"These blasted cashews," Luke said, his voice raising a little. "I come here once or twice a week for my Kung Pao chicken with spicy peppers, a nice portion of white rice and a generous dose of peanuts, thank you very much. Is that too much to ask?"

The Professor leaned back in the booth. "Too much to ask?" he said.

"Excuse me." Luke called the owner over as he passed by. "How come there're cashews in my Kung Pao chicken? That's not normal, is it?"

"No, not normal." The owner showed a row of teeth stained various shades of brown from drinking green tea and smoking unfiltered cigarettes. "Cashew nuts special, just for you."

"Oh, special just for me?" Luke said. "What's the occasion?"

"We close next week," the owner said. "You favorite customer. Do something nice for you before go out of business."

"Going out of business?" Luke said, looking around at the dining room full of customers. "Why?"

"Center City say so," the owner replied. He explained that the Centre City Development Corporation, the City's downtown redevelopment agency, had ordered the Rice Palace to renovate or close its doors and he couldn't afford to renovate to the City's specifications.

It was unfathomable. Luke was sitting in a pleasant restaurant with a robust clientele and someone other than the business's owner had decided to close the place down.

"I can't say I'd give a penny for your thoughts, because I don't have one," the Professor said.

Luke looked across the table at the clean-shaven Professor. His unruly salt and pepper hair and persistent cowlick made him a dead-ringer for the indefatigable comedian, Professor Irwin Corey, making his new Pendleton shirt and Levis seem like a poor choice.

Luke reached for water to wash away the lingering effects of a hot pepper. "I'm upset with this joint for putting cashews in my chicken, and it turns out they're a gesture to thank me for being a good customer. Who'd figure?"

"Didn't you know cashews are more expensive than peanuts?" the

Professor asked, finally allowing a slight grin to explode into a full-on smile.

"All I know is I prefer peanuts, is that so wrong?" Luke finally allowed a smile of his own. He didn't need the Professor to tell him he could be insufferable sometimes.

"Tell me more about you," the Professor said.

"What do you want to know?"

"Well, for starters, what did you do about Viet Nam?"

"Nothing," Luke said. "I was a sophomore in college the year Nixon pulled us out."

The Professor's astonishment showed. "That makes you only about twenty-four-years old," the Professor said. "You look a lot older."

"I turn twenty-four on April 23rd." Luke leaned back in the booth and waited for the Professor's response.

"No way," the Professor said, his words mixing with slight laughter. "You and Mr. Shakespeare share a birthday?"

Luke nodded and explained he'd finished his bachelor's and master's degrees in five-and-a-half years while wrestling in the A.A.U and working part-time. He admired the works of Joe Wambaugh and thought police work might give him something to write about. He'd also become a cop because he didn't want to teach children and, of course, as the Professor knew, he needed a doctorate or an MFA to teach college.

"I signed up for the civil service test and got lucky with my timing," Luke said. "I started the academy three weeks after college."

"Okay, but why literature?" the Professor said.

"What do you mean?"

"I mean why study literature and why Shakespeare in particular?" the Professor asked.

Luke had never really thought about it. "As far as the literature goes, I was raised in a land of absolutes. I'm not comfortable living in a land of absolutes. My dad's a fundamentalist preacher. He's a good man, but he can form a stronger opinion in less time, on less information, than anyone I've ever met. I enjoy the panorama of great ideas that come with an open mind, and books open the mind. As far as Shakespeare goes, he not only touches the soul, he does it with a conspicuous and contagious appreciation for the importance of language."

"How does your dad feel about your studying literature instead of the Bible?" the Professor asked.

"He thinks I'm going to hell," Luke said. "I'd like to give him some peace of mind about that, but I can't just shut off my mind and swallow everything he tells me."

"Does that mean you don't believe in God?" the Professor asked.

Luke paused, wondering if he wanted to head down this path without knowing what the Professor thought. He was the guy with the Ph.D. after all. "I'd like to hear what you have to say on that topic," Luke said.

"I asked first," the Professor said. "But I'll take a stab at it if you want. I didn't before, but I sort of think I do believe in God now. Only the God I believe in is a lot different from the one your dad keeps telling you about."

"What's your God like then?"

"I wouldn't classify him as my God exactly," the Professor said.

"Tell me anyway," Luke insisted, loosening up a little. He was sitting in a comfortable place, eating great food and talking to somebody who didn't absolutely insist the two of them had to believe the same way.

"My God, as you call him, comes from Jack London's short story To Build a Fire Builder, the Professor said. "Do you know it?"

"I know the story, but can't for the life of me figure out where you'd come up with a God from it," Luke said.

"Remember how the story opens with a man and a dog trudging along on the frozen Yukon tundra?" the Professor asked. "All the action pretty much goes on in the man's mind. He thinks about an old-timer who'd warned him it was too cold and too late to go out alone.

"He steps onto a shallow pocket of ice and his ankle gets soaked. He has to build a fire or die. He takes off his gloves so he can work, but his hands start to freeze. The dog's just lying there, panting and waiting for the fire to appear. The guy finally gets the fire started, but he's built it under a snow-covered tree. The flame melts the snow and it puts the fire out. The man eventually curls up and dies with the dog lying beside him.

"Once the dog realizes the guy's never going to get up and build the fire, he stands up and trots off into the wilderness to fend for himself.

"Most of us just sit around like that dumb animal, waiting for a fumbling God to build our fires for us," the Professor went on. "It's not that God isn't trying to take care of business. I think He's trying as hard as He can." The Professor leaned forward and lowered his voice. "Look at this mess we're living in." The Professor made his fingers into a steeple, put the tip of the steeple against his lips, and leaned back for dramatic effect.

"Now, this theory of an incompetent God makes more sense than the original sin whopper you've been told all your life," the Professor went on. "God screwed things up in the beginning by creating an imperfect creation. It's not Adam and Eve who messed up the world. You know what I mean?"

Luke answered the Professor's question with a dour expression that he held for several seconds before speaking. "Well Professor," he said. "That's a pretty wretched existence you've managed to get yourself into, don't you think?" He was about to ask if the Professor's vision of God was responsible for his drinking, but the dispatcher had another idea.

29

LUKE SPED OFF TO INVESTIGATE A BURGLAR alarm at a school, with the Professor in tow. Easing the patrol car to a stop a block from his destination, he told the Professor to stay behind and in the shadows as they walked.

The otherwise dark campus had a light shining in the cafeteria and Luke told dispatch to send a backup unit.

A side door opened and a shabbily dressed man stepped into the schoolyard. "Wait here," Luke whispered to the Professor. He turned down the receiving volume on his handie-talkie and tip-toed forward for a better look, telling the dispatcher to expedite his cover unit as the burglary suspect started jogging toward the fence in the darkest part of the campus.

Luke didn't know the location of his cover unit, but he wasn't about to let the suspect disappear into the night. He climbed the chain-link fence that surrounded the school stockade, leaving the Professor behind.

Thick metal links rattled and shook from the pulling and pushing efforts of his two hundred thirty pound frame as Luke scaled the eight-foot fence. He could hear footsteps digging into the distant gravel as he lifted himself over the top of the fence and jumped to the ground. He sprinted out of his crouch and snatched his portable radio from its holder, his breath quickening as he spoke into the radio, "Unit 5-John, I'm in foot pursuit of a 459 suspect, eastbound toward the baseball diamond."

Luke's arms pumped in unison with his legs. His biceps pounded and he gained ground with every step. He never thought in pictures. His thoughts came in insistent mental soundtracks and he could hear the voice of Lowell Perkins describing a lion pursuing a zebra as he pounced and knocked the suspect to the ground with a forearm shiver that sent him flopping to his belly, the momentum of the slide forcing his face into a skid against the gravel.

Luke snatched the skidding burglar off the ground by the scruff of his neck and the collar of his T-shirt. The twisting and struggling torso in his grasp ceased flopping as they went nose-to-nose and he ordered the dangling prisoner to stop struggling.

After Luke put the burglar behind the cage in the car, he led the Professor into the school and called off his cover unit. He lifted fingerprints from the three louvered window panes that rested against the exterior wall. He snapped photos of the point of entry; of a hamburger wrapper, of two empty chocolate milk cartons, and of a wadded up ice cream wrapper that all rested at the bottom of a clean cafeteria trash can.

The school janitor who showed up with the fancy title of Building Services Supervisor told Luke the food from the empty wrappers was all that was missing. Luke left his business card along with the phone number to call in case the janitor discovered any additional loss.

He pulled into a lighted spot in the faculty parking lot to fill out the jail booking slip and read the man behind the cage his "certain constitutional rights" from the back of his P.D. # 145 notebook. The suspect agreed to answer Luke's questions.

"Did anyone else come with you tonight?" Luke asked.

"No."

"Why'd you break into the school?"

"I needed something to eat."

"Why'd you choose the school?"

"I know there's food here."

"How?"

"I've done this before."

"When?"

"Two years ago."

"Same school?" Luke asked.

"Yes."

"Why haven't you been back since?"

"I was in prison."

"For the previous burglary at this school?"

"Yes."

"Are you a Fourth waiver?"

The question took the form of a code that cops and crooks shared, referring to the right against unreasonable search and seizure parolees voluntarily relinquished in exchange for an early release from prison.

"Yes."

Luke marveled at this straightforward conversation with an unsophisticated crook that made no effort to justify his crime to the cops. There was a miniscule population of smart criminals who worked the system to their advantage, but most of the ones patrol cops arrested were ill-educated, unsophisticated and downright stupid. "How'd you get in?" Luke asked.

"Same as last time," the admitted burglar told him. "I wiggled some of the louvered window panes until they loosened. Then I hoisted myself up and went through the opening."

Luke grabbed the steering wheel, a fulcrum to turn his body around in his seat and survey his prisoner. The space created by the missing louvers was mighty thin, but the prisoner was skinny enough to squeeze through. "That window's up pretty high," he said. "How'd you get down on the floor without getting hurt?"

"There's a ledge along the inside wall. I lowered myself onto that and jumped down," the burglar told him.

"What exactly did you do inside?" Luke asked.

"I had dinner."

"Did you take anything else?"

"Didn't want anything else."

"For what exactly is he being arrested?" the Professor asked as they sped toward the freeway. He obviously couldn't bring himself to finish a sentence with a preposition.

"Burglary," Luke said. "It's a burglary whenever somebody enters a locked building intending to steal something or commit any felony."

The Professor turned to face the man squirming behind the cage and the two men talked all the way to the watch commander's office. The Professor learned that the cuffed man amounted to a career criminal who'd spent more time behind bars than walking the streets a free man.

"What's going to happen to him?" the Professor asked Luke.

"He'll go back to prison," Luke said.

"For eating a hamburger and drinking some chocolate milk?" The tone in the Professor's voice ascended to accusation.

"He's going to prison for burglary," Luke said. "What he stole is irrelevant. Besides, even if he isn't convicted for this, they'll revoke his parole on the last burglary and send him back to finish his sentence."

Luke was sure he could feel a wall of resistance rising inside the Professor's stony silence as he drove the prisoner to jail.

30

"LOOK," LUKE SAID AFTER HE PUT THE burglar behind bars. "I don't write the laws. I just enforce them."

"I didn't say anything," the Professor told him.

"You didn't have to. I could just tell."

The Professor chuckled. "You not only think you're Superman, now you're a mind reader too. Somebody should create a comic book character to depict your secret powers."

"Get off my case," Luke said. He gripped the wheel tight and the two rode in silence for a while.

In the alley behind one of the Plaza's adult movie theaters, a man stood on his tip-toes, his face submerged in a dumpster as he rummaged through the City trash. His actions comprised a blatant violation of a section of the San Diego Municipal Code.

"Hey, cut that out," Luke shouted. "That's disgusting."

The rummaging man heard the command. Luke knew he heard it and he wasn't about to let him get away with ignoring him. "I said stop that," Luke shouted again.

Luke sprang from his car as the trash picker snatched a half-eaten hot dog, bit into it, grimaced and flicked ants to the ground. He scarfed another bite and reached into his pocket.

"Get your hands out of your pocket," Luke was done being ignored. "Come on, enough already." The guy either had his ears stopped up or was as arrogant as hell. Besides that, he could be pulling a weapon. Luke clasped the trash picker's wrist, pulled his hand from the pocket and turned the palm toward him, exerting enough pressure with his fingers to force the palm open, making it display its contents. It contained a packet of ketchup.

"I could've shot you," Luke insisted. "Why didn't you stop when I told you to?"

The trash picker pushed a shank of greasy hair off of his forehead, took a step back and sized Luke up. "I'm hungry and needed that hot dog," he said.

The confident answer rang out in a straightforward fashion, but it didn't make any sense to the young police officer. "You stop what you're doing when an officer tells you to. Do you understand me?" Luke said.

"I hear what you're saying."

Luke understood the line of communication. There was a world of difference between hearing Luke's command and a willingness to comply. "Why do you carry ketchup around?" Luke asked.

"I put it on stuff. Sometimes I make ketchup soup."

"Are you telling me…" Luke started to say.

The trash picker interrupted. "If I'm really hungry, I'll eat it on a leaf.

"You're under arrest for rummaging through city refuse," Luke said. "Turn around and put your hands behind your back." The Professor squirmed in his seat as Luke wrote a Misdemeanor Release Citation. "He's not going to jail?" he asked as Luke snatched the cuffs off so his prisoner could sign the bottom of the ticket.

Luke chuckled. "The jails are too crowded to book somebody for anything like this. It's sort of a game we play. These people sign their citations, but they don't go to court. The judge issues a bench warrant and, after they get several, we put them in jail where the intake deputy writes them another ticket with another court date. Eventually, the judge gets pissed off enough to sentence them to a work detail."

"These people?" the Professor said.

Uh-oh. Luke knew he'd stepped in it this time. "Yeah, you know, people who don't show up in court."

"That's pure crap," the Professor said. "You don't have any compassion for a guy who eats sandwiches made of ketchup and leaves?"

"I can't get bogged down with compassion for everybody I arrest," Luke said. "It's all I can do to enforce the law. You can't expect me to be anybody's savior."

The Professor was done holding his tongue. "I may be a worthless gutter drunk, but I can see more clearly than you think I can," he said. "You might as well be a trash collector if you can't care about starving people."

Luke's response blasted up from his gut and out his mouth like a shot from a cannon. "Give me a break. You can't just say you're a worthless drunk and then challenge me about how I live my life. What happened to you?"

The Professor looked out the window.

"Answer my question," Luke insisted.

"There's no easy answer to a question like that."

"I'll take a straight answer then."

"Don't go expecting some great revelation," the Professor said.

Luke refused to open his mouth. He'd learned silence was sometimes the best interrogation technique.

"I'm an inner tube with a slow leak ever since Nam," the Professor said.

"What the hell does that mean?" Luke could accept not getting an earth-shattering revelation, but not this nonsense.

"I can't stay full of anything. I can quote every philosopher you can think of," the Professor said. "I know the world's great literature and have studied every text somebody claims is holy. It's all just stale air that leaves me flat. Drinking myself out of my mind is better than that."

Luke stared defiantly, waiting for something better.

"Are you up on your Lear?" the Professor asked.

"King Lear, sure. I know Lear."

"I don't think you do," the Professor insisted. "Or we wouldn't be having this conversation about the way you treat other people.

"Lear's about a king who doesn't learn to be a human being until he's more than eighty years old and stupid enough to give his power away. Read it again, for real this time, and incorporate its wisdom into your life."

"Come on," Luke said. "It's all I can manage to try and sleep at night after doing this job. Don't go expecting me to be some kind of hero."

"I know I'm just a drunk, but look at you," the Professor said. "You're a great big tower of a man who thinks sweeping hungry people off the streets and into jail is a service to humanity. Do you know the Greek root word for hero?" the Professor asked, the crackling passion in his voice getting stronger.

"No," Luke said, "but..."

"But nothing." The Professor reached out the window, slapping his palm on the word "protect" in the slogan printed on its side. "It's even stenciled on your car. Protecting is only half of your responsibility; the other half is to serve 'these people' as you call them. Protecting and serving doesn't only mean supporting the power structures of society; it means using individual might to help people in need."

The acid pain of anger churned in Luke's gut. What about what he'd done for the Professor? He got him sober, took him home to clean him up and bought him a new set of clothes.

"Look at you," the Professor went on. "Sitting there with your muscles bulging and your head so full of penal codes you can't understand the simplest concepts. Like the good guys and the bad guys. You're supposed to be one of the good guys, Luke. That means not only protecting lives and property, but people's dignity too. This man you've got in your back seat here," the Professor said as he turned to look directly at the prisoner. "You not only think of him as homeless, you treat him like he's worthless and less than you."

"All right, that's enough," Luke shouted. Who did this ingrate of a drunken bum think he was talking to? "It's against the law to rummage through City refuse. It's also against the law to burglarize a school, even if it is to get food. It's my job to enforce those laws. I can't do it like you want without getting killed or fired."

"Do you remember when Lear tore his clothes off and crawled into the hovel with Tom O'Bedlam after he went crazy?" the Professor said.

Luke rolled his eyes.

"Lear was the most powerful man on the earth until he gave everything away. It took his seeing other hungry and naked people to realize they were like that because of him. Do you know what he said then?" the Professor asked.

"Yes," Luke answered, the anger in his voice giving way to exasperation. "He said, 'O, I have ta'en too little care of this.'"

"No!" the Professor shouted. "He didn't say it like that. You know the words, but he didn't just speak them. He bellowed them out from somewhere in the deepest part of his gut. The revelation shook his soul."

The Professor paused, giving Luke a chance to speak.

Luke stayed silent.

"Every classical tragic figure has one flaw that destroys them," the Professor went on. "Do you know Lear's flaw, Luke?"

Any first year literature student knew that answer.

"Pride," Luke said.

"That's the simple response. You can do better than that," the Professor said. "He was a putz. It's that simple. He should've been a great king, or at least a decent human being, but he only knew how to demand obsequiousness. Is that what you aspire to?"

Luke heaved a sigh. "Right now, I'm aspiring to finish my shift and take you home," he said.

"Give some thought to what I'm saying about Lear," the Professor exhorted.

"I don't have time for Lear right now," Luke said. The Professor had given him a headache.

"I've got one more quotation from Lear to throw at you," the Professor said, his voice filling the car like it undoubtedly had one of the lecture halls at UCLA years ago. "'*Thou hast seen a farmer's dog bark at a beggar?... And the creature run from the cur? There thou might'st behold the great image of authority: a dog's obeyed in office.*'"

Luke felt a familiar fist of pain at the back of his head as he struggled for a response. The perfect quips would show up too late.

"You think your uniform gives you the right to be obeyed. It shouldn't be the uniform that carries that authority," the Professor said. "It should be you as a human being and how you treat others that matters."

31

Spring 1979

"TONIGHT, WE'RE DOING THINGS A LITTLE BIT DIFFERENT," Sergeant Biletnikoff said as he carried a boxed videotape into lineup and set it on the podium. "The Chief has a few words to say about that fiasco in the park a while ago, but he can't make it to everybody's lineup, so Video-graphics made this tape." He lifted the box and shook it, the video rat-tling against the plastic insides.

"I want you all to listen up. This is important." Biletnikoff slipped the video into the slot. Chief Coleman appeared on the TV screen with his hands folded on top of his desk, in front of a paisley power tie.

"The investigation of the Mayor's complaint about the incident at the America's Finest City Rally is completed," he began. "As Chief of Police, I don't have the luxury the Police Officers' Association does of representing only you officers. I'm also responsible to the community and to the government. In my judgment, whenever there's an allegation that concerns the integrity of one of my officers, whether it's made by a private citizen or by the Mayor, I have a responsibility to investigate the complaint."

"Yeah, right," Francie blurted out. "What about those lying assholes over at the Mayor's Office? Who's investigating their integrity?"

"All right, that's enough," Biletnikoff said as he pushed the rewind button. "Keep quiet so we can get through this thing."

The Chief continued. "It was initially determined no wrong doing occurred on the officer's part and that technically, there was sufficient evidence to forward the battery charge for prosecution. So I signed the package over to the City Attorney's Office. In spite of what you may have heard, it's not true the Mayor ordered me to do anything."

The room exploded with laughter.

"He did request that the complaint be forwarded to the City Attorney's Office to be adjudicated there, which I already intended to do. He does not run the police department. I do."

Biletnikoff leaned forward, obviously anticipating the need to tell everyone to shut up after that comment, but no one said anything.

Luke thought the troopers were out of line. The reasonable ones respected the Chief and fully appreciated the difficult position Coleman was in. Trying to manage the Mayor's self righteous anger, while simultaneously implementing Councilman Cleveland's personal vendetta against the promiscuous homosexual behavior in the park, while also trying to keep the trust of the department's rank and file, was a Herculean feat.

Biletnikoff settled back into his chair.

"The City Attorney's Office reviewed the package and decided not to pursue the case in court. The City Attorney himself told me he'd have referred the case to a neighborhood mediation center if it had involved two less public figures."

"Hey, Denny," Shimmer said. "Did you know you was a public figure?"

"The POA has called for the U.S. Attorney's Office to investigate how we handled Mr. Goddson's copy of the citation, but it's my hope we can put this thing behind us and move forward.

"In conclusion, I want you all to know I have no problems with my officers engaging in picketing. That's your constitutional right, so long as it's done in a legal manner."

"Okay, that's it. Let's hit the streets," Biletnikoff said. "You plain clothes guys go get some coffee and meet back here in ten minutes."

"Can you believe that shit?" Francie said as the group filed out of the room.

"Unbelievable," Devree agreed.

"Bullshit!" Shimmer added. "I never heard so much pure bullshit in my whole life."

The officers stopped their sniping when they saw a gaggle of reporters assembled outside the lineup room. Murray headed up the group.

Sergeant Rood, who stood near the door, her arms folded, approached Denny as he emerged from the briefing room with Luke trailing along. "Congratulations," Rood said. "We didn't get the bastard convicted, but we did shove a little of his alleged power down his throat." She extended her hand for Denny to shake, and whispered, "Here's what to say when the reporters ask you."

She grabbed Devree by the elbow. "Thanks for giving me the heads up on all this," she whispered.

Denny glanced at a small piece of paper in the palm of his hand as the reporters questions started.

"I thought the Chief did a nice job of expressing himself," Francie said. "It's good to know we've got his support."

"Yeah, that's right," several others said.

"Maybe we can put this thing to rest," Devree volunteered.

The platitudes registered the public posture of the disgruntled family of officers who were angry at Mayor Pillson and Councilman Cleveland. But public disgruntlement now would make the Chief look bad. They were willing to spout their criticism behind closed doors, but not in front of the world.

Murray headed straight for Rood. "Sgt. Rood, will the POA withdraw its request for the U.S. Attorney to investigate the ticket fixing?"

"I think we can put this thing behind us so long as Officer Durango here doesn't object," Rood said. She nodded toward Denny. "But you can expect our officers to be visible at public gatherings and cognizant of their rights while we fight for decent wages."

"What's your take on all this Officer Durango?" Murray asked.

Denny glanced toward the cupped palm of his hand. "Mr. Goddson may be very nice, and under other circumstances, I'm sure I'd like the man." The political non-sequitur served as a media declaration that the POA would drop any requests for further action.

"Okay, you officers on patrol, hit the streets," Biletnikoff said. You plain clothes guys get back in here so we can get this show on the road."

Francie, Devree, Denny, Luke, Shimmer and several others filed back into the briefing room. Biletnikoff stepped to the front of the room. "As you know, we've been having problems with illegal activity in and around Balboa Park's bathrooms," he said.

"You're kidding," Devree spouted.

"You guys are going to do something about that tonight," Biletnikoff went on, doing his best to ignore Devree's heckling. "First, though, we're fortunate to have a representative from Councilman Cleveland's Office to give us a little training before we go out there. Go ahead Ms. Cleveland. We're all anxious to hear what you've got to say."

Everyone in the room except Biletnikoff, Denny and Luke lifted their eyes toward the ceiling and groaned.

"The Councilman's daughter," Francie said. "That's just great."

"Okay, knock it off," Biletnikoff ordered.

Denny edged his chair closer to fix his gaze on Cleveland's face. Strong cheek bones dominated otherwise plain features. She couldn't be considered a knockout exactly, but Luke knew her athletic carriage, together with her fully dressed female body, made her as enticing to Denny as a wrapped Christmas present under a sparkling tree.

Luke sat back and grinned, relishing the chemistry between Cleveland and Denny as part of his ongoing study of Denny's attraction to, and for women. Women enjoyed Denny's flagrant attentions the way a good book might appreciate being savored by an avid reader.

Denny's face splashed a carnivorous grin. His gaze traveled down Cleveland's torso, over her legs and back up to take her face in again.

He leaned forward, not licking his lips exactly, but giving the impression of a hungry cat about to feed on his kill.

Fidgeting under the intensity of Denny's gaze, Cleveland straightened her collar and stepped to the podium. "Well," she said, "I've never really done this sort of thing before. I must say, it's slightly intimidating." She glanced at Denny, adjusted her skirt and ran a palm over her hair, a nervous smile flirting with her lips.

"What's your first name?" Denny asked.

"All right, that's enough," Biletnikoff said.

"He just asked her name, Sarge," Francie said. "What's wrong with that?"

"It's all right," Cleveland said. "My first name's Tina." She looked down at her open-toed pumps and blushed.

"*This galant pins the wenches on his sleeve,*" Luke blurted out. "*This is the ape of form, monsieur the nice, That when he plays at tables, chides the dice, In honorable terms...the ladies call him sweet; The stairs, as he treads on them, kiss his feet.*"

"Shut up with that bullcrap!" Shimmer said. "Jeeesus criminy! With all the patrol squads in this whole damn city, you had to get assigned to us."

Luke grinned at Shimmer and settled back into his seat. "It's from *All's Well That Ends Well* and it fits the occasion," he said.

Tina Cleveland looked at Luke, then at Denny and straightened her skirt. "Okay," she said. "I'm sure you all know most of this already, but the Councilman's asked me to go over some of the pertinent laws. You'll most likely be using one of two penal code sections. Section 647 (a) makes it illegal to either commit or solicit a lewd act in a public place."

"No shit," Devree said. "Thanks for the scoop."

"Let the lady talk," Denny said. "I want to hear what she's got to say."

"That's not all you want," Shimmer said.

"Okay, okay. Knock it off," Biletnikoff said.

"Section 647 (d) is a little trickier. It makes it unlawful to loiter in the area of a public rest room with the intent to either commit or solicit a lewd act. Now, as you all know, specific intent crimes are harder to prove."

"Since we know this already, and you know that we know it, what are you wasting our time for?" Francie asked.

"Because the Councilman asked her to," Biletnikoff said. "Now shut up and let her talk."

Tina went on. "For the most part, it's easier to concentrate on either catching people in the act…"

"What act would you be talking about?" Shimmer asked.

"That would be the act of love, wouldn't it?" Devree said.

"Shut up," Biletnikoff hollered.

"Now, you might be surprised at whom you'll encounter," Cleveland said. She'd actually said whom instead of who. That caught Luke's attention.

"In recent weeks officers working this detail have arrested some famous sports personalities and a couple actors from shows over at the Old Globe Theatre," Tina Cleveland continued. "Just last week, the actor who's playing the Duke, Adolpho, I think it is, in *Measure for Measure* was…"

"Angelo," Luke said.

"What's that?" Tina Asked.

"The guy you're talking about played Angelo, and he's not actually the Duke…"

"Shut up!" Biletnikoff bellowed.

"Anyway," Tina said, flustered, "I guess you men know enough to get the job done without me rambling on."

"Nah, do you really think so?" Shimmer said.

"Way to go Jones," Biletnikoff said as Tina Cleveland made her way out the door. "You couldn't leave well enough alone, could you?"

"Sarge, could I go get a drink?" Denny asked.

"Don't let him go, Sarge," Francie said. "He'll be inside that woman's shorts inside of five minutes and we need him for the detail."

"All right," Biletnikoff said. "You knuckleheads keep your mouths shut for five minutes and I'll get you out of here. There's a couple other things you younger guys might need to know. Nobody's particularly proud of what they're doing in those restrooms up there, so they won't exactly be advertising who they are. They won't have any ID on them, but you can bet they'll have a car nearby with a wallet inside. Get inside their cars and find out who they are. Don't let anybody get away with being booked under a false name. And another thing, you guys stick close to your partners at all times. Some of these characters will try to get away because an arrest for a charge like this could ruin their lives. That's their problem though, not yours. They should know the risk, and you should know it could turn ugly."

"No shit," Francie said. "You're saying the sight of some asshole walking toward me with a pulsating dick in his hand could turn ugly?"

There was a unanimous guffaw.

"Okay, that's it," Biletnikoff said. "Oh yeah, one last thing, we have a reserve transport unit slated for our detail. Be sure your booking slips are complete and you have all the information for the report top sheet before calling for the jail run. Keep in service and make as many arrests as you can. Any questions?"

"Yeah, Sarge, could you go over that stuff one more time?" Devree said.

"Yeah, Sarge, some of that stuff ain't so clear," Shimmer agreed. "Could you just say everything over again?"

"Shut up and get out of my face," Biletnikoff said as he walked out with the troopers following along behind.

"What was on the note?" Luke asked Denny as they loaded their equipment into the trunk of an unmarked car.

Denny reached into his pocket, pulled the note out and handed it to Luke.

"Did you know about this deal before?" Luke asked.

"What deal?"

"You mean nobody told you what was happening here tonight?" Luke asked.

"Nobody told me anything. What're you talking about?"

"Somebody cut a deal," Luke said. "The Chief says there's enough evidence to file charges on the battery, but the City Attorney won't do it. Then he talks about the POA wanting an independent investigation of the ticket fixing, but he hopes it won't come to that. Then Rood gives you this note, basically telling you to adopt a conciliatory tone, after she tells the press she's dropping her request for an independent investigation. Everybody wins. Nobody loses. You don't think this is a coincidence?"

"I guess not," Denny said.

"You're just lucky somebody found that copy of the citation," Luke said. "It's what saved your scrawny Rican ass."

"No kidding," Denny said. "I'll be damned."

32

DENNY PULLED THE CAR INTO A SMALL parking lot at Balboa Park's northwest corner and jerked it to a stop near the other unmarked cars. The two rookies agreed Luke would take the first turn as the sexual enticement while Denny watched from a secluded spot.

Luke perched at the edge of a cold concrete table in a portion of the park with no artificial lighting, the splashing light of the full moon turning him into a solo actor on a stage, waiting for a cue from an absent stage manager. The moment oozed with creepy awkwardness.

He wore a new pair of Levis, running shoes, a purple T-shirt, a windbreaker and a San Diego Padres baseball cap. He glanced around trying to assure himself Denny was paying attention somewhere out there in the darkness as a fireplug of a man with a crew cut and an open-necked Polo shirt came his way.

"Hi. How are you?" the fireplug asked.

"Fine," Luke said. "A little cold, though,"

"Yes, it is a little cold," the man said. Then he grabbed Luke's crotch.

Luke had heard it would go down exactly like this, but he didn't believe it until now. "So much for foreplay," Luke said. He grabbed the wrist attached to the hand that was fondling him. "I'm a police officer, and you're under arrest."

Luke heard a low guttural groan and an "Oh shit!" before the man with the probing hand jerked his wrist away, pivoted and ran toward the crest of the canyon about two hundred yards away. "Denny, I've got a rabbit," he yelled as he took up the chase. Luke was fast enough, but in the time it took to leap from the table and look for Denny, the powerful runner had gained a lot of ground. "Stop or I'll shoot."

The top of a crew-cut disappeared over the horizon of the canyon and Denny was nowhere in sight. As Luke rounded the crest of the hill, the fireplug was standing there, his shoulders heaving from his wind sprint.

Luke pulled handcuffs from the pocket of his windbreaker and clicked them onto quivering wrists.

"Would you really"—there was a pause as the man panted to catch his breath—"have shot me?"

No harm could come from telling the truth now. "Not really," Luke admitted. "It was a bluff so I didn't have to chase you into the canyon."

"I should have kept running…"

"That pithy phrase seems appropriate for just about every one entangled in the machinations of this cruel world," Luke said.

"What?"

"Never mind. Where's your identification?"

"I don't have any with me."

"Where's your car?" Luke asked.

"I took the bus."

"Really," Luke said. "I guess I need to give you a ride home so you can prove who you are."

Out of options, Luke's prisoner blurted out the truth. "My car's up the street," he said. "My family doesn't have to know about this, do they?"

"I'm not making a point of telling anyone," Luke said. "I'll write up the paperwork and someone else will take you to jail. I won't see you again until we're in court, unless you plead guilty."

"What about my command? Do they have to know?"

"What did I just say? My job's done when you get to jail. You tell who you want to tell."

Luke's anger over his missing partner seethed higher with every step as he led his prisoner to get his identification, holding him by the biceps. He wanted to shout, "Where the hell are you Denny?"

"What's your name?" was the question he did ask while he rifled through the wallet he pulled from beneath the driver's seat. "Says here you're a Naval Commander. Commander Bryant."

"Yes, sir, and if the Navy finds out about this, I'll be court-martialed and kicked out of the service," Bryant said. Genuine trepidation infused the commander's words.

Luke could only imagine the Professor's lecture about the quality of mercy if he were here. He'd definitely outdo Portia's famous speech from *The Merchant of Venice* if he had the chance.

"I swear to God, Officer, this is my only time. Can't you give me a break this once? This would kill my kids." The efficacious plea for mercy almost worked.

Paul Devree, a prisoner of his own in tow, overheard the pleas and yanked on his prisoner's arm as a signal to stop. "Hey," Devree said, looking at Commander Bryant but intending his words for Luke. "We got you over in Palm Canyon for this last week and let you go."

"I'm sorry," Luke said. "You should've considered the consequences before you came down here." He escorted Commander Bryant to the prisoner staging area to start his report as Denny finally made an appearance.

"Hey, Luke, you and me've got dates for after work."

"Where the hell have you been?" Luke fought to keep his voice civil.

"Making a date. I just told you."

"This guy grabbed my crotch," Luke said as he sat the commander down. "And ran like hell when I went to arrest him. Nobody was around when I looked for my partner."

Denny knew not to say anything.

"What were you thinking?" Luke's controlled veneer was close to cracking. Leaving your partner in the lurch was borderline treachery and Denny could get in serious trouble if he made an issue out where the others could hear.

"Sorry," Denny said. "But you and me've got dates with Tina Cleveland and one of her friends."

Luke nearly choked on his anger. Denny should get in trouble for what he did, but he'd deal with that later.

"Tina Cleveland?" Luke said. "How'd you get a date with her so fast?"

"She came here to find us," Denny said. "Gave me some crap about wanting to see how the mission worked out, but she really came here..."

"To solicit a lewd act of her own?" Luke interrupted.

"Exactly."

Denny laughed and Luke cracked a smile. It was how all their arguments ended.

"You're coming along," Denny said. "She's bringing a friend, 'cause she thinks you're interesting.' Can you believe that?"

"I've got a date with the book by my bed," Luke said.

Denny put his thumb and forefinger together, wiggling his fingers in front of his face to simulate a fanning book. "Read this homie. You rode to work with me and can either come along or take a damn cab home."

"Here's how it'll go down," Luke said. "I'll take your keys and the divine Ms. Cleveland can ride you home."

"You got to start living man," Denny said.

Luke couldn't argue Denny's point. But he could communicate with a book and was clueless what to say to a woman he'd never met.

Loud shouting suddenly blasted out from the nearest bathroom.

Luke sprinted toward the ruckus, leaving Denny with the prisoner and the thudding and whacking sounds of a fight struck his ears as he got close.

"Hold the sonofabitch down."

"Ow. Shit. Ow," Luke could make out Shimmer's voice along with the sounds of bodies slamming against concrete and the distinctive thud of a head against a hard surface. He rounded the corner to see

Shimmer in a heap beneath the sink as Francie lost his grip on a shoe-less foot and a one-shoed man blasted out of a three-point stance for the doorway.

Luke knocked the man into a three-hundred-and-sixty-degree spin that ended with a thud against the concrete floor.

Reeling and dizzy, Francie tried to right himself and Shimmer lay in an unconscious heap on the floor.

Luke picked up Francie's radio from beneath the urinal and called for an ambulance as more officers ran in to help.

"Come on," Luke told his new prisoner as they walked outside. "Which one of these cars is yours?"

"The blue Mercedes."

"The one with the Happiness is family home evenings sticker on the bumper?" Luke asked.

"Yes sir. That's the one."

33

THE BOUNCER AT THE APACHE CLUB greeted Hartson and Francie inside the leather flap substituting for the front door and pointed out an old man at the bar. The old guy had clearly climbed the mountain that peaked at his eightieth birthday and was walking down the other side. He wore a collared white shirt with rolled up sleeves, open to the navel, and tucked into a pair of nylon running shorts. A gold medallion dangled from his neck and a pair of flip-flops rested against the metal bar that doubled as a foot rest.

"He keeps trying to pinch the girls," the bouncer told the officers as he led them across the floor. "I told him to leave and he told me to go fuck myself. I wanted to pick him up by those puny britches and toss him out on his ass, but the boss said to call you guys."

This had all the earmarks of an easy radio call. The geezer was an obvious nut case, but Hartson pegged him as a guy who'd be intimidated by the cops.

The trio approached the old coot from behind and Hartson tapped him on the shoulder. "Excuse me, Mr. O'Malley," he said. "Can we go outside so we can hear one another a little better? Your son here and I'd like to have a few words." Hartson jerked his thumb in Francie's direction.

The bouncer and the old guy looked appropriately confused, but Francie understood Hartson's shenanigans. It was the old, "here's your look alike act alike daddy routine" cops liked to break into when meeting a truly outrageous character.

Hartson, the bouncer, Francie and his new daddy, stepped into the sunshine. "What's the problem?" Francie asked in a polite tone.

"No problem, son," the old man said. "Just having a good time's all. No law against that, is there?"

Hartson couldn't pass up the opportunity. "You really are his son. I was just kidding because of the obvious resemblance."

Francie ignored him.

"No law exists against having a good time," Hartson said. "The problem is, sir, the manager doesn't want you back in there." Hartson paused to let his declaration sink in and got no sign that his statement registered. "We're going to have to ask you to leave."

The old guy's calm facade simmered for a few seconds before shattering into pieces. He looked at Francie, at Hartson, and back at Francie again, and started quaking in a slight body quiver that graduated into a full-on Joe Cocker imitation. The old coot—who wore a pair of shorts that belonged in a Nair commercial——ran to the base of a street lamp, threw his arms around it and pounded his head against its base. Blood gushed from his forehead with the first blow and got worse with each successive head butt until a steady flow of red sprayed the sidewalk.

Hartson tried prying the old guy's arms free. This was one strong old bastard and Hartson knew two things. It would be harder to subdue him than normal because he and Francie had to be easy on the old guy on account of his age. And he knew the gathering crowd wouldn't take kindly to two officers fighting with an old man bleeding buckets onto the sidewalk.

Hartson tried wrapping his arm around the geezer's throat, but the old guy backed him off with an open mouth full of sparkling dentures that searched for his bicep. "Grab his hair and pull his head back," Hartson said.

Francie did as Hartson said and the old coot started shouting for help from the crowd. Big trouble was brewing and Hartson told Francie to let go of the geezer's hair to make it seem a little less brutalizing to the aged son-of-a-bitch who was doing his best to chomp Hartson's arm off.

Francie pulled his portable radio to call for help, but the handie-talkie went skittering along the sidewalk.

Seizing his chance, the old guy let loose with a vicious backward head-butt, catching Hartson in the chin and sending him reeling backward. Then the geezer loosened his hold on the light standard and started biting enormous chunks out of his own forearm and spitting flesh onto the sidewalk to mix with the coagulating blood.

This amazing display shifted the crowd's attitude. The concerned citizens, who'd only recently been outraged at the physical treatment of the helpless old man, started declaring the officers too incompetent to effect a simple arrest. But nobody offered any constructive suggestions.

Hartson tried firming his hold on the geezer's neck to pull his head back and stop the public display of self-cannibalism. It didn't work. "Hit him in the stomach," he told Francie.

Francie hesitated.

"Hit him in the fucking stomach with the baton," Hartson said. Oh shit, he'd done it now for sure. Not only was he brutalizing this defenseless old man, he'd said a nasty word in public. He'd get complaints about that for sure.

Francie pulled his baton to push it against the old guy's abdomen, the action having its desired effect. The old guy reached for the baton, giving Hartson the chance to wrap his forearm around the old guy's throat without getting a chunk bit out of his bicep. He slung the old coot over his back, cutting off the flow of oxygen to his brain through the carotid artery.

From his vantage point, Hartson couldn't tell if the maneuver had its desired effect. It was Francie's job to shout out when the old guy lost consciousness. Hartson dropped the geezer onto the sidewalk, cuffed him and propped him against a knee to slap him on the back and snap him back to consciousness.

"Shit," Francie said as his sweat slathered the sidewalk. "Ain't nothing simple anymore?" His words came out in wheezing pants. "We can't take this old fuck to jail. They'd never accept him all chewed up like this, and we can't take him up to County Mental because they won't admit him without a medical release and we can't drop him off at the emergency room 'cause he'll go ape shit and tear the place up."

Hartson looked around, hoping nobody was tuned in to Francie's expletives. "So what do you want to do?" Hartson's belly heaved from exertion as he asked the question.

"We got no choice," Francie said. He looked at the ridiculous old coot with the cuffs around his wrists, the chunks of flesh missing from his forearm and forehead and the blood rolling along his wrinkled face. He shook his head in disgust. "We have to take this, this piece of work, up to the University ER and baby-sit him while he gets patched up. Once we get the medical release, which'll take forever because there'll be dozens of indigents forming a line around the block, we'll get the privilege of moving him over to Mental Health for the seventy-two-hour hold. The only good news is we'll have plenty of time to write our reports while we hold the old fuck's hand."

Hartson nodded in silence. It was the only workable alternative and a definite pain in the ass for two officers who just wanted to do a little foot patrol and pick up some easy numbers.

Francie's prediction of overcrowding came true as they neared the hospital. Mobs of prospective patients filled the parking lot, forming a sinuous line into the hallway. "Jeeeeesus, what a fucking zoo," Francie said. "It's a blinking nightmare from Hades here. We'll be stuck here until, until, hell, I don't know. We're just stuck here. That's all there is to it."

About five hours to the minute after they'd walked through the swinging doors of University Hospital's ER, the intake clerk let them know the old "gentleman" qualified for admission. It turned out he had a serviceable insurance policy and University Hospital had a perfectly good psychiatric unit only too pleased to accept patients with legitimate medical insurance. It was a situation they'd never encountered before.

"Shit!" Francie's voice mixed with exasperation and relief. "If we'd known they'd admit the old fuck, we could've cleared here a long time ago."

"It's your fault," Hartson said. "You should've taken care of your daddy yourself."

Francie told Hartson to bite the big one and a silent instant followed when both officers knew it was time for the tired joke to end.

34

FRANCIE GRABBED HIS FLASHLIGHT AND PUSHED himself out of the car with Hartson following.

The Plaza oozed with the usual denizens of the downtown night and Hartson reflected on the political hype and marketing slogans that touted San Diego as a modern "Camelot by the Sea," "America's Finest City," and a veritable "Eden by the Ocean." Which of the people on the Plaza, he wondered, best supported the notion that San Diego was paradise? Maybe it was the drunks huddled in the grass by the fountain? Possibly the Hare Krishnas bouncing, chanting and banging their drums and tambourines at the edge of the sidewalk? Was it the male prostitutes waiting for the public phones to ring with solicitations, or the heroin addicts scoring dope for money or sex? Was it the illegal immigrants who'd risked their lives crossing the border to wait for buses to La Jolla so they could perform menial jobs for too little pay, all the while under the threat of deportation? Was it the Bible-flailing preacher who threatened that everybody not believing like he did would spend eternity in hell? Was it the naïve runaways who thought life on the streets preferable to living with their screaming parents?

They were the least of his problems now. Two men were sharing a joint next to the fountain and a shiver of dread shot up Hartson's spine like a lingering neuralgia. The smaller guy seemed harmless enough, but his buddy, the one who looked like a metal skyscraper on a street of brownstones, might be under the influence of PCP. His shirt was tied around his waist and his chiseled torso moved like a gigantic robot constructed without the malleable joints and soft tissue necessary for fluid movement.

Hartson had encountered Phencyclidine users on the beat and the academy had taught him how the stuff had got onto the streets. It first showed up as a surgical anesthetic for conscious patients in the 1950s, but was discontinued after a series of psychotic patient outbursts. Veterinarians soon tried using it on large animals like horses and elephants, but it caused violent psychosis in the animals too.

Drug entrepreneurs eventually started manufacturing it and a new cottage industry was born. Street users ingested it by dipping cigarettes or marijuana joints into its liquid form and sucking it in with the smoke. Completely oblivious to pain and violently irrational, they transformed into malevolent super-beings; walking, talking, fire breathing nightmares for the cops who confronted and arrested them.

Hartson glanced over his shoulder to make sure Francie understood the potential danger. If they were lucky, it'd be a simple joint so they could write the guy a ticket and get the hell out of there.

The terror Hartson saw on Francie's face made him consider walking away.

After all, to most observers the two men just looked like they were sharing a joint. He and Francie could fake getting a radio call and get the hell out of there. The problem was, if the guy did turn out to be a duster and got violent, somebody would definitely get hurt. In Hartson's mind, his only legitimate response was to look out for the safety of the people on the Plaza.

He'd confront the smoking behemoth, but that didn't mean he had to like it.

He trudged forward, feeling a lot like a guy standing at the bow of a rocking boat and watching a monstrous storm rolling over the crest of the horizon. This particular storm took the form of a human being who stood about six-foot-eight. Although the muscular body displayed its athleticism, his stilted and jerky movements made him a look-alike for Boris Karloff in the Frankenstein movies.

"How're you doing tonight?" Hartson asked the question as soothingly as the fear in his voice would allow, intending his words to announce his arrival and avoid startling the gigantic duster who towered near the base of the fountain.

The small man nodded silently, but his enormous friend's hollow stare accompanied a rhythmic swaying motion and his voice carried a profound vibrato. "I hate cops." He repeated the pronouncement over and over in an ominous drawl, which was enough to convince Hartson the joint was laced with PCP.

Although he knew it, he also knew some defense attorney would try to convince an over-educated, under-experienced, black-robed jurist that sufficient probable cause didn't exist for an arrest. If he didn't get the probable cause, he'd be risking his life for nothing. The problem was, gathering the PC would almost certainly infuriate the giant angel duster.

"I'm going to have to ask you to undergo a couple of tests for me," Hartson said, mustering a mountain of deference in his voice. "You don't mind, do you? I'm going to move this pen in front of your eyes. I'd like you to follow the movement with your eyeballs, without moving your head. Can you do that for me?"

Hartson swiped another sidewise glance toward Francie who seemed a little farther away somehow. That couldn't be right. Fear was messing with his perceptions. Francie had to be ready to pounce on this enormous duster glowering down, his terrifying red eyes looking like a malevolent comic book character's, repeatedly muttering that he hated cops.

Hartson focused on his own actions, trusting his partner and roommate to do the right thing. He moved the pen in a slow, sideways motion in front of the duster's stony face, getting the expected result; horizontal nystagmus, an uncontrollable eyeball twitching at the extremes of the sideways movement. There was also the sweet odor of ether on the duster's breath that completed the probable cause necessary to make the arrest.

Hartson stole another furtive glance at Francie who seemed farther away somehow.

"I'm placing you under arrest for being drunk on drugs, unable to care for yourself or the safety of others." Hartson's words rang hollow in his own ears. What did they sound like to the rock cliff with feet that swayed in front of him?

Hartson reached for his cuffs.

He expected to see Francie pulling his portable radio and asking for cover units. What he saw, was his roommate getting into their police car and driving off.

He stood, frozen in a nanosecond's time warp that lasted an eternity. "Would you please turn around and place your hands behind your back with your palms together?" His request came in a whisper.

Luke knew Francie and Hartson were partnered up and wondered where Francie was going as he pulled into the vacated parking space, intent on asking Hartson's advice on an earlier arrest.

He heard a roar through his open window that sounded like a preternatural wind blowing through a rocky canyon. A collective gasp escaped from the crowd on the far side of the fountain. Luke sprinted from his car to see Hartson lying unconscious in the fountain, his head resting against a water spout, blood mixing with the oozing water and turning it red.

A spectacularly enormous person bent to pick Hartson up by the collar.

Luke climbed the assailant's back, wrapping his arm around an enormous neck to lift the giant away from the unconscious officer.

The man exploded backward, rolling massive shoulders out of Luke's grasp and taking a boxer's stance.

Luke ducked a punch and grabbed a massive leg. He drove forward, pushing his opponent toward his back, but got tagged by a quick downward right that sent him reeling before the duster drove a left hook toward his ear. Luke ducked. The roundhouse momentum pulled the duster off balance, giving Luke the chance for a double leg pickup. He lifted hard and drove blindly forward until they sprawled over a drunk who lay comatose in the grass.

The duster grabbed at Luke's gun as they rolled around and yanked it from his holster as they stood in unison. Luke shoved the barrel away from his chest. The first bullet dug into the grass. The second landed next to the first before they tumbled in a heap to the ground and the gun skipped along the sidewalk and into the fountain.

The duster crawled toward the gun. Luke jumped onto his back only to be shrugged off and clobbered with an uppercut. Luke could barely taste the blood filling his mouth as consciousness drifted away and he fell into a heap next to Hartson in the fountain.

Someone in the crowd had called dispatch and the arriving officers piled on top of the gigantic duster.

Luke's mind drifted back to him and he crawled toward the fray as officers flew into the air, arms and legs akimbo as they landed in heaps in and around the fountain. The duster grabbed another officer's gun to pull it from its holster. Someone was going to die if Luke didn't do something, but he couldn't get there in time.

He leaped into the fountain, the blood spraying from his mouth mixing with the spray of the fountain as he found the words from the scene when Banquo's ghost appeared to Macbeth:

Avaunt! And quit my sight! Let the earth hide thee! Thy bones are marrowless, thy blood is cold;
Thou hast no speculation in those eyes which thou dost glare with!

The world stopped rotating on its axis as the gigantic duster stared transfixed at the loony cop who spouted something crazy from the center of the bloody fountain.

Officers seized the moment and piled on, the sheer weight of their bodies driving the duster to the ground.

More bodies flew into the air, but Luke and Shakespeare had bought enough time. Luke piled on to wrap his bicep around the duster's neck and two officers grabbed the duster's legs. One of them, a finally conscious Hartson, hung on doggedly while other officers flew away and back and away again like erratic yo-yos.

Luke squeezed an enormous neck that felt like a slab of granite. He squeezed until time and space melded into a confused miasma that left him standing outside his body and watching himself in the fight. He squeezed until his arm went numb, until prying hands pulled his arms from around the duster's throat, until he watched himself re-enter his body, until he heard a chorus of voices yelling to him to let go so other officers could handcuff the unconscious prisoner.

35

"I DON'T KNOW WHY I LET YOU talk me into this," Luke said for the third time.

Denny turned his back on Luke's tired refrain. They were getting ready for an academy graduation dance at the police pistol range and Luke dreaded the tedium of another uncomfortable night in Denny's disco scene. Some wizard of wisdom had actually decided to throw a disco party at the firing range! How nuts was that?

Like always, Luke wanted to stay home and read.

He leaned against Denny's bedroom door frame with his arms folded, already knowing how miserable he'd be at this stupid party. He wanted Denny to know it too, and to appreciate his sacrifice.

Denny and Tina Cleveland would monopolize the dance floor while the other women marveled at Denny's odd mixture of graceful moves and animal magnetism, and the men would resent Denny for the way women responded to him.

Luke would stand at one end of the room like a Corinthian column and wait for somebody to approach him. He had no idea how to mix with a crowd, so he'd fold his arms and stand there, his turned-down mustache partnering with an uncomfortable frown to make him about as approachable as a reincarnated Rasputin.

He'd strike that ridiculous pose until Denny decided it was time to trade in his vertical la salsa dance for a horizontal mambo. Then he'd chauffeur Denny and Tina Cleveland home like a hired manservant where Luke would crawl into bed while Denny mamboed between the sheets at the opposite end of the apartment. Since it all amounted to a foregone conclusion, why not skip the preliminaries and stay home with his book so he and Denny would both be happy.

"Let's get on with it since you insist on dragging me off to this thing," Luke said. Watching Denny hand measure the magnificence of his Afro in the mirror amounted to about all he could stand.

"Perfection takes time, roomie," Denny countered. "Why don't you relax and let me do one of the things I do best?"

"You're right," Luke said. "Self-admiration is one of your finest skills. But when you're naturally gorgeous like me, getting ready doesn't take so much work."

"Yeah," Denny said. "If you're so goddamned gorgeous, how come there's never anybody in there besides you?" Denny tossed his perfectly coiffed head in the direction of Luke's bedroom.

"All right, but hurry up," Luke said, conceding to his inevitable fate and trudging off to the living room to leave Denny to primp in peace. He found the New Yorker he'd been saving for its cover article on "Britain's Romantic Poets" and flipped through the pages.

Insistent thoughts crowded his mind and obliterated his concentration as he tried to read. Was it possible for two people do be more unalike than Luke Jones and Denny Durango? They were definitely two halves of a human oxymoron.

Luke was a book learner with no practical street experience who flaunted his erudition to compensate for his ignorance of the real world. What he really needed was to learn how to get along with people without pissing them off.

Denny, on the other hand, joked that he had carried a book to school, once. He knew the language of the streets and he knew how to manipulate people. It was a sure formula for success as a cop. Plus, he knew he'd be able to figure out how to write a decent report one of these days.

Luke's father was a domineering Pentecostal preacher who ruled the family like a Caribbean potentate. He preached that God's plan called for a man and a woman to fall in love and deny their biological imperatives until a minister joined them in holy matrimony when they would "keep themselves only unto themselves" and then one of them would die.

Luke's mother died on his eighteenth birthday.

The cancer that eventually killed her started when Luke was two and he remembered her as an emotionally distant woman who was almost always too sick to take care of him.

Luke loved fine arts and he loved great books. He savored mellifluous language and the ebb and flow of experience and emotion in the hands of an expert writer.

On the eve of Denny's thirteenth birthday, his stepfather treated him to the neighborhood whore to celebrate his new manhood.

Although Denny's mother voluntarily turned a blind eye to her husband's infidelities, she was the one who wielded the family power stick. Since Denny was the oldest male child, she doted on him like a queen raising the heir apparent to a throne.

Denny roamed Bedford-Stuyvesant's streets and, in his spare time, joined in an unofficial partnership with New York City's public schools. Denny's job was to stay out of trouble and the school system's job was to grant a meaningless diploma.

What should have been a signet of accomplishment actually symbolized a double failure: the school system's unwillingness to maintain a set of minimum standards, and the Durango family's failure to educate a prized boy-child.

Luke's thoughts disappeared into his latest musings about how frustrating his evening would be as Denny finally swaggered into the living room, holding his hair pick to his lips like a microphone and singing along with the lyrics of a Bee Gees song wafting in from his bedroom.

The time had come for Luke Jones to put down his damn magazine and get with the program.

36

THE POLICE FIRING RANGE THRUMMED TO THE sounds of Marvin
Gaye's rendition of "Let's Get It On" as Luke walked in and Denny
made an entrance. Denny glided over to the corner where Tina Cleveland stood with a group of friends and Luke assumed his position near
the end of the bar.

For Luke, the police pistol range was about the worst place to hold
a disco party, even though the only necessary preparations involved taking down folding tables and chairs, stocking the bar and pushing in a
jukebox.

The floor was ancient tan linoleum with layers of wax wearing off
in various places, giving the entire room a distinctly dirty appearance.
A striking stone fireplace dominated the north wall where a group of
rookies huddled in animated conversation.

Several members of the Chief's senior staff had shown up to
demonstrate the department's interest in the new recruits. Hal Browner
fumed behind the bar, glaring at Denny. Luke didn't know Browner's
thoughts, but he could guess. Denny was an infamous womanizer who
was starting to do the bump and grind with Councilman Cleveland's
daughter where the whole world could see. He'd embarrassed the department at the America's Finest City Rally and now he was embar-
rassing one of the most powerful men in the city.

Luke surreptitiously worked his way into a spot behind a concrete column that stood close to where Browner talked with Sergeant Biletnikoff.

"Everybody knows this Durango is a marginal employee," Browner said. "We should have fired his ass a long time ago."

Luke wasn't sure if Browner knew Biletnikoff was Denny's immediate supervisor, but he'd be willing to bet he did based on what Browner was saying.

"I'm told he has photographs of naked women in his locker," Browner went on.

Luke kept a wary eye on the dance floor as Denny crotch danced with Tina Cleveland in the middle of the crowded room. Everybody knew Denny was sleeping with her, and Denny didn't have enough sense to consider the impact of his shenanigans on Cleveland's feelings or the embarrassment to the department.

"Who does he work for?" Browner asked Biletnikoff. His tone said he already knew the answer. It would certainly explain why Browner had sought Biletnikoff out behind the bar.

"He's on my squad," Biletnikoff said.

"I hear this Luke Jones kid carries him," Browner said. "Some of my people say he helps with his reports. Is that true?"

"I'm not sure," Biletnikoff told him. He fidgeted from one foot to the other. "But I'll keep my eye on it." Luke knew Biletnikoff was shifting his feet on dangerous ground. Biletnikoff did know the truth, but obviously hadn't seen anything wrong with it until that moment. Admitting that to Browner would be stupid.

"This department would be better off without that piece of shit, I can tell you that much," Browner insisted. He poured a tumbler of scotch and soda down his throat and slammed the glass on the bar.

Browner's comments didn't amount to ordering Biletnikoff to fire Denny exactly. No one could accuse him of that. Termination for incompetence rested in the hands of an officer's immediate supervisor. "When's his probationary period over?" Browner asked as he snatched a refill from Biletnikoff's hand.

"He's got a few weeks to go," Biletnikoff said. "He's only been with me a few months and I've been on vacation and at training schools part of that time."

"I'd take a good hard look at him before I'd let him pass probation if I were his boss," Browner said. "Of course, I wouldn't focus on that mess back at the America's Finest City Rally. That's already been handled."

Browner glared at Biletnikoff, seemingly waiting for a response, although there was nothing to respond to really. Browner could claim they were only having a friendly conversation if anybody ever questioned his motives.

"He hasn't exactly been a model employee," Biletnikoff said. "I'll go through his personnel jacket and see what I see."

The smile Luke saw on Browner's face clearly showed the Assistant Chief thought Biletnikoff had a pretty good idea. It also told him Denny was in trouble.

37

SERGEANT CONSTANTIN BILETNIKOFF KICKED HIS flip-flops onto the floor of his locker, slid out of his beach shorts and pulled his uniform pants off a hanger. No doubt about it, he had to face the blunder he'd committed by letting Luke Jones and Denny Durango stay on the same squad. It had allowed Luke to carry Durango. Denny's inadequacies would have stood out like a Doberman in a Chihuahua kennel if Luke hadn't helped him all the time. Fortunately, it wasn't too late. He could fire a probationary officer easily enough. None of the brass would care. They'd have no interest in keeping a marginal employee who'd already embarrassed the department.

He knew one thing for certain. Deputy Chief Hal Browner, the ultimate reviewer of discipline for Central Division, certainly wouldn't second guess him when it came time to review the termination package.

Biletnikoff's decision to go after Denny wasn't influenced by the looming Lieutenant's exam or the fact that Browner could push his promotion. Nothing he intended doing was for self-serving reasons. Terminating an incompetent employee might be the most important thing a sergeant ever did.

Biletnikoff finished dressing, strolled into the lineup room and took his place at the podium to give out assignments and cover crimes from the night before. "Durango," Biletnikoff said once he'd covered the preliminaries. "I need you and Shimmer to handle security on a movie set over at Sixth and B Streets."

Biletnikoff parked a block away and pulled his binoculars from the glove compartment.

Several motor officers from Traffic Division had already cordoned off the six hundred block of B Street before Denny and Shimmer arrived. The motorcycle cops' job was to control traffic around the set and the patrol officers were there to keep the groupies and lookie-loos away.

The motor officers had parked their Kawasakis parallel to a catering truck that bisected three horizontal parking spaces. Shimmer followed their example and Denny parked next to him, completing a line of illegally parked police vehicles.

The filming of Scavenger Hunt was about to begin and the newspaper articles had said the low-budget comedy involved a cast of aging television actors competing in a high-stakes treasure hunt.

Biletnikoff had been right. Denny's behavior was ridiculous. He actually asked Scatman Crothers to pose with him for a photograph.

Biletnikoff could tell the Scatman was annoyed. Sure, he took the trouble to clasp Denny's hands and grinned about as wide as the Joker in the Batman comics when the bulb flashed. But that didn't matter. It was Denny's job to keep people from annoying the actors, not to annoy them himself. That wasn't the half of it. He made a pig of himself when the crew offered up the catered spread filling several tables near the set.

Sure, all the other officers had a plate of food, but they were veterans who had enough sense to know when to quit.

Biletnikoff had attached the zoom lens and gotten the pictures he needed. He snapped Denny posing with the Scatman and he caught Denny wolfing down the catered food. He clicked repeatedly as Denny had the gall to talk to other actors on the set. Denny definitely didn't stay out of the way and Biletnikoff had the proof on film.

When the movie cameras rolled and all eyes were riveted on the action, Biletnikoff unlocked the trunk to Denny's patrol car and pulled out his equipment bag. He rifled through it, found the envelope that contained the photographs of women in various states of undress he'd been told about, and pulled out the three depicting Tina Cleveland wearing a smile and a crimson bow in her hair.

Biletnikoff correctly predicted that Denny would hang around the set too long after the filming wrapped. Once Shimmer and the motor cops had secured the scene and the catering truck was gone, Biletnikoff took a few pictures of Denny's car as it sat alone on a downtown street blatantly taking up two normal parking spaces.

More than mere pictures, Biletnikoff's photographs were quite literally the pictures that supported a thousand words. Those words, as written in Biletnikoff's report, said Denny had interrupted the day's filming. Not only that, he'd blatantly ignored the California Vehicle Code with his illegal parking. It was a clear case of a probationary officer using poor judgment and behaving in a manner that could only be construed as "Conduct Unbecoming an Officer."

Biletnikoff was clobbering Denny with the dreaded CUBO offense and supporting everything he wrote with photographs. He'd constructed his house-of-cards termination on a foundation of half-truths and downright lies. But no one who'd care could possibly know it.

He called Denny into his office the next day to deliver the news. "Officer Durango, I'm sorry to have to inform you, I'm recommending your termination as a San Diego Police Officer."

Denny wobbled like a dazed boxer enduring a mandatory eight count. He couldn't believe Biletnikoff's words. His reports had continued to get better. He'd made several arrests recently that only somebody with his street savvy could make. What had he done? Why single him out?

Biletnikoff showed Denny the termination package. His presentation started with copies of Shimmer's field training evaluations that recommended his termination way back in the first training phase.

Denny's thoughts started to spin.

Sure, Shimmer had written that Denny wasn't a salvageable employee back then. But that was months ago and Denny'd done nothing but improve since then.

Biletnikoff showed Denny the Scatman photographs and the pictures of the illegally parked police car along with his narrative report. It said that Denny had been such a nuisance he'd ruined the entire day's shoot, at an enormous cost to the production company.

This was flabbergasting. Those guys at the set had loved him. The Scatman had put his arms around him. None of this rang true.

"This is all extremely serious," Biletnikoff assured him. "You do have the right to representation and to a Skelly hearing."

"A Skelly hearing?"

"An appeal to the Commanding Officer," Biletnikoff said. "I have to tell you though, you're still on probation and there's no way you'll prevail in this thing. If you ever hope for another job in law enforcement, you should resign before you get fired.

"I'll take you over to personnel right now if you want," Biletnikoff said. "Or I can hold on to this package for a few days if you want a little time to think it over."

What should Denny do? Luke had warned him something bad was coming. He'd know what to do, but he'd flown up to the Oregon Shakespeare Festival for a few days.

"I'd like a little time to think about it," Denny said.

38

LUKE HAD LOVED HIS TIME AT THE Oregon Shakespeare Festival. He went to plays, took long walks along Ashland Creek in Lithia Park and actually played pool with Romeo and Juliet in a bar right after their show. He'd also spent some time thinking about how tough it was to be a rookie.

Luke knew Biletnikoff was gunning for Denny and the note Denny left him on the kitchen table had confirmed that something happened while he was gone. He'd talk to Denny about it as soon as he could.

There was also a message waiting on his machine from Andee Bradford. She wanted to talk to Luke about what she'd told him on the Plaza a few weeks ago. She kept getting hit on by senior officers with veiled threats to get her fired if she didn't cooperate with their advances. Luke had seen how guys treated her and he believed everything she'd told him. She wanted her job as much as Denny wanted his, but was threatening to quit if the harassment didn't stop.

Luke had told her to take the threats head on, that she should spend more time with her peers after work. After she'd had a few drinks and developed a little camaraderie, she'd become one of the guys just by showing up and they'd eventually get tired of screwing with her and leave her alone.

He was exhausted and hungry now though and had a more immediate problem of his own—to kill the last hour of his eternal graveyard shift. The local breakfast joints were opening and he could stay out of service, grab some breakfast and roll into the station. That was the smart thing to do, but he decided to go back in-service and request a code-7 so he could officially eat in peace.

"Negative, 5-John," the dispatcher shot back. "I need you to investigate an 11-46 behind the auto repair shop at Seventh and Market Streets. RP says the victim's a white male, between forty and fifty-years-old. He's slumped against the exterior wall to the rear of the shop."

Luke was starting to understand why the senior guys ate when out of service instead of asking for a meal break. If he'd done that, communications would've saved the call for a first watch unit.

Handling dead body calls was a total drag with no potential upside. They took hours under the best of circumstances and now, he'd not only have to skip breakfast, he'd also be several hours late getting to bed. He'd just completed his second overnight shift in a row with all day court in between and hadn't closed his eyelids for thirty-six hours.

Luke eased toward the ramp leading off the Motor Machine's rooftop parking lot. When the business was closed, officers wrote reports up there and some even napped on those interminable graveyard nights when they couldn't stay awake. Its seclusion was perfect.

Only a few civilians knew it existed and an enormous generator stood in the middle of the lot. With the San Diego-Coronado Bay to the south, and no high rises to the east or west, the north represented the only direction for potential sniper fire and the generator prevented that possibility.

Luke played the call out in his mind as he stopped at the top of the ramp to put his paper work inside his metal clipboard. As first officer at the scene, he'd verify the guy was dead and make a preliminary decision about potential foul-play. In this case, with the body lying outside, no witnesses, and his status as a rookie, he'd have to call Sergeant Biletnikoff to consult on his decision. It was bound to be a miserable experience.

Luke stepped out of his car and into the early morning light as the sun climbed past the top of the concrete garage behind him. The shop's janitor, who Luke knew always arrived a half-hour before the business opened, came out the front and shook Luke's hand. "He's over here, around back." The janitor wiped donut crumbs from his mouth and stuffed a dirty mechanic's rag into his back pocket.

The dispatcher had said to investigate a report of a body, so Luke had a pretty good idea what to expect. He just hoped it was something natural that wasn't too gruesome.

His wish was granted.

It was just another drunk who'd died alone in the middle of the night, one of the many indigent downtown alcoholics who drove police officers, paramedics and ER docs nuts with their filth and squalor. But the Pendleton shirt looked familiar.

The Professor's rigid body was positioned exactly the way it was the first time Luke saw him in Balboa Park. Luke squatted to check the Professor's vital signs. This time, the nearly supine man in front of him was dead, and the can of Olde English 800 in his grasp was empty.

Once Biletnikoff arrived and concurred with Luke's decision about a natural death, he'd call for the Coroner's Office to claim the body. That would end the San Diego Police Department's official involvement with the notorious drunkard at his feet.

Luke told the janitor to go about his business. "I'll take care of everything from here," he said. It was the straightforward comment of a cop doing his job and precisely what Luke intended to do.

Luke pulled a cigar from his equipment bag. He tugged the plastic wrapper off, lit the tobacco and leaned against the wall, hovering over the Professor. The Professor's body only stunk a little this time, but the situation reeked.

How many times had he made himself a fool over the dead man at his feet? How about the time he'd gone over Biletnikoff's head to press the Lieutenant about the Professor's ride-along? Only he would have the balls to go over his immediate boss's head about that one. He'd gotten away with it too, but not without making Biletnikoff his enemy.

How silly had he looked when he'd marched the Professor into the apartment to tell Denny he intended to clean him up and let him sleep on the couch? How absurd was their argument when he told his roomie that if Denny could keep his parrot, he could keep the Professor?

Keep the Professor?

If Denny could keep a pet, Luke could keep the Professor. How stupid had he seemed when he tracked down the Professor's brother to demand that he take care of his sibling?

Once the name-calling had subsided, the Professor's brother told him they both had trust funds from a family endowment and money was deposited into their accounts every month. The Professor could have it whenever he wanted.

Biletnikoff pulled up to find Luke puffing on the cigar and expecting a smirk on his boss's lips. What Luke actually got came as a surprise. "I'm sorry," Biletnikoff said. "I know he meant a lot to you."

Biletnikoff's words carried no hint of insincerity and challenged everything Luke believed he knew about his immediate supervisor, just like the job challenged all his notions about what was good and bad and right and wrong.

"Why don't I call another unit to wait for the coroner?" Biletnikoff asked. "Maybe you should grab a cup of coffee and clear your head."

"This is something I need to do myself," Luke said.

When the Coroner's Deputy arrived, Luke told her how to reach the Professor's brother, gave her his department issued business card and said he'd claim the body if the brother declined.

He was disgusted with the Professor himself. He could only imagine how his brother would feel. Luke knew the brother would decline to claim the body of the man who'd been a boy, a soldier, a student, a professor, an anonymous public drunk, then a mentor who challenged everything Luke believed, a known drunk who refused Luke's help, and a dead man clutching the only thing that really mattered to him. The empty can of Olde English 800 was clearly his best friend.

The call from the coroner's office came three days later. Luke telephoned the Bradbury Mortuary to arrange to have the body picked up and cremated.

He set the brass urn on the seat beside him the next day and accelerated toward the G Street Pier that jutted into the ocean where cool breezes whipped through to inter-mix with the stench of fish from a tuna cannery. The breezy aroma of the fresh breezes commingled with the stench of the dead and dying in an incessant battle to rule the air over the waters of the San Diego Bay.

It was the perfect spot to spread the Professor's ashes.

Luke sucked in the pungent stench as he pulled his dilapidated Mercury Tracer into a parking stall next to the Tuna Fisherman's Association Headquarters. He tucked the urn under his arm to stroll to the end of the pier, pulled the top off and tipped the ashes into the breeze. As the ashes spread over the ocean, Luke quoted something he knew the Professor would appreciate from the end of *Oedipus Rex*: "*Count no mortal happy till he has passed the final limit of his life secure from pain.*"

39

Luke and Denny marched into Biletnikoff's office together.

"I know Denny's not exactly a model employee," Luke said. His soft opening seemed to surprise Biletnikoff, who'd obviously prepared for a fight, and left Denny with his mouth gaping.

"I can work with him," Luke said. "He's a good street cop who just needs to work on his report writing."

Biletnikoff looked like he might explode for a second before bellowing his response. "What the hell makes you think you can take responsibility for a marginal employee? You're still wet behind the ears yourself."

"I'm not trying to make this thing about me," Luke said. "I'm trying to talk about Denny's ability to do the job."

"Don't kid yourself for a second this isn't about you too," Biletnikoff said. "I've got enough trouble on my hands with you challenging senior officers all the time and going over my head whenever you feel like it. Now you're telling me how to do my job? The last thing I need on top of dealing with you is an incompetent cop. I've gone through Denny's personnel record and Shimmer was recommending his termination way back in field training."

"Shimmer?" Luke said. "He's an idiot and you know it."

Luke was always ready for a confrontation when conciliation didn't work and Biletnikoff was clearly unwilling to negotiate anything.

"Denny wants a Skelly. You know as well as I do the termination package he told me about won't hold up."

Luke squared his shoulders and looked into Biletnikoff's eyes. He could care less about his own probationary status. He knew right from wrong.

"Let me ask you something," Biletnikoff said. "As his roommate, are you aware Denny uses a department camera to take inappropriate photographs of women?" It was more than a question. It was a threat to discipline Luke if he knew about it and hadn't told anyone.

"I'm never around when Denny takes his pictures and I don't know what camera he uses," Luke said. His confidence apparently convinced Biletnikoff he was telling the truth. But he couldn't believe what he was hearing.

"Is there any truth to that Denny?" Luke asked.

"Any truth to what?"

"Did you take pictures of women with the department's camera?" There would have been a way around this if only Denny'd told him about it.

"Well, I guess I sort of did that," Denny said.

"Why don't you tell us why you'd do something like that," Biletnikoff said.

Luke wanted to knock the smile off Biletnikoff's face.

"I carry my equipment bag home with me every night and I carry the camera in the bag," Denny said.

"Whose film did you use?" Biletnikoff asked.

"Sometimes I used department film, but other times I bought film and used it for work," Denny said.

Luke couldn't believe his ears. Denny was standing there admitting he'd used department property to take pictures of naked women and acting like he couldn't see anything wrong with it. Worse than that, Luke could have been prepared to deal with it if Denny'd only told him.

There must be more to it.

"There's nothing about this in the termination packet," Luke said.

"I was trying not to pile on," Biletnikoff said. "I've told Denny I'm willing to hold off on submitting this thing if he decides to resign."

That was it, his real agenda. Even with those stupid pictures, Biletnikoff knew he didn't have enough to fire Denny. He wanted Denny to quit. He'd made this whole termination package up to please Chief Browner and he wasn't about to get away with it.

"That's not enough to fire him and I think you know it," Luke said. "I'd like to hear what the other cops at the movie set have to say about what went on there, then we'll see what we'll see at the Skelly hearing."

"Well, let's see," Biletnikoff said. "There were a few motor cops and another patrol guy there. Let me try and think who that was. Oh yeah, that's right." Biletnikoff turned to Denny. "Wasn't Shimmer there with you?"

Biletnikoff had obviously not interviewed the motor cops at the movie set for his termination packet because they wouldn't be critical enough to support his outrageous conclusions. Shimmer was his ace in the hole. Biletnikoff knew Shimmer would back him if it meant getting rid of Denny.

Luke wanted to vomit. Biletnikoff was playing a damn good Iago. But once they got to the Skelly hearing, the Captain would see what a shoddy investigation Biletnikoff had done.

Luke motioned for Denny to follow him out the door.

"Maybe you should see these before you go." Biletnikoff tossed a white envelope on the desk. Several photographs slid out and onto the desk top.

"How do you think Councilman Cleveland would feel about those going public?" Biletnikoff asked.

Luke stood transfixed. He'd been sure he was right about Biletnikoff not having enough to fire Denny. Hell, in the real world he was right. But not in this strange world where naked pictures of a city councilman's daughter got tossed onto desk tops in a police sergeant's office.

"You should tell Denny to resign," Biletnikoff said. "It'll save you a lot of personal grief and his chances of getting another job in law enforcement would be a lot better, don't you think?"

Luke had walked into a trap because Denny hadn't had enough sense to prepare him for it. What was worse, Denny had made it impossible for Luke to help him.

Luke knew Denny's job meant the world to him. He'd been living the dream of a lifetime and now Luke was part of his worst nightmare. Denny was a simple soul really who couldn't possibly fathom the hatred of a Hal Browner, the self-serving manipulations of a Constantin Biletnikoff or the unspoken power of an outraged city councilman. His inability to comprehend those things was as much his fatal flaw as his unwillingness to keep his pecker in his pants. It didn't matter that Denny had spent half his weekends writing the practice reports Luke gave him and was really getting the hang of it.

Why had Denny done something so stupid?

The question boomeranged and the answer smacked Luke in the face. It was only partly Denny's fault. Yes. It was true Denny's dick controlled his behavior, which turned him into a moron sometimes. But that was only part of it.

Biletnikoff hated Luke for going over his head to the lieutenant about the Professor's ride-along and he hated him for speaking his mind all the time. Luke was a rookie on probation and he needed to act like it. Of the two of them, Denny was the most vulnerable, the easiest to cut away from the herd. Biletnikoff knew getting rid of Denny would hurt Luke almost as much as it hurt Denny.

"I think you should go down to personnel and turn in your badge," Luke told his roommate.

Tears welled in Denny's eyes.

"I can walk down there with you if you'd like," Luke told him and Biletnikoff seemed to think that was a darn good idea.

Luke and Denny turned their backs to walk out.

"Before you go," Biletnikoff told Luke. "I'm partnering you with Shimmer so you can benefit a little from his experience."

40

HORTON PLAZA SHUCKED AND JIVED LIKE any other night. Hare Krishnas bounced and begged for change. Pickpockets worked the bus stops and pimps huddled with prostitutes. A preacher proclaimed San Diego a modern day Sodom and bellowed that God's vengeance was drawing near.

Charles Henreid drove past the freak show on his way to die. He slammed his front tires into the curb and piled out of the car.

Three transvestite whores argued over a baggie of marijuana in the doorway of the Golden West Hotel. Henreid stomped past several street punks as they jerked a nearly comatose drunk to his feet, rifled his pockets and called out for Henreid to give them a quarter or they'd take all his money. Which was what they intended to do anyway once he handed them the coin.

Henreid ignored them.

Tripping over his feet, he dropped his keys, along with the half-empty Jack Daniels bottle that fell from his belt to shatter against the sidewalk. He picked the keys up and tried inserting one into the keyhole, but the key ring slipped from his fingers and into the puddle of whiskey. The downward motion as he bent to pick them up again sent his thoughts into a spin cycle that tumbled together in a heap of confusion. He fell to his knees, found the keys and started to stand.

He could see his wife screwing up her nose earlier in the day. She didn't care that he'd really changed his life this time and she had no intention of giving him another chance. Couldn't she have let him finish a sentence? Was she too stupid to understand everything would be better this time?

"I've saved up enough money for first and last month's rent on a nice apartment," he told her. He had a really good job and was close to starting his own business again. If she'd let him finish one lousy sentence, he'd tell her how gambling didn't control his life anymore.

Had she actually said she couldn't respect anybody she couldn't trust and that she'd found someone else? Would his daughter be raised by another man? What other words came out of her mouth? Had she said she hated him?

None of it mattered anyway. He knew what he had to do to make things right.

Henreid inserted a key and turned his wrist, but nothing happened, so he tried the other keys. None of them opened the damn lock and it was no wonder because he remembered now, the contractor he used to work for took them away when he'd laid him off right after Henreid's meeting with his wife.

He knew how to get in and it was better this way anyhow. This would definitely trigger the burglar alarm. The cops would have to come and investigate once he shattered the window. They should've let him kill himself a long time ago.

Henreid turned toward his truck, all the while cursing his stupid life and his stupid wife and his stupid self and those stupid cops who'd taken his livelihood from him and messed up his chance to kill himself. How could he have been so goddamned stupid as to think his bitch of a wife would ever take him back? He was a moron that was for sure.

Henreid lifted a hammer from his toolbox as the street thugs finished their mugging and called out in unison, ordering Henreid to give them his money.

Henreid turned toward them, the shadows splashing against his reflected smile in the window creating a macabre mask. He gripped his hammer tight. He'd be happy to take these punks out if it came to that. He stomped toward them and they marched away like a shoddily disciplined drill team.

Henreid lifted the hammer near his ear, smashed the glass door and walked in to the laundromat he'd finished renovating earlier in the day.

41

AS FAR AS LUKE WAS CONCERNED, their getting interrupted by a radio call was a damn good thing for John Shimmer. It had taken him months to recover from his injuries in the park restroom and he'd obviously forgotten Luke had saved his ass. Just exactly where did this chump get off now that he was back at work, saying Luke should go fuck himself? Not only was Shimmer just a street cop like anybody else, he was part of the reason Denny got fired and now he had the nerve to tell Luke he was the car commander. Luke was supposed to sit in the passenger seat with his mouth shut and do what Shimmer told him.

No scenario in hell could make things play out that way.

The radio call temporarily kept Luke from speaking his mind.

He acknowledged the call and set the transmitter down. It was his first flagrant act of defiance since Shimmer had told him his only jobs for the shift were to write the reports and follow orders.

Luke picked up the receiver again to announce their arrival as Shimmer drove past Caruso's Italian Restaurant. "Unit 2-King, 10-97," he said and beamed a toothy grin in Shimmer's direction.

Shimmer took another stab at seizing control. "Let's get one thing straight, rookie. I'm senior officer in this car and you do what you're told. Are we clear on that?"

"Look," Luke said, "you sit over there in the driver's seat and command that. If you want something, you can ask me nicely and I might consider it. Are we clear on that?"

A moment of hard silence followed until Shimmer finally pushed his car door open and stepped into the street while Luke stepped into the gutter.

The officers hugged the fronts of the adjacent buildings as they crept through the shadows, trying to not make any noise.

Light splashed onto the sidewalk from the interior of the laundromat and the officers heard footsteps crunching on broken glass. They cleared their holsters and posted on opposite sides of the door. Luke took charge and nodded. Shimmer nodded back with an exquisite look of exasperation on his face.

Luke stepped through the doorway with Shimmer following close behind. The snapping of broken glass sounded beneath their boots.

Henreid glowered at Shimmer then he smiled at Luke.

Luke saw Henreid better tonight than he ever had before. His biceps could have been sculpted of marble. His Rugby shirt accented pronounced pectorals and his close set eyes nearly disappeared under a single bushy eyebrow.

Broken chairs, chunks of stucco, loose bricks and scattered carpenter's tools littered the floor. Henreid threw a pipe at Shimmer that clanged against the doorframe.

Luke's reality instantly distorted into a slow motion movie.

Why didn't Shimmer shoot? He was the senior officer and the one who should shoot this guy who'd already thrown a pipe a couple inches away from his head.

Henreid went off like a Hollywood Apache. He hopped. He hollered. He bounced on the balls of his feet and screamed things Luke couldn't understand.

Luke knew Henreid well enough to know he didn't want to kill anyone. He wanted to die.

Henreid threw another pipe at Shimmer's head.

Luke retreated, the barrel of his gun riveted at Henreid's chest, waiting for Shimmer to pull his trigger. But Shimmer shuffled backwards.

Luke could wrestle Henreid into submission if he could only get his hands on him. There was no need to kill him if Luke could just get a little closer. Luke could barely hear Shimmer barking orders for Henreid to stop, to give up, that they wanted to help him.

It wasn't fair that Luke might have to kill a guy he'd taken on a ride-along. Shimmer's years of patrol experience clearly made him the one to know when to shoot.

Henreid threw bricks and he threw hammers. He threw screwdrivers. He threw wooden stools. He stalked toward Shimmer.

Luke shouted out his own orders for Henreid to give up.

Objects flew and the officers retreated.

"Shoot me!" Henreid screamed. He hit Shimmer in the chest with a clock radio and barely missed with a wrench.

"Shoot me, asshole," Henreid bellowed. "You're going to have to shoot me." Henreid smashed a bar stool against the cement floor, knocked the top free from the legs, and hurled the thick wooden seat like a Frisbee. It smashed into Shimmer's neck. He clutched his throat and tripped over a brick.

Henreid hovered. He cocked a leg from the bar stool above his head, a home run hitter about to uncork a wicked swing and Shimmer's head was the baseball.

Luke heard a muffled explosion and he saw fire belch from his gun. He watched a .38 semi-wadcutter bullet fly through the air. The round smacked into Henreid's chest by his armpit before Henreid turned toward him.

"You asshoooooooole," Henreid bellowed. "You shot me." He looked at his chest and he looked at Luke. "You fucking shot me." He was coming for Luke now with the bat still poised for a home run swing.

Luke saw another muzzle flash and he heard the whooshing explosion in Henreid's neck an instant before a third bullet slammed into Henreid's shoulder. He didn't recollect firing the third shot. He never heard the bang and he never saw the flash.

Henreid toppled to the ground.

Luke rushed forward to render first aid.

Shimmer called for help over the radio. "Unit 2-King," he said. "Shots fired. Suspect down. Send us a supervisor and an ambulance."

42

THE LAUNDROMAT SWARMED WITH COPS. Reporters crowded together outside the doorway.

Among the first to arrive, Hartson watched Biletnikoff order officers to escort the reporters farther down the block. Then he told Hartson to assume command.

With the lieutenant's exam only two weeks away, now would be a really bad time for an ambitious sergeant to screw up a sensitive investigation. It was true that supervising the initial stages of any homicide scene required following a relatively simple set of procedures. But police shootings always brought intense internal scrutiny because of the potential for negative press.

Hartson had to give it to Biletnikoff. His solution to the problem was foolproof. If Hartson messed anything up, Biletnikoff could claim he was developing a subordinate's career. Hartson's name sat at the top of the Sergeant's list and supervising the scene would not only give him valuable experience, it would insulate Biletnikoff from potential fallout.

Hartson put Shimmer in the back of a patrol car, ordered him not to talk to anybody, and posted a rookie nearby to keep people away.

He issued the same order to Luke as he took his gun, but the order ate at his guts. He wanted to sit and talk to Luke, to tell him he'd done the right thing. That he was stuck in an ongoing nightmare of necessary standard procedures that would all go away one day.

He posted a rookie near Luke to keep others away instead and placed a trainee outside the doorway, issuing him an impossible order. "Do not let anyone in here but essential personnel."

The trainee blinked nervously.

"Do you know what essential personnel means?" Hartson asked.

A pair of blank eyes stared back.

"It means only the Homicide guys can get inside here now. I don't care if the Chief shows up. You look him straight in the eyeball and tell him he ain't allowed inside unless he intends to take charge of the investigation personally."

Hartson knew the order was patently absurd, that the trainee wouldn't challenge any high-ranking officer wanting inside the laundromat unless he had balls the size of the ones Luke Jones carried around when he was a trainee. But it was the right order to issue and Hartson had met his responsibility. "Anybody gives you any trouble; you refer them right over there to Sergeant Biletnikoff." Hartson nodded toward the patrol sergeant who stood on the sidewalk amidst a throng of reporters.

Hartson made Paul Devree the incident scribe, which was a dubious compliment. Scribes needed superior decision-making skills backed up by the experience necessary to cope with the inevitable chaos and stress of a hectic scene.

More importantly, scribes were the final line of defense against the powerful interlopers that would inevitably get past the sentinel outside the door. Scribes had to demand the names, ID numbers, and assignments of everybody who showed up at the scene and write it on his log. Everyone with their name on the log had to write a report detailing his or her role in the investigation. It was the mandatory report that deterred a lot of unnecessary meddling.

Everyone understood that the personnel log had to be accurate since opposing attorneys in subsequent court actions could allege incompetence or cover up, and the press reports would definitely turn ugly if that happened.

Hartson kept a folded arm vigil on the proceedings.

Could he have saved Henreid if he'd only had the guts to tell him quitting gambling wouldn't win back his wife? What if he'd let Henreid jump that night up on the Concourse? One thing was for sure—Luke wouldn't be dealing with killing him tonight.

He knew he'd done the right thing that night and he knew Luke knew it. Enough nonsense, he had to focus.

He wasn't surprised that Biletnikoff faced off with the news cameras even after relinquishing command of the scene. The inevitable phone calls after the television face time were a lot of fun and Biletnikoff could argue how important it was for somebody with proper experience and savvy to handle the press who always demanded access to a department spokesman even though state law mandated that virtually nothing of consequence could be divulged this early in an investigation.

Biletnikoff assured the reporters it was premature to make any further comment. But yes, more information would be forthcoming, and no, he couldn't give out the names of the involved officers yet.

Watching the charade provided a passable distraction for Hartson who'd otherwise have to focus on the frigid reality at hand. His former trainee, who'd become his trusted friend, now had to deal with the emotional devastation of killing a desperate man whose struggle he respected in order to save the life of a partner he hated.

43

THE HOMICIDE TEAM SERGEANT ASKED Biletnikoff for the scribe's log.

Biletnikoff hollered out to Hartson, who yelled out to Devree, who presented a page from his notebook before the Homicide lieutenant asked for a quick briefing.

Hartson started to say what he'd learned, but Biletnikoff muscled his way in front. It was a spotlight moment and Biletnikoff clearly wanted the beacon even though the briefing was normally the responsibility of the scene supervisor.

The team sergeant designated a detective as scene investigator. That detective, teamed with a laboratory criminalist, took pictures of Henreid's body, of the debris, and of the smashed glass. They measured Henreid's distance from the walls and the doorway before detailing sketches of the laundromat and its contents.

A forensic pathologist and the "body snatcher" from a privately contracted company sealed a bag around Henreid's body. They lifted him onto the gurney and a detective followed to attend the autopsy.

The Homicide sergeant assigned two detectives to escort Luke and Shimmer to the Homicide office.

"Son, I'm Detective Hensen and I'll be driving you down to the office where you'll be a little more comfortable." The surreal words hitting

Luke's ears poured out of a Dover Cliff of a man with wing tips as big as clown shoes. The words echoed in Luke's head.

Luke felt like a character in a science fiction novel set in an upside down universe as he sat inside the detective's copper-colored Dodge Aspen. Luke dwarfed nearly everyone in the real world, but, in this altered reality, the man in the adjacent seat made him the little man.

Hensen stood nearly seven feet tall and weighed about as much as a small sedan. In his mid-forties and old enough to be Luke's father, he assumed a paternal role that apparently came easily to someone whose physical presence dominated his environment.

Hensen's thinning hair was tamed with a dab of hair cream and combed straight back to plaster against the top of his head. His ears supported silver-rimmed glasses and his tramp steamer of a body dominated the cab of the car as he slouched as low as possible into the seat, his head pushing against the lining of the ceiling.

The car holding Shimmer eased through the police garage behind Hensen's car and they pulled into a parking area surrounded by the brown stucco buildings of an aging Spanish hacienda.

Police Headquarters held sway over Dead Man's Point, State Registered Landmark number 57, a graveyard for sailors who'd died during Don Juan Pantoja's mapping expedition of 1782. Situated at the southeast corner of the intersection of Market Street and Pacific Highway, it rested where corporeal land merged with the Pacific's waters in a preternatural feeling of calm.

Palm fronds floated in the breeze beside a tower roofed with desiccated red tile. Police cars peppered the cobbled courtyard and the interior of the buildings exuded ill-tended Spanish elegance as Luke and Hensen walked past the SWAT armory that sat adjacent to the retired city jail. Once overflowing with drunks and vagrants, the jail presently flowed over with storage boxes stuffed with discarded public records. It was here the once stylish Spanish buildings hid their filthy little secret. The cells gave refuge to scores of rats that left their droppings during the daytime hours and raided the rest of the building at night.

The detectives ushered Shimmer into a Homicide interview room while Luke sat motionless in the waiting area, staring into nowhere. For the first time in his life his thoughts bombarded him with mental pictures.

He saw Henreid finishing a picture perfect home-run swing, but the head exploding against the impact belonged to Phillip McGrath, the Headless Horseman he'd encountered his first day on the job.

A distorted Henreid walked through a fun-house mirror to warn that Luke would visit this altered reality again as Luke sniffed the stench of the boiling witches' brew and Macbeth's weird sisters circled a spewing pot. Their mouths worked, but nothing came out.

Sergeant Farren escorted Luke into the interrogation room. Luke could have been waiting for minutes or he could have been waiting for hours. Farren pushed the door closed behind him as Lieutenant Berend waved Luke into a chair and fussed with a cassette recorder. He set the recorder in front of him and looked at his notes. "This is May 8, 1979," he said into the recorder. "I'm Lieutenant Jim Berend recording an interview with Officer Luke Jones regarding his shooting of Charles Henreid. Present with us in the room is Sergeant Bob Farren."

Berend turned his attention to Luke. "Before we ask any questions, I'd like to explain a few things you'll need to know. Homicide Team II is investigating the shooting. Afterwards, the DA's office will review our findings to verify the thoroughness of the investigation. Now, there isn't any statutory mandate for the DA's review, but the practice has developed in nearly every California County over the years.

"The purpose of the review is to assure the public that peace officers perform their duties in a manner commensurate with their authority. Now, the process determines the legality of the shooting, not the wisdom of the officer's actions or whether there was a better way of dealing with the situation." Berend reared back in his seat. "Do you have any questions so far?"

Luke shook his head.

"Because of their independence, experience and access to criminal justice agencies throughout the county, the DA's office is the logical agency to conduct the review and make sure our investigation is both thorough and impartial.

"Are you sure you don't have any questions?" Berend asked.

"I'm sure."

Berend snatched a butterscotch candy from a bowl in the middle of the table, unwrapped it and stuck it in his mouth. "Once the DA has reviewed our investigation, they'll send a letter to the Chief, summarizing the facts and providing a legal analysis of the use of deadly force. Now, typically, these letters are released to the press.

"Do you understand all this?"

"Yes," Luke said.

"Okay," Berend went on. "Before we ask any questions, there's one last thing I need to explain. Probably the most important piece of evidence for the DA's review is what you say about the shooting. You're the only witness who can relate the information available to you when you pulled the trigger. It's up to you to communicate a picture of what happened, tell us about any inferences you drew from the victim's actions and articulate your motivations. In other words, tell us why you had to kill..." Berend flipped through his notebook for a second. "...Mr. Henreid. Let us know how he constituted a threat to either you or your partner. Is all that clear?"

Luke knew it was more than a question. It was a supplication for proof of Luke's competence to continue with the process.

Luke nodded.

Berend shifted uncomfortably in his seat and turned the questioning over to Sergeant Farren.

"Okay," Farren said. "Officer Jones, could you please tell us about what you perceived and felt at the time of the shooting?"

From somewhere Luke found the words to describe the shooting.

He turned on the television at home sometime later to stare at the last half of Tyrone Power's black-and-white version of *The Razor's Edge*. The station's broadcast day ended with the movie.

Luke didn't move. The bright visual snow and insistent roar of the audio signal assaulted the room. But Luke sat still.

Sergeant Biletnikoff was on the other end of the line when the phone rang early in the morning. "Luke, did you get any sleep?"

"Are you there?" Biletnikoff asked.

"Yes."

Luke tasted his rancid breath.

"Hey, take a few days off," Biletnikoff said. "Think up some fancy quotes for lineup." He paused, apparently waiting for a chuckle. "Then I'll have you work the front counter until the shrink clears you."

"The shrink?" Luke said.

"Yeah, didn't anybody tell you? Here's how it all works. First, you take a few crazy days, but don't worry. You'll get paid. Then you work light duty until the investigation's completed and the shrink releases you to go back into the field." Biletnikoff paused. "Look," he went on, "if there's anything I can do to help..."

Luke dropped the phone into his lap.

Biletnikoff and help; those two words didn't go together.

44

Luke found Francie holding court in a circle of tables in the One-Five-Three Club and sitting next to Andee Bradford, his former trainee. Luke knew Francie wasn't part of her problem, but discomfort still wrinkled her forehead and showed the effort it took to try to fit in.

A chorus of greetings interrupted Francie's raucous story as Luke sat next to Hartson, who dispatched his current trainee to fetch Luke a beer.

The trainee handed Luke a Coors and sat a little outside the circle. "Go ahead on," Devree prodded Francie as Luke settled into his chair.

Francie shifted nervously. "Anyways," he went on, "I'm assigned to work the Heights this night because somebody's called in sick. I get this radio call and, I'm not shitting you now, dispatch says, 'Contact the woman about a stolen pork chop.' So the lady tells me she went shopping earlier in the day and then got her hair done. She comes back later and finds somebody's stolen her pork chop from her refrigerator."

Francie sipped his beer and bummed a cigarette from Devree.

"So the lady goes sniffing around the hallway and smells a pork chop cooking. A woman in a nearby apartment's stolen from her before, so she calls the police.

"I knock on the other lady's door and ask to be let inside. I go in the kitchen and sure enough, there's a pork chop in the frying pan. I go back across the hall, bring the victim in, and hold what you might call a stove-top lineup, because I don't have time to take pictures of other pork chops for a proper photo array."

Most everybody at the tables burst into laughter.

"'Can you ID this pork chop as the one you bought earlier today?' I say to the lady, and she tells me 'Sure, that's the one, all right.' Only I don't feel too good about making a pinch, so I get them to agree to split the pork chop after its done cooking. I'm a regular fucking Solomon."

Francie puffed his cigarette and sat back in his chair, relishing the laughter around him.

Luke took it all in, listening in his unique style of imparting motive and thought to others the way he used to listen to his father's sermons as a kid.

Francie reveled in the outward acceptance of his peers. His love for attention made him swallow what he really wanted to admit, that his wife had been right to leave him, that he'd been stupid when he got seduced by the adrenaline rush of police work. He'd discovered his cowardice too late, wanted to publicly apologize for abandoning Hartson with the PCP suspect and was shocked Hartson hadn't spilled the beans, especially since he'd moved out of their apartment two days later.

Francie wanted to declare himself an outcast in this company of brave people who did a job taking courage and patience and integrity; all qualities he'd discovered he lacked. He ruled the room with his laughter and his stories instead.

"Anybody want to hear a good Biletnikoff story?" Devree asked.

"Who's Biletnikoff?" the trainee outside the circle wanted to know.

"A Philistine," Luke said.

"What's a Philistine?"

"A Philistine is one of the unwashed masses you don't know and therefore don't like, or somebody you know well enough to hate his guts," Luke said.

"You mean an asshole," Hartson said.

The laughter was spontaneous and universal and Hartson downed the dregs of a scotch and soda as everyone took another sip of beer.

"I'm minding my own business at the Plaza one day," Devree began. "Biletnikoff pulls up and tells me to get in, hands me a stopwatch and tells me to time him. Without saying another word, he drives to Queen's Circle, puts the car into park and tells me to stop the watch. 'How much time did that take?' he wants to know. 'Twelve minutes,' I tell him. Then he says, 'You remember the other day when I called you to bring me a ticket book up here?' 'Yes,' I tell him. 'I remember.' 'That took you fifteen minutes,' he says. 'Three minutes longer than it took me just now. I want to know what happened to those three missing minutes!'

"Can you fucking believe that? He actually says to me, 'I want to know what happened to those three missing minutes,' like the whole fucking universe revolves around his sorry ass. I should have told him I stopped to take a dump because it was more important than his stupid ticket book."

Luke sipped his beer and surveyed the laughing audience, settling his gaze on Hartson who fought the urge to admit drinking had cost him his family. He should set his drink down right now and go home to fight for his wife and kid.

Luke knew Hartson didn't denounce Francie as a coward because exposing him could be his salvation. The only way to redemption for your sins was for someone else to offer absolution. Hartson wanted to stand up and admit he was having an affair with Shimmer's wife and the thought of it disgusted him. He asked Luke if he wouldn't mind picking up another round of beers instead.

Luke was happy to oblige.

Shimmer intercepted him half-way across the room and told him he'd buy the next round. Everybody in the room stared in disbelief as he came back with a full tray of beers and sat in the middle of the circle.

He wanted to say he'd emotionally abandoned his wife after their son drowned. That he couldn't live with the knowledge a woman had died because he couldn't kill her husband fast enough to save her. He needed to make things up to his wife and he needed to atone for his incompetence as a cop. It didn't matter that nobody else blamed him for the woman's death.

He wanted to shout out he couldn't bring himself to shoot Henreid because he wanted to die himself that night. He wanted to say it all, but he said none of it. "Say, did I ever tell you guys about the night I arrested Mr. Clean?"

No. He hadn't told them, and it was a damn good story, too. He relished the laughter that surrounded him and, for the first time in months, started enjoying the company of his compatriots. Luke Jones had saved his sorry life and it was about time he started doing something with it.

It was Hartson's turn to tell a story. He handed his trainee a twenty and dispatched him to fetch another round of beers.

Hartson leaned forward and motioned for everyone to lean into the center of the circle. "This one's about that one over at the bar," he said and he whispered his story of how he'd taken his unsuspecting trainee to a silent burglary alarm and made him climb a ladder to check out the roof. "I took the ladder away and left the poor kid with no way down," Hartson said.

Everybody in the huddle started to laugh, except for Luke.

"Wait, it gets better," Hartson said. "He switches over to the tactical frequency and asks a unit with a trainee to come and help him. So I wait and order the trainee not to interfere. I want to see how resourceful my guy is. You know what I mean?"

Everybody but Luke and Bradford nodded in appreciation. Luke wasn't a fan of hazing of any kind and knew it still might make Bradford quit her career.

"So what happened?" Devree asked.

"As I'm about to put the ladder back up, I notice he's standing on the edge of the roof. Before I can holler to stop, he jumps over to the telephone pole that must be six-feet away."

A peal of laughter filled the room.

"It's not funny," Hartson said. "I thought the dummy'd break his neck."

Howls of laughter started again.

Luke stood, went to the bar, bought a beer and handed it to the trainee as Shimmer hoisted a beer into the air.

"Hey, Luke," Shimmer said. "Quote us a little something from Shakespeare."

The request landed in the room like a concussion grenade.

Luke stood dazed.

"Go ahead and quote us some Shakespeare," Shimmer repeated.

Never one to miss out on an invitation like that, Luke bounded on to the bar and surveyed his audience, giving himself time to recover from Shimmer's request. He wished Denny were there and wanted to declare his regret over the part he'd played in Denny's termination. He wanted to say Denny might still be around if only he'd learned to keep his mouth shut and play by the unofficial rule that senior officers and supervisors had the right to screw with rookies.

He glared down at Francie, wanting to shout out his cowardice, but he knew stewing in the lingering acids of Francie's regret was far worse. Shakespeare had gotten it right in *Julius Caesar* when he wrote, "Cowards die many times before their deaths; the valiant never taste of death but once." Cowardice kept you in a perpetual state of hiding, in a secret place where self-hatred killed your soul over and over again. It was what Francie deserved.

Luke looked down at Bradford, his academy classmate, wanting to denounce the rude behavior and sexual innuendos of some of the guys in the circle that had nearly made her resign. She was a good cop who should be left alone to do her job, but Luke had learned his lesson about meddling in the affairs of others.

He wanted to trumpet his despair over killing Charles Henreid, but he knew he wasn't going to say any of it. He decided on the perfect quotation for the absurdity of the occasion instead, a bit of gibberish from Polonius in *Hamlet*:

> *To expostulate*
> *What majesty should be, what duty is,*
> *Why day is day, night night, and time is time,*
> *Were nothing but to waste night, day, and time.*
> *Therefore, since brevity is the soul of wit,*
> *And tediousness the limbs and outward flourishes,*
> *I will be brief...*

"Whoa, wait a minute," Shimmer demanded.

"What the fuck is that?" Francie asked.

"You're not making any sense," Devree said. "Can't you give us something that makes a little sense?"

Hartson laughed an uproarious laugh. "You go get 'em, Luke," he said.

"That's just pure nonsense," Shimmer chimed in again.

"It's a *sui generis* bit of nonsense," Luke said, deliberately choosing a phrase they wouldn't understand to underscore the absurdity of their situation.

"Bullshit!" Shimmer shouted. "Can't you say something that makes a little sense?"

"All right," Luke conceded, "but, I think I'll go to London for that one."

Luke relished the confused expression on the faces looking up at him.

"I mean Jack London," Luke said before he spoke.

If you suppress truth, if you hide truth, if you do not rise up and speak out in meeting, if you speak out in meeting without speaking the whole truth, then you are less true than truth.

"Oh, for cripes sake," Shimmer said. "What the fuck is that nonsense? Would you please get down from there?"

Luke was speaking at their invitation and wasn't ready to quit yet. Jack London had a little more left to say.

Let me glimpse the face of truth. Tell me what the face of truth looks like.

His audience pelted him with bottle caps, wadded up napkins and straws as Luke towered above them with a wry smile playing across his lips. "You guys asked for it," he said.

45

THE DA'S OFFICE FINALLY SENT A LETTER to Chief Coleman declaring Luke's shooting of Charles Henreid a "Justifiable Homicide." The accompanying report exonerated Luke's actions, but offered the opinion that Luke should have considered "other non-lethal options" before pulling the trigger.

Luke never saw the letter or the report, but he did read about them in the *San Diego Union* newspaper he found on his doorstep. He knew they were the final impediments to full duty and wondered exactly which options that punk of an assistant DA had in mind.

Just exactly who was right, he wondered. Was it Lieutenant Berend who'd implied that Luke should have shot sooner? Was it Shimmer and some of the others who hailed him as a hero? Or was it the assistant district attorney who'd probably never confronted real physical danger in his life?

Luke picked up another account of the DA's findings in the afternoon *Tribune* that sat on the table in the lineup room when he reported for work. "San Diego Police Officer Luke Jones," it read, "has been cleared in the fatal shooting of Charles Henreid. The District Attorney's office returned a finding of justifiable homicide. Jones shot and killed Henreid during a burglary in the Golden West Laundromat. Henreid, who was unarmed, died of multiple gunshot wounds."

There was a simple period at the end of the final sentence, but Luke could see the implied question mark hovering over the paper. It trumpeted doubt about whether Luke should have pulled the trigger and an accusation about a police officer's needless shooting of an unarmed man.

Luke tossed the paper onto the table.

A familiar fist of pain squeezed the base of his head, exacerbating the ruthless headache that hadn't relinquished its grip since the shooting. The same fist had squeezed his head in the Headless Horseman's den and seized him as he spread the Professor's ashes over San Diego Bay. It nearly blinded him when he told Denny it was best to resign.

Luke knew he could wrestle the fist into submission. That he'd never give in to it. It would figure that out sooner or later and leave him alone.

He sat through lineup, picked the local section up, rolled it into a cylinder, stuck it under his arm, walked into Biletnikoff's office, and announced he needed a sick day.

He'd submit to the pain this one and only time, and never again. "I have a headache," he told Biletnikoff. "I'll be back tomorrow."

Luke bought a fifth of Jack Daniels and a package of Garcia Y Vega cigars at the Gaslamp Liquor at Ninth and Market Streets, picked up a book of matches from the counter and headed for the G Street Pier where he sucked in a lungful of the stench of dead fish.

He sat on the hood of his car, gazing at the super structure of an aircraft carrier with the number 64 emblazoned in enormous white lights at the North Island Naval Air Station. He gulped another breath of the putrescent air and walked to the brim of the pier, the toes of his boots teetering over the edge as he stared into the water's blackness.

Luke tore the plastic wrapping off his box of cigars, wadded it into a tight ball and pulled out a smoke. Holding it tight between his lips, he rolled the *Tribune* into a tighter cylinder and lit the match he used to set the newspaper alight before flaming the tip of his cigar. He held the Jack Daniels into the wind and spoke into the night. "If you can hear me, Professor," he said, "say this one along with me. 'I have been studying how I may compare this prison where I live unto the world.'"

The quotation came from Richard II and was the same one Luke and the Professor had shared the night Luke threw the Professor in jail. It wasn't exactly a salute to a departed friend. It was an act of defiance. The Professor had deliberately thrown down a gauntlet the night of their ride-along. He'd made Luke's life and job harder to endure. He'd sucked Luke into a meaningful friendship and demanded that he reach out to help others. Then he slapped away every effort Luke made to help him. Then he drank himself to death before he could help Luke figure out how to live with killing Henreid to save Shimmer.

How could he "Protect and Serve" to please the Professor and live to tell about it? He had a job to do and he intended to do it.

It was the best he could do right now, and the Professor could be damned.

He took a puff from the cigar and gulped his Jack Daniels.

A cold breeze whipped his face. He pulled his jacket collar around his throat, knocked the cigar's ashes into the ocean and watched the newspaper burn.

~

About the Author

T.B. Smith served as a police officer for twenty-seven years with the City of San Diego and San Diego Unified School District Police Departments, retiring as a lieutenant in 2003, after being injured in an on-duty traffic accident. He's a graduate of San Diego State University, where he studied English Literature and creative writing. He currently lives in Ashland, Oregon, where he enjoys attending the Oregon Shakespeare Festival.